CRIMINALLY COCOA

As if being in New York City for Easter isn't exciting enough, Charlotte Weaver is helping her cousin, Bailey, on the set of her first cable TV show, *Bailey's Amish Sweets*. Charlotte notices odd events intended to make Bailey look bad . . . and realizes her cousin has a dangerously jealous rival. Can she find out who—before someone's sour grapes turn fatally bitter?

BOTCHED BUTTERSCOTCH

Mother's Day is a sweet and busy time at the candy shop Bailey King runs with her Amish grandmother. This year, Bailey's parents are visiting, and for Mother's Day Tea at the local church, Bailey's whipping up her mom's favorite: butterscotch fudge. All's going well, until a sticky-fingered thief makes off with the money raised for a local women's support group. Can Bailey find the culprit before events boil over into disaster?

CANDY CANE CRIME

Thanks to her new cable TV show, Bailey's shop has more orders than she can handle this Christmas. Fortunately, her beloved Cousin Charlotte is organizing the Candy Cane Exchange, pairing sweet notes with a peppermint treat. Charlotte is delighted to discover she may have a secret admirer...until she sees something underhanded going on beneath the merrymaking. Can she stop a local Grinch before the holiday, and her fledgling romance, are ruined?

Visit us at www.kensingtonbooks.com

Also by Amanda Flower

Amish Candy Shop Holidays

An Amish Candy Shop Mystery

Amanda Flower

Kensington Publishing Corp.
www.kensingtonbooks.com

KENSINGTON BOOKS are published by
Kensington Publishing Corp.
119 West 40th Street
New York, NY 10018

Copyright © 2021 by Amanda Flower

All Kensington titles, imprints, and distributed lines are available at special quantity discounts for bulk purchases for sales promotion, premiums, fund-raising, educational, or institutional use.

Special book excerpts or customized printings can also be created to fit specific needs. For details, write or phone the office of the Kensington Sales Manager: Kensington Publishing Corp., 119 West 40th Street, New York, NY 10018. Attn. Sales Department. Phone: 1-800-221-2647.

The K with book logo Reg US Pat. & TM Off.

First Print Edition: October 2021
ISBN-13: 978-1-4967-3736-6

Printed in the United States of America

Criminally Cocoa

Chapter One

"Cut! Cut!" the director Raymond Reynolds yelled. He was a tall, loose-jointed man, who braided his hair into a ponytail at the back of his head. Before meeting him, I didn't think I had ever seen a man with a braid before, and I couldn't stop staring at it. In my community only little girls braided their hair, never grown women and certainly never menfolk.

Bailey King froze in place. She was halfway through giving instructions on how to weave a chocolate basket for a candy display. Bailey made tempering the chocolate and weaving it over the bottom of a bowl look easy. She held a strip of chocolate in her hand, and it fell on the top of the almost complete basket.

She was frozen like a doe I had seen once paralyzed by the headlights of my father's buggy back in Holmes County. Not that we were anywhere close to the rural Ohio village at the moment. We were inside a New York City skyscraper standing on a television soundstage. It was a new world for me, being on a soundstage, also known as a set. I had heard it called both. I have learned so many new words since coming to the Big Apple, which is what Bailey's friend Cass called the city when we first arrived at the airport. She said to me, "Charlotte Weaver, welcome to the Big Apple!" and I had no idea what she meant. My ears were still ringing and my legs were still be wobbling from being on my first airplane flight, and I thought she'd misspoken until I saw the same phrase all over the souvenirs in the airport gift shop.

Cass had made a big deal out of my coming to New York City because it was my very first time. Bailey lived here before moving to our little Amish village of Harvest. In Harvest, she was an outsider, or at least she was at first—now she fits into the village just fine. I don't think I would ever fit into the big city, not in my plain dress, with my bright red hair wrapped up into a bun at the nape of my neck and covered with a white prayer cap, sensible black sneakers, and apron. Everywhere we went those first few days, I thought people stopped and stared, but after a week I stopped noticing. There were too many other wonderful things to see in the city, and I wanted to see all of it.

It was this want to know that was the reason I wasn't baptized into the Amish church yet. Now, during *Rumspringa*, I could try new things and ask questions. When I was baptized all those questions would have to stop and I would have to live my life by the edicts of the district bishop whether I agreed with him or not. I'd already left my family's Amish district months ago, so that I could play the organ, an instrument I dearly love. Cousin Clara's district lets me play music, but they won't let me avoid making a choice about my faith forever.

Bailey scooped up the piece of chocolate and placed it on a piece of parchment paper. Her long dark hair, which was curled and styled for the camera, fell into her eyes.

The set was almost identical to Swissmen Sweets' kitchen back in Harvest, except for a few "additional things" to make it seem more Amish— or at least what the *Englischers* from the network considered Amish. For one, there was a blank-faced doll on the shelf next to the spices. Clara King, Bailey's grandmother, would never keep such an item in her working kitchen, and Bailey told the producer so. My *maam* would never have done such a thing either. The kitchen wasn't the place for dolls. Dolls were for little girls to play with quietly out of the sight of their mother, who would be busily preparing supper to feed ten people. Feeding everyone every night after a long day working on the farm was a production, and my mother didn't like the children under her feet.

None of this mattered to Linc Baggins, the show's executive producer. He wanted things called "props" to give the set an Amish feel. I was learning that how the set "felt" was very important to everyone who worked on the show. Before this, I had never thought about what a room felt like at all.

"We have to do something to indicate this is an Amish show," Linc had argued with Bailey. It was all quite fascinating, really, learning so much about the *Englisch* world. What's more, I was gaining insight into what the *Englischers* thought of *us*. For one, they all believe that every Amish person lives on a farm. A lot of them do, but certainly not all. I grew up on a farm, but many Amish live in town and run shops, like Cousin Clara, or work in a factory. With land scarce, owning a farm in Holmes County was quite a feat for an Amish or *Englisch* family.

As strange as my ways were to the New Yorkers, their ways were even stranger to me. For a girl who had never set foot outside of Ohio, everything about this production was like a trip to another planet. I knew very well that I was in the same country as I always was, but the lights and noises and even the smells were so different that it drove me to distraction. At home, the most noise you would hear was the moo of a cow that might have escaped from a neighboring farm. With all the noise and activity in New York, I didn't know whether most of the people living here would even notice if a cow started walking down the street.

The set was only half of the room that I was in. The other half was where most of the people were. It had a concrete floor, metal fixtures, and uncomfortable folding chairs that didn't invite you to sit at all.

Three cameras were pointed at Bailey; one was on a track and moved every few minutes. Two other smaller cameras were placed on tripods. Teven, the cameraman, blew his uneven bangs out of his eyes every few seconds, and the light brown strands dangled in the air for a moment like pieces of thread. It made me wonder why he would grow his hair that way when it so obviously annoyed him. I'm sure it was for fashion reasons, something that my Amish sensibilities couldn't quite grasp. I was raised to appreciate practical and plain dress.

Linc clapped his large hands together, and they made a *thwack, thwack, thwack* echo off the mock walls of the set. His clapping jarred Bailey out of her stupor, and she carefully picked up the piece of chocolate she'd placed on the parchment. "That was marvelous. You got it just right on the first take, Bailey. You are a natural! We aren't going to need the entire six weeks to film if things go so famously well."

Bailey blushed, and her bright blue eyes, so like her grandmother's, my cousin Clara's, sparkled. She looked as happy as I have ever seen her back in Harvest. She was one of the best candy makers in the world. I don't know enough candy makers to make such a judgment, but Jean Pierre, her mentor, told me so last night, and since he had a chocolate shop named after him in this big city, I guessed that he was in a position to know. Even if Bailey wasn't so good with candy and chocolate, I could see why she would be on television. She was pretty. Everyone back in Harvest, Ohio, thought so, Amish and *Englisch* alike, especially Deputy Aiden Brody, her boyfriend. Aiden was smitten with Bailey because of her brains and her beauty. Bailey had helped Aiden out on a case more than once.

She brushed her wavy brown hair over her shoulder, and her bright blue eyes were thoughtful. As she moved her hair she sent her long earring swinging back and forth. She wore a different pair of long, dangly earrings almost every day.

I wondered what it would be like to have so much of one thing that in a month you could wear something different every single day. That certainly wasn't my experience. I had four dresses. Well, five if you counted my Sunday church dress, which I only wore every other week. The other dresses were plain and dark colored. Only one of the dresses was different. It was lavender, and I bought the fabric after I left my strict district and moved in with Clara above Swissmen Sweets. In Clara's district, lavender fabric with no adornment was acceptable. It never would have been accepted in the community in which I grew up.

"Don't you think things are going well, Raymond?" Linc asked.

The director, who had yelled, "Cut" just a moment ago, nodded. "I do." But he didn't sound all that happy about it.

"Buck up, man! We have a hit on our hands. We will have the Pioneer Woman shaking in her boots by the time *Bailey's Amish Sweets* hits the airwaves."

Raymond got out of his chair. "Well, I believe it's too early to start making announcements about dethroning any other stars from cable. We have a very long way to go to make this show work."

Linc folded his arms over his broad chest. He wasn't a big man. In fact, he was shorter than either Bailey or me with a square build. Bailey said he looked like a hobbit, which she thought made his last name of Baggins even funnier. She tried to explain to me why it was funny, but I just didn't get it. Must be another odd *Englischer* thing like putting dolls in a kitchen.

"You're pessimistic to your very core, Raymond. You must admit that Bailey has the knack for TV." Linc sniffed. "We're both going to be working on this show for a very long time because Bailey is a star. She might be the biggest star we've signed in the last year. I'm already having visions of her Bailey's Custom Candy Making line of dishware and kitchen gadgets."

"I suppose," Raymond said grumpily. He didn't look too pleased with the idea of kitchen gadgets or anything else Linc said. In fact, in the whole time that Bailey and I had been in New York, I'd yet to see the braided director smile.

Bailey noticed me standing off to the side of the set and crossed her eyes at me. I had to clap my hand over my mouth to stop from laughing out loud. She always had a way to lighten the mood and make me laugh. I owed a lot to her, and when she'd asked me to come with her to New York to be her candy-making helper on her television show, I couldn't turn down her invitation. I can't say it was an easy choice. No. It was quite controversial because as an Amish woman, there were certain things I couldn't do, and one of those things was to be on television. However, I wasn't baptized into the church yet, so I could be on TV without getting into too much trouble. Even so, I knew many of the strict Amish back in Holmes County thought I was up to no good. Clara wasn't keen on the idea of me doing this, but Bailey knew how badly I wanted to be a part of the show, and, somehow, Bailey convinced her grandmother that she needed my help.

"Your friend seems to be doing very well for herself," a woman cooed in my ear.

I dropped my hand from my mouth and jumped, spinning on my heels to see Maria Langston standing behind me. Maria was at least ten years older than Bailey and had a voice that sounded worldly and knowing. She also moved as silently as a cat, and her black hair was tethered into a ponytail at the back of her head with black ribbon. In the three weeks that Bailey and I had been in New York filming, Maria had managed to sneak up on me countless times, and every time she did, she made sure to make a comment about Bailey.

I took a big step away from her because the tall woman and her thick makeup made me a little nervous. She always acted like she knew something I didn't, and I wondered if one of those things she knew was about me.

"Bailey is good at everything she does," I said, shuffling back two more steps.

Maria examined her painted nails. Her nail polish was metallic, and I could see my reflection in them, which was a little distracting. "You think a lot of Bailey, don't you?" Her lip curled slightly. "And Linc certainly thinks she is God's gift to television."

"*Gotte's* gift?" I asked. "I don't think anyone would think that about anyone."

She laughed as if I was making a joke, but I didn't see what was so funny. *Gott* bestowed gifts on people, this I knew, but he didn't make people the gifts.

Maria leaned in. "Just remember this, Amish girl. Television isn't kind to anyone. One day, you can be on top of the world, and the next you are forgotten like you were never born. Attention spans are short in this business. Bailey won't be Linc's darling girl forever. Someone else will take her place, and she will be cast aside like last week's news. Then, she can run back to her precious Ohio and lick her wounds."

She stalked away on her black platform shoes, and I let myself breathe again. Later, when I looked back on everything that happened, I realized two things: Maria was a very short-tempered woman, and that was the day things started to go wrong for Bailey.

Chapter Two

Bailey stood under the bright lights of the set while I watched from the side. She was comfortable in front of the camera. She stirred the chocolate in front of her in a double boiler, which was a pot filled with boiling water with a glass bowl in the pot hovering just above the water, and smiled at the giant lens. "My Amish grandfather was the one who taught me to love candy making. He had a wonderful knack for putting flavors together. He was the one who taught me to make fudge. I don't think I would have ever been able to work in chocolate in New York without him, which is strange to say considering he never visited the city in his life. I feel blessed that I can continue his traditional Amish candy making in our shop, Swissmen Sweets, and that I can share those sweets now with all of you. I think my *daadi*, which is Pennsylvania Dutch for grandpa, would be surprised by where I am now, but I like to think he would be quite pleased too."

Even though pride was considered a sin by the Amish, I knew that Jebidiah King would be so proud of Bailey now.

The service crew had already put lunch out on the table for the day. A little before noon every day, lunch just appeared on a long table just off the set and anyone could go and grab a bite while they had time during the filming. My stomach rumbled, and watching Bailey make candies had only made me hungrier.

Another interesting thing about the food table was the startling number of choices. Even if everyone on the crew ate twice their fill, there would be more than enough left over for the next day, but the next day there was always something new. What did they do with the leftovers? The Amish would never let this much food go to waste. It would be given to neighbors, church members, and friends. Everyone would go home with plenty.

There was no one at the food table at the moment, so I inched over to it. I couldn't believe how much of it was untouched. I was tickled to see that there were bagels. I picked up one of the bagels, cut it in half, added cream cheese and lox, and took a bite. It tasted like nothing I'd ever eaten in Holmes County, and I think, just for that reason I liked it. I had had one every day since the production started.

I took another bite, and cream cheese smeared onto my cheek. I was just about to grab a napkin to wipe it off when a hand appeared, holding a napkin out to me. I took it without a word since my mouth was still full of bagel. I wiped my mouth and chewed as quickly as I dared without choking.

Finally, I swallowed, forcing the bit of bagel down my throat, and looked up to see a young *Englisch* man staring at me with a half smile on his face. I knew that he must be from the crew because he wore all black as most of them did. I thought I might have seen him a few times in the weeks that Bailey and I had been on the set, but I couldn't be sure. Other than Maria, the crew members gave me no notice and hardly spoke at all. In many ways, the crew reminded me of Amish children, who were taught not to disturb their parents and be seen and not heard. Not all Amish children were raised like that, but it was the way I had been brought up.

"You have cream cheese on your cheek." He picked up another napkin and dabbed at my cheek. I jerked away.

My face turned the same color as my hair. It was one of the many times that I wished I didn't have red hair, but the Amish don't dye their hair. I had never had any other color.

"Like the bagels?" he asked as he tossed the napkin into the wastebasket at the end of the table.

I nodded.

"I heard that this was an Amish show. Are you in costume every day to be authentic?"

"Costume?" I looked down at my lavender dress and white apron. My blush intensified. I had been so proud of this dress when I put it on.

He covered his mouth. "Oh man, I'm sorry. Are you, like, really Amish?"

I wrinkled my nose. "I have to get back." I wrapped up my bagel in a second napkin. I was no longer hungry, but I couldn't bring myself to throw it away. I was just too Amish to do that. Bailey had a little refrigerator in her green room (another word that I had learned since coming to New York). I planned to tuck it in there.

"I'm Todd Bray." He held out his hand to me.

I frowned at it. In my community, a man does not extend his hand to a woman he doesn't know, but I reminded myself, I wasn't in Holmes County any longer, and I most certainly wasn't in my strict district.

I gave him my hand and let him squeeze my fingers before I pulled away. A strange expression crossed his face, but I wasn't going to bother to explain to him why a handshake would make me uncomfortable. He was *Englisch*, and he wouldn't understand.

"Are you going to tell me your name?" he asked.

I lifted my chin. "I don't know why you would want to know it since I'm Amish." Even as the words left my mouth, I grimaced. As my father used to tell me, I should think before I spoke. I had a tendency to say the first words that came into my head. Most of the time those words shouldn't be shared. "I'm sorry. That was rude."

He laughed. "I like your honesty. It's refreshing, especially when you work in television."

I wrinkled my brow. "What do you mean by that?"

"Everyone here is trying to get ahead, and sometimes that takes deceit. Even your friend."

I blinked at him. "Bailey? Never. Bailey is one of the most honest *Englischers* I know." Granted, I didn't really *know* that many *Englischers*, and the customers in Swissmen Sweets didn't count—

"Englisher?" he asked. "What does that mean?"

I frowned. There I went speaking too much of my mind again. Maybe my father had been right, and it would be much better if I stayed quiet.

"Oh, please don't be like that," he said when I started to step back. "I know I put my foot in it before, but I didn't know you were really Amish. I thought you were an actress that they'd hired to play the part. We're in television. They can hire anyone to play any part."

"Well, I'm not an actress," I said, feeling annoyed. "My name is Charlotte."

"See, that wasn't so hard. It's nice to meet you, Charlotte."

I pressed my lips together. "I'm not shaking your hand again."

Todd laughed.

"Quiet on the set," Raymond bellowed. He glared at us, and I felt myself cower.

Bailey blinked in the bright lights. She seemed to lose her train of thought when the director screamed at us.

I frowned. I didn't want to be the reason Bailey lost her train of thought.

"Rolling!" the director yelled.

Bailey gave a quick shake of her head and began talking again. "The next step is to add the marshmallow cream to your chocolate over the double boiler. In Swissmen Sweets we make our own marshmallow cream, and it's much easier to do than you might think. If you go online to Gourmet Television dot com, you can find the instructions on how to make it there. Today, I had some ready to go."

Just as she walked to the other end of the set to pull her marshmallow out of the cupboard, there was a loud bang and the sound of shattering glass.

I found myself on the ground with Todd on top of me. I rubbed the back of my head where it had connected with the floor. "What happened?"

Todd climbed off me. "Something blew up."

"Blew up? Bailey!" I jumped to my feet but found that my legs were just a little bit wobbly.

I spotted Bailey crouching on the floor. She looked stunned as she gripped a tea towel in her hands.

A crew member grabbed a fire extinguisher and blew white foam all over the set.

"Stop that! Nothing is on fire, for Pete's sake! Turn off the stove!" the director shouted.

"Is anyone hurt?" Bailey jumped to her feet. "Is everyone okay?"

I glanced around the room. I saw Bailey, Teven the cameraman, Raymond the director, Todd—I felt myself blush just remembering how close to me he'd been on the floor— and Maria. There was no one else there.

After I counted all the people, I looked around the set. There was chocolate everywhere. Even a huge smear of it over the lights and ceiling. Pieces of glass were scattered over the stovetop and on the floor around the island where Bailey had been standing just moments before the explosion. She could have been badly burned—or worse.

"The double boiler exploded," Bailey said, staring at the chocolate dripping from the ceiling. "At least no one was hurt."

"Look at this mess," Raymond said. "How on earth are we going to stay on schedule? It will take days to clean this all up." He glared at Bailey. "I knew it would be a disaster to work with a country bumpkin."

Bailey set her hands on her hips. "Excuse me? Who are you calling a country bumpkin, you egoistical—"

"Cripes!" Linc stepped onto the set. I wasn't sure where he had been when the boiler blew up, but not anywhere close by. "What happened?"

"Your famous chocolatier doesn't know what she's doing and almost got herself and the rest of us killed by rigging a death trap on the set."

"I did no such thing." Then Bailey closed her eyes. I knew she was reciting all the different kinds of chocolate in her head. It was something she did when she was trying to stay calm. She opened her eyes again.

"That's not fair. I'm a chocolatier and have worked with chocolate for over a decade. This is the first time an explosion has ever happened!"

"Was the heat on too high?" Todd asked.

Bailey scowled at him. "I wouldn't have put it on high."

Maria was at the stovetop. She wore oven mitts on both of her hands. Each mitt was streaked with chocolate. "The burner was on high."

"I didn't turn it to high," Bailey said. "I wouldn't keep it up that high when the chocolate was already melted. It would scorch the chocolate and make the taste bitter."

Linc frowned. "What are you saying?"

Chapter Three

"I—I don't know," Bailey stammered. "I just know that someone made a mistake. I don't think it was me. At least, I didn't change the temperature."

Linc rubbed his chin. "Well, it will be easy enough to see what happened if we play back the film."

"That won't help," the director said.

"Did you have the camera rolling?" Linc asked.

"We can play back all you want," Raymond said. "But she was the only one anywhere close to the stove. We were all sitting well back for a long shot to get the view of the entire kitchen set."

"Okay, okay," Linc said. "We will have to close up the production for the day. I'll call someone to come in here and clean the place."

"It's going to take forever," Maria said. "How do you get chocolate off of a ceiling?"

"Any lost days will hurt the schedule," Raymond said. "The schedule was already too tight as I told you countless times."

Linc puffed up his chest. "I'm the executive producer. Let me worry about the schedule."

"What do you want to me to do?" Bailey asked. "I can help clean."

"You're not cleaning," Linc said. "You're the star. Todd and Maria can get started cleaning up the glass and dishes until I can get a professional company in here."

Bailey looked as if she wanted to say something else, but Linc was faster. "Bailey, let's meet in your green room and talk about the recipes for the rest of the show. I'll call the writer and ask her to come in. At least we can do some planning if not actual filming."

After that, Linc marched away with his phone next to his ear. Raymond went after him, complaining about what a mess the explosion had caused and how the show was doomed.

Bailey watched them go with a frown on her face. I hurried over to her. "Are you sure that you're not hurt?"

"Only my pride."

"How can your pride be hurt if it's not your fault?"

"I should have noticed that the burner was on high." She bit her lip. "Even so, that should not have caused an explosion. The glass bowl must have been cracked."

"Cracked?" I asked.

"It's the only way I can think of that the double boiler would have exploded. If the heat was on high and the pressure built up too much under the cracked bowl, it would shatter the bowl. I should have looked at the pot and bowl before starting."

"But you didn't set the stove that way."

"That doesn't matter, Charlotte. I should have checked. Had I been at home, I would have checked because I wouldn't be relying on someone else to set up my candy-making area for me. I should have looked everything over instead of trusting that it was right." She took a deep breath. "I'm the expert in candy making; I should have noticed."

I wanted to argue with her more on that point, but she patted my shoulder. "I'm going to go into my green room and get my recipes ready for when Linc comes back. I at least want to give the impression that I'm a professional."

"And you are," I said.

"I love you for saying that." She walked away from me toward the green rooms.

That's when I realized I was still holding my bagel. I tossed it in the wastebasket.

"Hate to see such a good bagel go to waste," Todd said.

I instantly felt guilty and brushed off my hands. "I've lost my appetite." I looked around the set, and the mess was daunting. "Do you and Maria need help?"

Todd put his hands on his hips. "I won't turn that away."

Maria came onto the set and put a trash bag in my hand. "Here. Just toss anything that's broken or ruined." She gave Todd another trash bag and kept one for herself.

I swallowed and nodded. I stepped around the island that had the stovetop where Bailey had been working. I didn't dare touch anything near the stove just yet since it was all still too hot. The smell in the space was an odd mixture of chemicals and burned chocolate. Neither of those scents was appealing, and together they made my stomach turn.

There were several dishrags that were so splattered with chocolate that I knew not even my *maami* would have been able to get the stains out. I knelt behind the counter to pick them up with the intent of tossing them into my trash bag. As I did, I noticed that the stove knobs seemed to be on upside down. I frowned. Could that have happened from the explosion? They were just below the burner where the pot blew, and since the pot and the glass bowl had exploded upward, hitting the ceiling—the dark chocolate stain on the white ceiling was proof of that—I didn't think that was the case. Maybe since the knobs were on incorrectly, Bailey had turned the burner up to high.

Could the stove have been tampered with? And if it had, did the person who'd done it know that the chocolate scene was to be a long shot, which meant the only person at risk of being hurt was Bailey? I shivered. I had to be wrong about this, I told myself. I just had to be.

Maria came around the side of the island and found me squatting in front of the stove knobs. "Are you going to help or hide on the floor?"

I grabbed the ruined towels and tossed them into my trash bag as I popped up to my feet.

Maria rolled her heavily made-up eyes and started putting salvageable dishes in the sink to soak on the other side of the set.

Todd threw a pan into his bag. "Don't worry about Maria. She has a chip on her shoulder that is at least a thousand pounds. She might not like you—"

I looked over my shoulder at the other woman, who had a scowl on her face as she stacked the dishes in the sink. "She doesn't like me? What did I do to her?"

He laughed. "Nothing. What I was going to say was she might not like you, but she doesn't like anyone. There's no use worrying about it or trying to change her mind." He glanced down at the stove knobs while holding a piece of glass in his hand. "What were you looking at back here?"

I twisted the edge of my trash bag in my hand, wondering if I could trust this young *Englisch* man I had just met. He had protected me from the explosion. As awkward as it was to have him on top of me, his action could very well have kept me from getting hurt. "Does anything look strange to you about those knobs on the stove?"

He frowned and peered at the knobs. "They aren't on right. That's odd. I'm sure whoever installed the stovetop would have noticed that and corrected it right away."

"I wonder if Bailey just assumed that they were on correctly and set the temperature accordingly."

"You don't think Bailey made a mistake with the heat?" he asked.

"Bailey wouldn't have made a mistake like this." I paused. "That can only mean one thing..."

"What?" Todd asked.

"I—I don't know," I said realizing the mistake I'd made in speaking aloud.

He shook his head. "You do know. You think someone was up to something."

I bit my lip, feeling afraid to even consider the thoughts that were flying through my head. "What if someone did this because they wanted to stop the show? Because it's stopped now. Or because they wanted to ruin Bailey?"

"We all work for the show." Todd arched his brow. "Why would anyone want to halt production? Why would someone want to do that?"

I shook my head. "I don't know. It's a ridiculous idea. I shouldn't have said it." I regretted speaking my thoughts out loud—again, and regretted even more that Todd had heard. I didn't know him. I didn't know if I could trust him.

He removed his phone from his pocket and took a photo of the stove knobs.

"What are you doing?" I asked.

"Taking a photo, so we know what it looks like after they replace this. I think you are onto something, and it had to be someone here today. I can tell you it wasn't like that when Maria and I set up the scene this morning."

I shivered and stared at him.

He held up his hands. "It wasn't me if that's what you're thinking."

I didn't say anything.

"I found something too." He held up the piece of glass. "Look at this. Look at how clean the edge is, like it's been cut. That didn't happen on accident."

"Bailey said that she thought the glass had to be cracked in order to make it explode like that."

He shook his head. "I don't think it was cracked. I think it was cut and possibly by whoever tampered with the knobs. Someone wanted to make sure that there would be an accident in the kitchen."

I felt sick. "How would they cut the bottom of a glass bowl?"

"With a diamond or a file, really anything to make a crease. That glass bowl wasn't particularly thick. It was ingenious, really."

I took a step back from him.

"You can't possibly think I did this, can you?" he asked. "Why would I tell you that and get myself in trouble?"

I sighed. "I'm sorry. This whole thing is so confusing. Bailey is just about the nicest person you will ever meet. I don't know why anyone would want to cause her any trouble."

"Maybe they don't want to cause her trouble, but they do want to get the show off the air like you said."

I frowned at him. "Why are you telling me all this? And why are you trying to help me?"

"Maybe because you look like you could use some help." He smiled.

I scowled. "I don't need any help from you. And why would you want to help me?"

"Okay, maybe I could use the distraction. There's not much for me to do around here between setups." He looked around. "Although Maria and I will be busy for a while getting the place put back together. As you can see, I don't have the most exciting job in the world. I prepare the set for cooking shows. It's not what I wanted to do when I went to film school, but everyone in the industry has to start somewhere, and for me that somewhere is at the bottom. I've been out of film school for nine months and I have already moved up some. I don't have to fetch the producers' coffee any longer, for one. I guess I want to occupy my time while I wait for my next big chance."

"You want to help me because you're bored." I played with the hem of my apron.

He laughed. "I guess so."

I shook my head. "I need to talk to Bailey."

He held up a hand. "I don't think you should tell her."

I frowned. "Bailey is my friend. Of course I need to tell her what's going on."

"But you don't know for sure," he said. "Do you really want to worry her like that? Her confidence is already shaken from the explosion. She can't continue filming thinking someone is out to get her. She won't be able to keep her focus on the show."

He had a point, even though I didn't like it in the least. I didn't want to cause Bailey any more stress than she was already feeling, and I knew her too. Bailey had been tangled up in more than one crime investigation, and she couldn't help poking her nose in something that didn't feel right. If she knew someone was tampering with her set, she would be bound and determined to find out who it was, which would drag her attention away from the show. She really needed to put all her focus on the production right now.

"You and I will keep a lookout for her," Todd said. "We will make sure nothing like this happens again, so that she can concentrate on her job, which is filming this show."

I decided not to say anything to Bailey just yet. I needed to know if my hunch was right first.

Todd crossed his arms over his chest. "Even if you're not saying it, I can tell by the look on your face that you agree with me."

I frowned at him again. I hated that a person I had just met could read my feelings so well, not that I was hard to read. My mother always said I wore my emotions on my sleeve. That had gotten me in trouble back in my old district too. It was not the way of an Amish woman to show when she was upset. Clearly, I wasn't doing a great job of being an Amish woman. Then again, I never have.

Chapter Four

Everything was so big, so bright, so loud, so...everything. I still hadn't become used to it even after being in the city for weeks. My fascination with the bright lights and tall buildings didn't amuse Bailey this morning the way it usually did. She was on edge. The day before, Raymond had said the show would never make it on the air. Considering what had happened, I wondered if he might just be right.

As I followed Bailey and Cass down the busy sidewalk, I found myself studying the faces of the people passing by. Most were so focused on where they were going that they took no notice of me or of anything around them. It was so different from back home. If I walked down the street, I would see so many people I knew. It was hard to be anonymous in such a small town and even more difficult in the Amish community, but as far as I could tell, the people I passed here didn't know each other, and Bailey's friend Cass, who'd lived and worked in this city all her life, didn't know them either. Things could happen here that no one would have any knowledge of, and the thought made a chill run down my spine.

Suddenly, the big city felt like a very unsafe place to be. Yesterday, Bailey could have been seriously burned or even killed had she been leaning over the chocolate when it exploded. It could have been an accident, but then I remembered those knobs and what Todd had said about the glass bowl and how people in the television business wanted to get ahead. Would they be willing to hurt someone else to do that? I was very grateful that we weren't going to the studio that day. What could possibly go wrong in a park? Nothing came to my mind.

I hurried to catch up with Cass and Bailey. Cass was a fast walker. In fact I had never seen anyone walk so fast in all my life. She seemed to glide in and around the other people on the sidewalk instead walk by them. Her moves were effortless. I, on the other hand, felt like my father's bull trying to get out of the too small gate in his pen. I brushed up against or bounced off everyone I passed. I got a good number of dirty looks for my missteps.

"Bai, you are going to have to chill out or you won't be able to pull yourself together for the camera today." Cass stopped in the middle of the sidewalk and put her hands on her hips.

Cass was just about the most interesting person I'd ever met. She had black-and-purple hair and a sharp tongue. She was also the only one who could calm Bailey down other than Deputy Aiden Brody. Since Aiden was in Ohio, Cass was the one taking care of Bailey.

"Cass," Bailey said. "You don't know. You weren't there. The double boiler exploded! There was glass and chocolate everywhere." Bailey shook her head. "I can't believe that I missed there was something wrong with that boiler."

Cass started walking again. "You can't be expected to notice everything. You're the star of the show. The crew is supposed to set up your station for the shoot. Your job is being able to talk and look like you know what you're saying while doing it."

"Clearly I didn't if the boiler exploded." She rubbed her forehead. "I have made chocolate thousands of times with a double boiler, and I have never had it explode."

"There's a first time for everything," Cass said.

"That may be, but I'm a chocolatier; this is what I do. If I can't use a double boiler, what use am I?"

"Overdramatic much?" Cass asked.

"I'm not being overdramatic. Someone could have easily been burned or cut. It's a miracle that no one was. What if someone had been hurt?" Bailey asked.

I reached out and squeezed Bailey's hand. "If it's your fault, then it's my fault too. You brought me here to help you with the show. I promise to keep a closer eye on things." I made an internal vow to do this as well. I wasn't going to let any more accidents happen on the set. Clara would be so disappointed with me if something happened to Bailey while we were in New York. Not to mention that Aiden would be beside himself.

Before Bailey could respond, Cass asked in her rapid-fire way, "How did it happen? Was something off about the setup? Were the pot and bowl the right sizes?"

"I don't know what happened; the setup looked fine to me." Bailey edged around a man walking a dog on the sidewalk.

Bailey seemed to read my mind, saying, "Don't tell Aiden. Either of you. He has enough to worry about being a deputy, not to mention all the trouble Sheriff Jackson is giving him."

Sheriff Jackson was the sheriff of Holmes County and Aiden's boss. He'd just won reelection in the county because there was no one brave enough to run against him. I had a particular dislike for him because of his negative attitude toward the Amish. He'd never met an Amish person he respected, and because of that I couldn't respect him. If it were not for Aiden's presence in the sheriff's department, the Amish in Holmes County would be in real trouble, because any time that Sheriff Jackson could blame some wrongdoing on the Amish, he did.

Bailey and Cass expertly moved through the pedestrian traffic and seemed to think nothing of it at all. I, on the other hand, kept muttering, "Excuse me" as I bumped into one person after another. A cluster of schoolchildren stepped between my friends and me and cut me off from them. By the time the children passed by, Bailey and Cass were half a city block ahead of me.

"What's with the flying nun?" asked a man I'd just bumped.

The woman with him chuckled.

I wrinkled my nose, having no idea what he was talking about. Flying nun. It sounded like another one of those *Englisch* riddles to me. I ran to catch up with my friends, bouncing off three more people as I went, my bonnet strings flying behind me in my haste.

"Hey, watch where you are going!" a woman shouted at me.

"I'm so sorry," I called over my shoulder. When I finally reached Bailey and Cass, I was out of breath.

Bailey eyed me as we came to stop at a crosswalk. "What happened to you?"

I gasped. "What's a flying nun?"

Cass turned to me. "Where did you hear that?"

"A man said it as I passed him on the sidewalk. I don't understand what he meant." I squinted in the sun. New York was a lot brighter than I'd expected it to be. The sunlight reflected off the shiny buildings and hit me in the eye.

"Never pay attention to what people say about you on the street," Cass advised.

I wrinkled my nose again. I wanted to know what his words meant. I felt like it might be another one of those times that Bailey and Cass were so in sync with each other that they forgot I was even there.

Bailey must have noticed my face. "He's just making a reference to a movie. It's a stretch, but your Amish clothes are slightly reminiscent of the clothes a nun wore in that movie."

"Oh. So he was being unkind?"

Cass patted my shoulder. "Welcome to city life, my girl."

I frowned.

The light in the crosswalk changed, and I followed them across the street. A line of waiting taxis was just inches from us. As soon as we made it safely to the other side, the traffic light changed, and the taxis took off like a shot out of my father's hunting rifle.

Cass stopped at the entrance to Central Park. I knew that because there was a sign on the wall. She turned to face Bailey and me. "Okay, yesterday was a bit of a mishap with the mess."

"Mess?" Bailey asked. "More of a catastrophe. The double boiler *exploded.*"

Cass rolled her eyes. "I know that, Bailey. You're really going to have to let that go and move on. I'm moving on."

"You weren't even there," Bailey grumbled.

Cass grinned. "And I have something up my sleeve that will have them forgetting about the silly double boiler in no time."

Bailey narrowed her eyes. "What?"

"You will know it when you see it."

"Now you really have me worried." She turned to me. "Charlotte, do you know what she's talking about?"

I shook my head. The day was warmer than I had expected, so I removed my black bonnet and tucked it in the canvas tote bag on my hip. I adjusted my prayer cap on the top of my red hair; my hair was coiled at the base of my neck to make sure the cap was in the exact middle of my head.

Cass shook her head. "Since the set needs to be cleaned and chocolate has to be scraped from the rafters, I came to your rescue as your superagent, and called Linc. I proposed that we use today to get some exterior shots of you with candy for promo and the like. One of my sous chefs from JP Chocolates should already be here with all sorts of delectable candies for you to pose with." She smiled brightly. "I had an apprentice make an entire batch of chocolate Amish buggies! I went for kitsch. People love kitsch."

I began to see why Cass and Linc got along so well. This kitsch sounded a lot like his "props."

"Annnd," she went on, "I have another ace up my sleeve. Just wait. Your show is going to be bigger than *The Great British Baking Show!*"

This wasn't the first time that Cass has called herself Bailey's agent. I wasn't sure what an agent was exactly, but Bailey said it was a role that Cass had given herself to help Bailey with the TV stuff. After which, Cass told me that she was my agent too.

Bailey laughed, and the anxiety that had been etched on her face since the double boiler incident smoothed away. However, the laugh died on her lips when a voice rang out in the park.

"Bailey!" a sweet southern woman called.

Bailey spun around to Cass and said, "Are you kidding me?"

Cass grinned. "The show must go on."

Chapter Five

Juliet Brody hurried over to us along the paved path inside the park. She was beaming and carrying her black-and-white, polka-dotted potbellied pig, Jethro, in her arms. Both Juliet and Jethro always looked like they were ready to go on a fancy outing, but today, they looked like they were here to be in the movies. Juliet's hair was pinned to the back of her head in an elaborate design, with twists and pinned curls, and she wore a pink-and-white polka-dotted dress with enough tulle under the skirt to cause it to puff out one foot from her body. Over the dress, she wore a white fur shrug as it was still March and there was a bite in the air. Jethro, too, wore his best: a pink-and-white polka-dotted bow tie made from the same material as Juliet's dress.

I glanced at Bailey, and she stood there with her mouth hanging open. I think this was one of the few times since I'd known her that she didn't have anything to say.

Cass shook Juliet's hand. "I'm so glad that you could make it to New York. How was the flight?"

"It was divine!"

"We are so happy you're here," Cass said. Bailey remained speechless.

"Well, when I got your call that Bailey needed Jethro's help on the show, I said to Reverend Brook, 'Reverend, I know it will be a great hardship for the church if I leave for a few days, but Bailey needs me and Jethro is going to be a star.' Of course, the dear man was so very understanding. He knows how important Jethro is to Bailey."

Bailey and I shared a look. We both knew that Reverend Brook would do anything for Juliet because he was sweet on her, as Clara would say. Juliet was sweet on him too, but they thought they had fooled the village into believing they were just church friends. Nothing could be further from the truth.

"I—I—" Bailey stammered.

Cass clapped Bailey on the shoulder. "You've rendered Bailey speechless; she is so excited that you're here!" She cocked her head. "But as adorable as that bow tie is on Jethro, it has to go. It takes away from his Amishness."

"Pigs aren't Amish," I argued.

Cass waved away my comment. "Fine. It takes away from his plainness. We need a plain pig like you'd see back home."

Juliet hugged the pig to her chest. "Jethro is the furthest a pig could be from plain."

Cass sighed. "You know what I mean. You might need to lose the fur too, Juliet. Around here, passersby might find it to be offensive."

Juliet touched the fur on her shoulder. "Oh, this. It's not real fur. It's synthetic. I would never wear real fur. What kind of person do you think I am?"

"That's a relief," Cass said, and then she clapped her hands. "Look, there is the production crew and Linc from the network." She pointed across the path to an open green field. A large white trailer was parked in the field with Gourmet Television emblazoned on the side. It reminded me of the production van from the network that had been in Harvest over Christmas.

"Juliet, what are you doing here?" Bailey managed to find her voice.

"Oh." Juliet beamed. "We did it. We were actually able to keep my arrival in New York a secret. Let me tell you, it wasn't easy for me not to just pick up the phone and call you. To make matters worse, I had to keep the trip secret from my son Aiden too because I know that he would have told you."

"I hope that he would," Bailey muttered.

"Oh, I know that Aiden would have loved to come with us too, if he had known, but he never would've gotten away from work. My son works like a dog for the county, as you know."

"How on earth did you get here?" Bailey asked.

"By plane, of course."

"With Jethro?" Bailey asked.

Juliet sniffed. "He is my comfort pig. I have to have him with me at all times. I can't fly without him. I hate flying. I never told you that's how I got Jethro."

"You got him from flying?" Bailey asked.

"No." Juliet laughed, and it sounded like the jingle of bells. "Several years ago, I had a flight out to California. I was going to see an old friend from college whom I hadn't seen in over thirty years, but I was afraid to fly. My friend told me about comfort animals. She said that everyone in California has one. They are super on trend. Well, I thought that was great, and I started to look for an animal that would give me the peace I needed when I fly." She placed a hand to her chest. "And I can't tell you what it was like. I met Jethro and the rest is history. It was love at first sight."

"I'm just trying to imagine how Jethro might have been received on the flight by the other passengers," I said.

"Oh, today? Today, we had the pleasure of flying in Jean Pierre's private plane."

Jean Pierre was the former head chocolatier at JP Chocolates, where Cass worked. He was also Bailey's mentor.

Bailey shot Cass a look. "Jean Pierre knew too. Now, this is all beginning to make a lot more sense. Cass, can I talk to you for a moment?"

When they stepped away, I greeted Juliet and scratched Jethro under the chin. The little pig closed his eyes as if in a moment of sheer bliss.

Across the grass where the production crew was standing, I saw Maria watching us. There was a frown on her pretty face, and her eyes were narrowed. Her stern expression made me shiver. I wondered what had happened in her life to make her so angry looking. Clara's bishop always said that people are angry for a reason, and that helping them find that reason will speed their healing. I pressed my lips together. I didn't think I wanted to help Maria. My goal over the next several weeks was to stay away from her.

Todd, who was standing next to Maria, waved at me. I felt myself blushing. I hoped that he didn't think I was staring at him when I had been looking at her. From the lopsided smile on his face, I knew that he did.

I looked away and straightened my apron.

"Yes," Linc said as he came toward us with Todd a few steps behind him. "This is just what we need to breathe life back into this production." He waved behind himself at the director. "Raymond, come here and meet another star of this show!" His voice boomed. Not for the first time I wondered if Linc should be the director and not Raymond since his voice seemed to carry much better than the other man's. People walking their dogs through the park glanced our way, but not a single one of them stopped. If there had been such an uproar in Harvest, everyone, both Amish and *Englisch* alike, would have come running to see what the commotion was. I supposed in New York, commotion was part of the everyday.

Raymond was speaking to the cameraman Teven—I always paused when I heard the cameraman's name. *Englisch* was not my first language, but the name reminded me of the number seven; perhaps it was intended to be "Steven" but somehow someone had dropped off a letter.

Teven turned slowly, his mouth drawing down when Linc called his name. Linc said something more to Teven and reluctantly followed Linc to where I was standing with Juliet and Jethro. Bailey saw him coming, so she and Cass joined us as well.

Raymond stopped in front of Juliet and held out his hand. "It's nice to meet you. You don't look Amish either."

"Oh, I'm not the star that Linc is talking about." Juliet blushed. She held Jethro up to the director's face. "Jethro is."

Raymond took a big step back. "Is this a joke?"

"I *told* you," Linc scolded him. "The footage we shot in Harvest included the village pig."

"They have village pigs in Ohio?" Raymond scowled.

"He's not really the village pig," Juliet corrected. "He's my pig, my comfort pig."

Raymond narrowed his eyes. "Of course it is." His hands shot to his hips as he turned away from Juliet and squared off with the executive producer. "Linc, really, what are you trying to turn this production into, some kind of petting zoo? I'm a serious director and should be treated as such."

"Yes, yes, Raymond, we all know about your illustrious career shooting antacid commercials. You were going nowhere before I signed you to direct for Gourmet Television. It would serve you well to remember that."

Cass winced. "Harsh," she whispered in Bailey's ear just loud enough for me to hear.

Linc beamed. "Jethro will be a great addition to the publicity shoot."

Raymond folded his arms. "We should be shooting the show today, not photographs." He shot a look at Bailey. "But since someone made a miscalculation in the kitchen, we aren't able to do that."

Cass stepped in front of Bailey. "I hope you aren't implying that my client was in any way responsible for yesterday's incident. She's not the one who sets up for the shoot; your crew does that."

Raymond looked as if he wanted to say something scathing back, but Linc stepped between them. "Let's not go back to that old argument now. What's done is done. No one is at fault. It was a freak accident in the kitchen. No one was harmed, and the set will be as good as new tomorrow for the six a.m. call."

I glanced at Bailey and saw that she was biting her lower lip. It was a habit she had when she was upset or nervous. She still wasn't over the incident from the day before, and I couldn't blame her for that. Also, I peeked at Maria again. Maria was someone who was responsible for setting up. Maybe she knew more about the double boiler incident than she was letting on. I made up my mind to keep my eye on her.

Chapter Six

"Hold the spatula out to the pig! Great! Great! That's the shot." The rail-thin photographer looked over his shoulder at Linc and Raymond. "These publicity shots are going to kill. The pig really makes it." He spoke in a thick German accent, and I wondered if I said a few words to him in Pennsylvania Dutch whether he would know what I was saying. I knew a little bit of High German because our church services back home were conducted in that language, but I was too timid to speak at all to this sophisticated man.

"Bringing the pig in was a great idea," Todd whispered to me as we watched the photo session. "It was a big surprise when Linc told us this morning."

I glanced at him. "This might be a shock, but it wasn't a big surprise to me or to Bailey. It's seems that Jethro has a knack for always getting tangled up in whatever Bailey is doing."

He cocked his head. "Why's that?"

I pressed my lips together and wondered if I'd said too much.

"Come on," Todd said. "You can't leave me hanging as to why the pig is here. I thought we were friends."

I blinked at him. "I haven't known you long enough to think of you as a friend."

He chuckled. "I love your Amish honesty. I have to say, Charlotte, it's so refreshing to meet a straight shooter like you."

"A straight shooter? Like shooting a gun?"

He shook his head with a giant grin on his face. "You're honest. That's hard to come by in this business. That's all I mean." He put his hands in his pockets and rocked back on his heels. "So tell me about the pig."

I took a breath. "Jethro is Juliet's pig, and Juliet is the mother of Bailey's boyfriend, Aiden. Juliet *really* wants Aiden and Bailey to get married, so she seems to show up everywhere Bailey goes to remind Bailey of that. Wherever Juliet goes, so does Jethro, and ever since Juliet learned that Bailey was getting a television show, she has been adamant that Jethro needed one too." I shrugged. It was the best I could do explaining Jethro's role in Bailey's life.

"Interesting dynamics you have in Amish country."

I nodded absently.

"I wanted to tell you, too, that I have been keeping an eye out for more trouble like I promised."

I turned to look at him. "You mean like the explosion."

"Yes, I double-checked everything today, and nothing can hurt Bailey or anyone else on set. I have your back, Charlotte."

I nodded even though I had no idea what he meant when he said that he had my back. "Did you find anything strange at all?"

He shook his head. "And I've been keeping a close eye on Maria too. Her behavior hasn't changed at all. She's still her normal irritable self. If I ever saw her smiling, I would know something was most definitely up."

"*Gut*." I nodded. "Maybe what happened yesterday really was an accident. It's possible that the knobs on the stove could have been accidently bumped, and that's what caused them to turn upside down like that. Also, maybe the bowl was just cracked on the bottom like Bailey thought, so it could have all been an accident."

He removed his hands from his pockets. "The more I think about it, the more I believe it was just an accident too. So glad that no one got hurt, but you should probably put what happened behind you."

"Todd!" Raymond cried from where he and Teven stood.

"Duty calls," he said with a smile and sauntered away.

I watched him go. As much as I wanted to believe what had happened yesterday was an accident, I couldn't shake the image of those upside-down knobs out of my head or the piece of glass that Todd had shown me. I couldn't shake the idea that someone had done it on purpose with the intention of hurting Bailey.

Juliet walked over to me and gave a happy sigh. "This is such a dream come true for Jethro. I have to pinch myself over it."

"Jethro dreamed of being on TV?" I asked. As far as I knew, pigs didn't have big dreams, or televisions, but I knew the *Englisch* understood animals differently than the Amish did.

"Yes, of course, he and I share the same dreams. We're so interconnected, you see, that we want the same things." Juliet smiled.

"Oh," I said, but I didn't understand her at all.

"Can we get a few more with Bailey holding the pig in one arm and the chocolate-covered spatula in the other?" Cass asked. "I want some tight shots that show the affection between the two of them."

"Oh yes," Juliet said. "That's wonderful."

Bailey gave Cass a look.

"I'm just trying to sell you the best way I know how, darling," Cass said.

"Thanks," Bailey muttered and picked up the pig, holding him close to her face. She held out her spoon to the pig, and Jethro pressed his chocolate-covered snout onto Bailey's cheek. Bailey laughed.

"Did you get that?" Cass shouted.

The photographer pumped his arm.

"That's the one that's going on the side of buses," Linc said. He and Cass gave each other a high five.

"Buses," Bailey whimpered.

Raymond cleared his throat. "Now that you are finished with your little bit of fun, I think it would be a good idea to get some opening film for the show here."

Bailey handed Jethro back to Juliet. "I'm okay with that. Has anyone heard the status of the set?"

"It's just about ready. The cleaning crew is doing a knockout job. Maria went back there to oversee things." He looked at the photographer. "Do you have what you need?"

"I have more than enough," the photographer said. "Bailey, you are a natural in front of the camera, and that pig is on another level. I'd shoot him any day of the week. He's a star."

Juliet looked as if she would burst with pride at the very idea that her pig was a star. "Maybe we can discuss headshots for Jethro?"

He nodded enthusiastically, and Juliet followed the photographer to a spot by a tree where he'd left his tripod.

Bailey smiled and walked over to where Cass and I were standing. "I'll admit that I had my reservations, but, Cass, you are a genius. Bringing Jethro here was a great idea, and I think everyone has forgotten what went wrong yesterday."

Cass gave her a thumbs-up. "Remember this if you remember nothing else in show biz: always trust your agent."

"You did wonderfully, Bailey," I said. "Everything is going to be fine now. You're doing great."

She laughed. "You are a chief encourager, Charlotte. Are you sure you were never a cheerleader?"

I blinked at her. "There aren't any Amish cheerleaders."

She laughed. "I know. I was teasing you, but, seriously, thank you for everything you do and for coming all this way to be on the show with me. It means a lot."

"I'm happy to do it. You know that."

The photographer came back with his camera and a sparkle in his eye. "I think I need just one more shot to put this film to bed."

"What's that?" Bailey asked, taking a step forward because she assumed, as everyone else did, that he wanted to take another photograph of her.

"Not you." He pointed at me. "Her."

I pointed at myself. "Me?"

"Charlotte?" Bailey and Cass asked at the same time.

"I'm not sure…" I trailed off. How did I explain to a man like this that it was against my beliefs to have my photograph taken? He wouldn't understand it; not many *Englischers* did.

Bailey stepped in front of me. "I don't think that's a good idea."

At the same time, Linc clapped his hands. "I think it's capital."

Bailey took another step. "But—"

Linc smiled at Bailey. "Now, Bailey, you are the star of the show. Charlotte isn't going to steal your thunder."

"That's not what I'm worried about…"

I cleared my throat. "It's okay. I'll do it."

Bailey looked at me. "Are you sure? This photograph could potentially show up in more places than just on television."

"I know it could be on the side of buses," I said with a brave smile.

Bailey pulled me aside. "Charlotte, you have already done so much for me and for the show; you don't have to do this, if you aren't comfortable."

I straightened my shoulders. "I want to. I'm not baptized yet, so I can do it at least in Clara's district. It would have been a giant no-no in my old district, but so was playing the organ and a whole host of other things. That's why I left."

She bit her lip.

I smiled. "Bailey, I'm trying to decide whether to be Amish or not for the rest of my life, and experiences like this will help me do that." Here was another aspect of my religion and culture that few *Englischers* could truly understand. This period of my life, prior to my baptism, this *Rumspringa*, wasn't just about trying things and seeing the world beyond Amish country. It was about choice. Ours was not a religion in which we expected our followers to be blind to the world. No, we were encouraged young people to *see*—and then we had to choose.

"If you're sure..."

I smiled. "I'm sure."

"Are we settled on this?" the photographer asked impatiently. "The light is perfect now. I don't want to lose it."

"We are." I stepped forward and took Jethro from Juliet's arms. I held the pig to my chest.

"Great." The photographer wiped at his brow. "Good. Let's move before the light does. I'd like the pig to walk beside Charlotte—is that your name?"

I nodded and clenched my hands.

"Right, I would like the pig and Charlotte to walk across the grass like they are on a Sunday stroll."

"On a leash?" Bailey asked.

"No, I want the pig to just walk alongside the girl. The leash will ruin the shot."

"Can you edit the leash out?" Bailey asked. "Jethro has a reputation for running off, and we wouldn't want him to get lost in the park."

"Everyone thinks you can edit anything in and out of a photograph. That may be true, but I'm a purist. I would much rather not put something in my shot that I will have to take out later. Not if I can avoid it."

Bailey looked as if she wanted to argue more, but then Juliet spoke up. "Don't fret about it, Bailey. Jethro will behave perfectly. He won't run away here. He doesn't know this place. He might be more apt to run away at home, where he always knows how to get back to the church."

"Good, good," the photographer said and pointed to me. "Go about ten yards from where we are standing now, set the pig on the ground next to you, and walk."

"Walk? Just walk?"

"Yes." He nodded. "I will give you more direction if I need to then."

I took a deep breath and did as I was told. I didn't look at Bailey before I headed out into the field because I didn't want to see the concern on her face. I wasn't doing anything wrong. I wasn't baptized into the Amish church yet and could do more or less what I pleased. I'd never been the focus of a camera before. I didn't know what it would feel like. Or how I'd feel seeing a photo of myself afterward.

As I set Jethro on the grass next to me, I patted his head and whispered: "Be a good pig and stay with me. Don't run away, okay?"

He looked up at me, and I heard the click, click of the camera.

The photographer waved at me. "Don't look at me. Be natural like you were being. Now walk!"

I started to walk, and Maria stepped onto the grass next to Linc. The two spoke for a moment. I glanced down at Jethro. Much to my amazement, the pig walked next to me like we went on strolls like this all the time, just the two of us. We never had.

I glanced back at Linc and Maria. Maria's penetrating gaze on me was distracting, and I stumbled over a bit of loose turf.

"Charlotte," the photographer shouted with his thick German accent. "Pay attention. You were doing so well. Don't let what is going on around you take your attention away!"

I nodded, and Maria walked out of the park. A second later, a loud horn honked, and Jethro took off.

Chapter Seven

I wasn't sure which was worse. The prospect of chasing a terrified pig through Central Park in my Amish clothing or listening to Juliet wail over losing her comfort animal.

Bailey asked me to stay with Juliet as she and Cass went running into the park looking for Jethro. I felt better when I saw Todd run into the park, too, to search for the little pig.

As much as I wanted to join the search, I knew I would help much more by keeping Juliet calm, not that I thought I was doing a great job at that.

Juliet clung to my arm and cried. Between her tears she said, "This city is so big. How will we ever find him? He's a country pig. He doesn't understand how life in the big city works. How will I ever get along without him, and oh, Reverend Brook will be so brokenhearted if something happens to Jethro. You know how he loves that pig so. Why, I wouldn't be the least bit surprised if he jumped on the next plane to be with me during this difficult time. He is working hard getting ready for the Lenten season, of course, but he cares deeply for all his parishioners and would want to comfort any of us in our time of need, even me."

Despite the stress of the situation, I couldn't help but internally smile at the thought that even at such a time as this, when her pig was missing, Juliet insisted on acting as if she wasn't an extraspecial parishioner to Reverend Brook. Everyone knew how they felt about each other. Why did they insist on hiding their feelings for all these years? Neither of them was married.

I patted her hand. "I know, but let's wait before we tell Reverend Brook. It's no use worrying him until we are sure."

"Hey!" Todd cried, running toward me at top speed. "This way. A cyclist said he saw Jethro down this path."

Juliet ripped her arm from my grasp and took off shouting Jethro's name. I took a breath and ran after her. The path started behind a thick stand of trees. I came to a halt when I reached the other side of the trees. The path was wide, more like a buggy trail that any walking path that I had ever seen, and it was so crowded. Hundreds of people walked, ran, skated, rode bikes, and cruised on skateboards on the path.

"Where's Jethro?" Juliet asked. She was crying now. I patted her arm and searched the path, and then finally I spotted Todd, who was talking to a man on a bike. The bike was bright red and decorated with silver handmade pinwheels all over it that twirled in the breeze. The man wore glasses with lens as thick as my hand. My face fell. How could a man with such difficulty seeing spot a black-and-white pig the size of a toaster in this crowd?

Todd shook the man's hand, and the cyclist turned his bike around and pedaled off in the opposite direction.

"That was Mac," Todd said. "He's a fixture in the park. If something odd is happening, he notices. He said that he saw Jethro running down the path dodging walkers and runners like his curled tail was on fire."

"Let's go after him!" Juliet cried as she tore down the path shouting the pig's name.

"Won't she scare him by crying and calling his name like that?" Todd asked me as we followed her.

I frowned. "I don't think it will help much to tell her that. Juliet really loves that pig."

"I can't imagine loving anything that much," Todd said in a quiet voice.

I glanced at him but decided not to make a comment on his statement. I barely knew him. I bit my lip.

"Charlotte." Bailey called my name as she and Cass ran down the path. "We heard that someone spotted Jethro over here?"

"Mac saw him," Todd answered for me.

Cass nodded. "Then it must be true. Mac sees everything that happens in his section of the park."

"His section of the park?" I asked.

Cass laughed. "The park is too huge to see what's happening in every corner, so different eccentrics have different spots and see different things."

My forehead crinkled, and Cass patted my shoulder. "It's okay if you don't get it. This city can be quirky even for people who have lived here their whole lives, but I wouldn't change one thing about it. It's my home. Not everyone will get it or love it, but I do."

As she said this I felt a pang of homesickness for Harvest, not just for the village but for my family. In my mind's eye, I could see my mother in the kitchen and my father in the barn as they always would be this time of day. Just as not everyone understood New York City, not everyone understood the world I'd grown up in either. It made me think that I was more like Cass than I'd ever thought possible.

Cass stared. "What is Juliet doing?"

Juliet was standing in the middle of the wide path crying to anyone who would listen about her missing pig. She yanked on their sleeves as tears ran down her face. More and more people gave her a wide berth.

Cass nodded at Bailey. "This is you, girl. I think you're the only one who will be able to calm her down this time, Bailey. You'd better go."

Bailey sighed, walked up to Juliet, and put her arm around the older woman's shoulders. Juliet cried and buried her face in Bailey's shoulder. Juliet and Bailey spoke quietly beside the path for a moment, and Juliet seemed to calm down.

Cass shook her head. "Bailey does have the magic touch when it comes to Juliet. I'm sure that will come in handy for both her and Aiden."

Bailey and Juliet walked over to us. Bailey's arm was around Juliet's shoulders while Juliet's head drooped down in defeat. "We have to find him," she whimpered.

"Todd said someone spotted Jethro on this path," I reminded her. I glanced around for Mac or Todd and didn't see either. Where would Todd have gone? Why had he left without saying anything? My brow wrinkled.

"Where's Todd?" Cass asked.

"I—I don't know," was all that I could say.

Bailey patted Juliet's upper arm. "We will find him." I couldn't ignore the fear etched on her face, though. Bailey was worried, and I was too.

"That little bacon bundle couldn't have gotten very far," Cass said. "I mean, how far can he run on those little legs? Don't forget. Someone did see him running this way. He's probably passed out from exhaustion by now. He doesn't strike me as an animal that gets much exercise."

"Oh," Juliet moaned. "I think I'm going to be ill."

"Not helping, Cass," Bailey said.

"Did someone say something about a lost pig?" A young man in a silver jumpsuit and in-line skates cruised up the sidewalk with Jethro in his arms. I had to blink twice to make sure that was what I was really seeing because it was such a strange image.

"Oh my Lord!" Juliet cried and ran up to the man. She grabbed Jethro from his arms so quickly, she almost sent the man reeling on his skates.

He was able to regain his balance just in time for Juliet to throw her arm around his neck. "Thank you, thank you so much. You don't know what a hero you are for reuniting me with my Jethro!" Tears streamed down her face, making black rivulets of makeup drip off her chin.

Cass handed her a tissue. "Clean yourself up, Juliet. We are still on a publicity shoot."

Juliet dropped her arm from the man's shoulders and dabbed at her face with the tissue. "Yes, right. Thank you for the reminder, Cass."

Cass shook the man's hand. "Thanks for finding the little sausage. You stop by JP Chocolates sometime, and you get a box of our famous truffles on the house."

The man grinned. "I love chocolate. I'll stop by today."

Cass nodded. "You do that. Tell them Cass sent you. I'll call ahead and let them know you're coming. What's your name?"

"Nole."

"Okay, Nole. I'll take care of your chocolates. Just pop in the shop and they are yours."

He pumped his fist and skated away.

Tears continued to stream down Juliet's face, and she kissed Jethro on the head over and over again.

"Juliet, please, get a grip," Cass said. "You're making a scene. One big enough that New Yorkers are staring."

Juliet sniffed. "If it hadn't been for that awful loud sound, Jethro would never have run away. He's a very good pig. So obedient."

Cass snorted and Bailey sighed at that comment, but I couldn't help thinking that just maybe Juliet was right. Jethro had been fine walking next to me on the grass. It was only when the sound came that he bolted. Also, I couldn't forget that the sound happened just as Maria left. Could she have done it? I shivered. She was also on the set during the explosion, but so were a lot of people, including Bailey and myself, and we were the only two I could be one hundred percent certain didn't do anything to cause all the problems that we'd been having.

I glanced at Bailey as the four of us—well, five, if you counted the pig who was cradled in Juliet's arms—walked back to the lawn where we had left Linc, Raymond, and the rest of the team from Gourmet Television.

Should I tell Bailey my suspicions? The thought ran across my mind. I knew if I did, it would distract her from her work, but shouldn't I warn her that something odd was going on during the production of her candy-making show? Doubt crept in. What if I was wrong and Bailey started accusing people or snooping around the set? She might lose this opportunity because Linc and Raymond would think she didn't trust them.

No, I wouldn't tell her yet. Two odd things happening did not mean someone was trying to make trouble.

Chapter Eight

"Charlotte, this way." Bailey pulled on the sleeve of my coat the next morning as we made our way back to Gourmet Television Studios. The night before, Linc had called Bailey and said that the set was as good as new. Since the show was behind schedule from the lost day and a half, the call time—another new *Englisch* TV term—was just as the sun was coming up over the giant buildings. Bailey groaned when it was time to get up, but rising early was no trouble for me. Back home on the farm, I had always risen before first light to feed the chickens and let the sheep out into the pasture. Now at Swissmen Sweets, I woke up at four o'clock to make candies for the day. Bailey rose early too to make the candies, but she still didn't like it.

I tripped forward on the uneven sidewalk. The toes of my black sneakers caught on the cracks. I might have fallen on my face if Bailey hadn't been holding my arm so tightly.

She looked over her shoulder and smiled nervously at me. "Sorry, I'm just in a rush. I want to get there early. We can't have any more mess-ups with the show."

I knew what she meant.

I watched in amazement as the sun poked through the buildings and its beams reflected off the countless windows, making a kaleidoscope of light sparkle in front of my eyes. Growing up on a farm, I had seen a thousand beautiful sunrises in my life. Ones that burned the dew off the fields and painted iridescent colors on the clouds, but I had never seen a sunrise like this. I wasn't sure I could go back to Holmes County at all after seeing this. The city was more than I could ever have imagined, and it just a small piece of the whole world. If I stayed Amish, I would only see a very small portion of it. If I became *Englisch*, I could see it all. It was one of those moments when I was most torn. It would be hard to leave my culture, but there was a yearning inside me to do and see more. I couldn't describe it, and not many in my community truly understood; the ones who did left.

"Charlotte, we have to keep moving." Bailey tugged on my arm again.

"Right," I said dreamily and let Bailey pull me along the sidewalk around the many people making their way to work. None of them seemed to be as mesmerized by the sunrise as I had been. Maybe, I thought, my sunrise back home, the one they didn't know, would be the one to stop them in the middle of their tracks. Perhaps, I thought, everyone grew numb to the beauty that surrounded them; only when something is different does it stand out.

I followed Bailey to the building where Gourmet Television was filmed. On the first day we were on the set, I was surprised to learn that there were many businesses in this one building, maybe even dozens, including lawyers, other television networks, and more. On that first day, I stared at the building directory by the elevator and was overwhelmed by all the business names. That was so different from back home where each business seemed to have its own *much* smaller building. Bailey told me it was because New York didn't have open land like Holmes County did for its many businesses. New Yorkers might not have room to spread out, but that didn't stop them from building *up*. Story upon story straight up into the air. I'd never seen anything so tall as the buildings there.

That first day was over three weeks ago now, and I had learned so much since, I was surprised that my mind didn't just stop working. I now knew words like director, filming, and playback. None of those words were part of my Amish life. And I knew how to get from Cass's apartment, where Bailey and I were staying while we were in the city, to Gourmet Television. I never would have believed I would know that when I arrived at the airport.

I followed Bailey through the glass door. The floor was polished, and there was a man stationed there every day with a little hat who bowed at us. There were so many people around us, walking at a fast pace. Their shoes made a *tap, tap, tap* on the marble floor. My own plain black sneakers didn't so much as squeak.

For the most part, the fancy-shoed people didn't pay any attention to Bailey and me.

"This way, Charlotte." Bailey's voice was as sweet as ever, but I heard the hint of nervousness in it. She wanted today to go off without a hitch. In Bailey's words, she "had one more shot at getting this right." Television wasn't very forgiving and didn't give second chances, or so she said.

The elevator opened, and half a dozen people got out before Bailey and I could get in. There was no one else waiting to go up, and we were alone. I could feel Bailey's anxiety. She made me nervous with all her fidgeting.

We stood in the elevator, and for the hundredth time Bailey pulled out her recipes for the candies she would be making. It was what she had been doing all night. Her mouth moved as she quietly recited her ingredients.

"I can't have anything go wrong on the set today. The network is putting a lot of money into producing these episodes, and I have to be on top of my game."

I held my simple black purse in my hands. It was my first purse. Bailey had bought it for me before we came to New York. She said I would need something to carry my things in on the airplane, and she gave me the purse as a gift. She said it was the plainest one she could find.

Even though it was black, it seemed so much fancier than the cloth tote bag that I carried. The zipper had a black leather tassel on it. I loved that tassel. Throughout the flight, I played with braiding and unbraiding the individual cords. The activity seemed to keep me calm. I had never been on an airplane before, and takeoff and landing felt so strange. Bailey let me sit by the window to look at the clouds, but I spent more time playing with my tassel than looking outside. I didn't need to be reminded how high up we were.

The elevator dinged, and the doors opened. We were in the hallway that was just outside the soundstage area.

"Bailey, there you are! Come, come, we have to get you into makeup." Linc stormed toward the elevator. He wore a V-neck sweater over a white button-down shirt and appeared to be uncomfortably hot.

"What's the rush?" Bailey asked. "Charlotte and I are here a whole hour before I'm supposed to be in the makeup chair."

"That was the original call time. Didn't you get my text? Right now is the call time."

She looked at her phone. "I'm sorry. It must have come when we were in the subway."

He pressed his lips together. "It doesn't matter now. Just get to hair and makeup. Stat. The reason for the earlier time is I have had the most wonderful idea."

"Ohh-kay," Bailey said and waited.

He rubbed his hands together. "What's coming up in a few weeks?"

"Ummm," Bailey said.

"What *candy* event is coming up in a few weeks?" he emphasized, barely able to contain his excitement.

Bailey was still blank faced.

"Easter?" I asked.

Linc pointed at me. "Bingo. Easter. Easter is one of the biggest candy holidays of the year, so we need to get you on the air."

"But the show doesn't air until the summer," Bailey said.

"I know that, but this is the time of year when we should let people know that the show coming. Last night, I realized that this would be the perfect time of year to start promoting your show and getting your name out there. That's why I made the earlier call time. We want you to have a five-minute recipe that we can sprinkle in between programming during Easter week. It will be a great way to introduce you to our audience. We want you to be plastered all over the network, so that by the time the show begins, the viewers will already feel like they know you and want to tune in. I just know *Bailey's Amish Sweets* will be the breakout hit of the summer. I can barely wait to see the ratings roll in."

"That is a great idea," Bailey said.

I couldn't have agreed more. Easter candies were some of my very favorites to make. I wondered which one Bailey would choose—there were so many. My favorite was fudge eggs filled with marshmallow cream.

"Do you have an Easter recipe that you can do for the camera from start to finish in five minutes?" Linc asked.

The chocolate basket was definitely out in that case, I thought.

Bailey thought for a moment. "It doesn't get much easier than a bird's nest. Do we have some pastel-colored candy-covered chocolates, the small ones that look like birds' eggs, and pretzel sticks?"

He clapped his hands. "I knew you would think of something. I will send Todd out to pick up the ingredients you need straightaway. And I have even better news. We are going to have a special guest for this demo."

"Please tell me it's not…" Bailey trailed off.

The elevator door opened, and Juliet floated through with Jethro in her arms.

"Jethro," Bailey murmured.

Chapter Nine

Juliet beamed. "We came as quick as we could. It took the bellhop ages to hail a taxi in front of the hotel. A man stole the taxis the bellhop called in right out from under me. Of course, I was beside myself when he did that. The nerve! And here I'm standing on the side of the street with this terrified little pig in my arms." She shook her head as if trying to dispel that bad memory.

"If I'm cooking on the counter, how is Jethro going to be in the shot?" Bailey asked.

"I've already thought about that," Linc said, "and we brought in a high bench for the pig to sit on. Charlotte can be with you on the set to make sure the pig stays in line. You won't mind doing that, Charlotte, will you?"

I shook my head.

"Great. Now off to the makeup chair for both of you."

Before I knew it, I was in a makeup chair between Jethro and Bailey. Juliet circled about the pig. "Can you put a little powder on his nose to take off the shine?"

The makeup artist didn't seem to be the least bit surprised by Juliet's request and brushed powder on Jethro's snout.

"My life is so weird," Bailey groaned on the other side of me.

I wasn't going to argue with her about that. Her life *was* weird, and mine was weird by association.

The makeup artist was quick about her work, and before I knew it, she was packing up her kit. I looked in the mirror. "I can't even tell I have makeup on."

"That's the point," the artist said. "We want you to look Amish."

I frowned a little and felt a twinge of jealousy at how big Bailey's blue eyes looked with mascara and eyeliner on. I wasn't going to admit that to anyone other than myself, though. I followed Bailey back to the set with Jethro in my arms.

I gasped. The set looked just as it had before the double boiler incident. The only changes were the addition of a high bench that was level with the counter for Jethro to sit on and the Easter decorations. Decorating a working kitchen for Easter was something neither Clara nor any other Amish woman would ever bother to do. It wasn't practical.

Bailey stared at the stuffed bunny on the spice shelf. "Ummm, this isn't really Amish."

"It will be fine," Linc said. "The viewers need to know that this is an Easter spot."

"Won't they know that from what I'm making?" she asked.

"We need to drill it home to them."

Bailey looked around at all the pastels and flowers in the space. "I'd say you have accomplished that."

Maria was at the counter putting the last touches to Bailey's cooking setup. Todd was there too. It was the first time that I had seen him since the park. He caught me staring and smiled.

A flush filled my cheeks, and I looked away, feeling like the shy girl in my one-room schoolhouse back in Ohio all over again.

The director was back in his chair. "Let's make short work of this promo because we are still behind on the main schedule."

"Yes, of course," Linc said. "But you know, Raymond, shoots like these are important too. We have to give the audience a reason to watch the show. Not that I doubt they will want to. This is going to be an amazing hit. I hope we are all ready to work on *Bailey's Amish Sweets* for years to come."

Just as he had the last time Linc said something similar, Raymond made a face.

"Everything is ready to go," Maria said, stepping away from the island. "Todd was about to put out the candies and pretzels you wanted."

"That's great." Bailey stepped around the side of the island. "This should go pretty quickly. I just need to make a quick caramel, which has only three ingredients."

"Perfect for a promo spot," Linc said, and then he turned to me. "Here. Put the pig on the bench, and I want you to stand beside him."

I placed Jethro on the high bench. He looked around the room with a little trepidation on his piggy face.

Juliet waved from beside the camera. "I'm right here, baby. You're doing great. You're a star!"

"She's talking to the pig," Bailey whispered to me.

I laughed. "I know she wasn't calling you or me baby."

Jethro sat back on his haunches. It seemed that Juliet's encouragement was all he needed to settle in.

"Let's start rolling," Raymond said. "We have a busy day, and I don't want to be here all night."

I patted Jethro's head. Across from me, I could see Maria just off the set. She had her arms folded across her chest, and she was glaring at Bailey. She definitely didn't like my friend. Should that give me more reason to think she was behind the odd things that were happening on *Bailey's Amish Sweets*? Todd stood a little away from her and caught me looking again. He gave me the thumbs-up sign and grinned. I frowned.

"Rolling in five!" Raymond shouted.

I took a deep breath and put a smile on my face. My only job on the set was to look Amish. I knew that was something I could pull off.

A few minutes later, Bailey stirred the caramel she was making on the stovetop. "If you don't have time to make your own caramel, you can always buy it. Not that my Amish grandmother would ever let me get away with that. She is a firm believer that caramel and fudge should be made from scratch. However, if you want to cheat a bit—and if you do, I won't tell my grandmother—then you can actually buy Amish caramel sauce from Swissmen Sweets. We have a new online store, and you can order whatever you need in a pinch. I know how hard it is to make time for those extra things." She peered into the pan. "It's looking great. I'm going to turn the heat down and get the pretzels and the candies ready for our nests. Charlotte, can you open the bag of candies and pour them in a bowl? Make sure you keep them out of Jethro's reach."

"I'll do my best." I laughed and picked up the bag of candies. They were pastel-colored chocolates just as Bailey had requested. Todd had gotten her everything she wanted.

As I opened the bag, Bailey picked up a plastic container of pretzels with a screw-top lid. Like most cans and jars on the set, it had been previously opened. Bailey said that the crew did this so she wouldn't struggle to get something open on film, which might result in the costly reshoot of a scene.

I started pouring the candies in the bowl as Bailey pulled the lid open. A cloud of black powder puffed around her face, and she sneezed so hard she stumbled backward. Startled, I threw the bag of chocolates in the air, scaring Jethro. The pig leaped off his bench and bolted for Juliet, who was standing by Teven. The pig miscalculated and ran into the legs of the camera's tripod, knocking it to the floor with a crash.

When the black powder cleared, the camera was on the floor in two pieces, bird's egg candies were all over the set, and Bailey was still sneezing.

Chapter Ten

Raymond threw the stack of papers he had been holding on to the floor. "This is ridiculous!"

Bailey continued to sneeze, and her eyes were watering terribly.

I touched her arm. "Are you okay?"

She shook her head. "I need fresh air." She stumbled off the set.

I peered at the pretzel container. It lay on its side, the pretzels spilling out onto the counter, and they were all covered with a fine black powder. I didn't touch the powder, but I leaned over it and sniffed. Almost immediately, I sneezed.

"It's sneezing powder," a voice said beside me. "We used to use it in film school when we needed to sneeze for a scene but couldn't work up the sniffles on command."

"Sneezing powder?" I asked. "Why would there be sneezing powder in a container of pretzels?"

"They didn't come that way, I can tell you that. I bought them and gave them to Maria to set up the scene for the promo."

Maria again. She had to be behind what was going on at the show.

Bailey stumbled back onto the set. "I'm so sorry. I don't know what came over me. I don't have allergies, and I'm not sick."

I grabbed her hand and showed her what I'd discovered. "It's not your fault. Someone put sneezing powder in the container."

Her eyes were bloodshot. That sneezing powder must be strong stuff. "Someone did this on purpose."

While Bailey and I were looking at the evidence of tampering, Linc and Raymond were arguing about the broken camera. "Who's going to pay for this?" Raymond said, pointing at the camera. "Because it's not coming out of my paycheck."

"You don't have to worry about that, Raymond, and we can have another camera here in a half hour. This isn't a disaster."

"Everything related to this show has been a disaster from start to finish!" the director shouted back.

"Jethro has a bump on his head. Does anyone care that poor Jethro has a bump on his head?" Juliet asked. "Can we get a vet here?"

Bailey rubbed her forehead. "I think I'm getting a headache."

"I can see why," I said sympathetically.

"I need a vet," Juliet said.

"The pig looks fine to me," Teven said. "What about my camera?"

Everyone looked down at the very expensive video camera that was now in pieces on the floor.

Raymond took charge. "Okay, I'll make some calls and we can borrow another camera from another set that is not currently filming." He pointed at Jethro. "But I want that pig off my set!"

Juliet held Jethro in her arms and glared at Raymond so fiercely that her expression would have scared me half to death if she ever looked at me like that. "How dare you be so unkind to Jethro? It wasn't his fault. He was frightened. You should not treat the star of the show so poorly."

"He's not the star," Raymond shot back.

"I—I—how—I will call Jethro's agent and let her give you a piece of her mind!" Juliet sputtered.

It was a real threat considering that his acting agent was Cass, and I personally found her a little bit scary.

Linc stepped in between them. "Raymond, that's a good idea. Get a new camera. Also, you and Teven go through the film to make sure we didn't lose anything in the accident."

"It should still all be there," Teven said. "The lens is broken, but the recording should be intact."

Linc nodded. "Good, good." He snapped his fingers, although I didn't know whose attention he was trying to get since we were all looking at him. "Let's reset the scene so we can start filming again as soon as the new camera arrives."

"I texted a friend of mine," Teven said. "A new camera should be here in about forty minutes."

"Good, good," Linc said. "That's not too much time lost."

"Every minute counts with this production. Some of us have other, more important things to do than this—this..." He sputtered and trailed off as if he couldn't think of a word that would describe whatever "this" was. I had a feeling it wouldn't have been a word that I'd learned growing up Amish.

"I want the pig out!" Raymond said finally when he regained a bit of his composure. At least he could speak again, so that was something.

Linc glared at Raymond. "You seem to want a lot of things, Raymond. I don't see you getting any of them."

Raymond turned bright red from the base of his neck to the top of his forehead. I had never actually seen someone's face turn red like that. Instinctively, I took a step back.

Bailey started sneezing again and covered her mouth. "Excuse me." She ran back in the direction of her green room.

I started to follow her.

"If Bailey is sick," Juliet said, "who will take care of Jethro? I can't do it by myself in a strange environment."

Who was she kidding? She could barely do it back home. "She's not sick. Someone..." I trailed off. I couldn't tell Juliet about the sneezing powder, especially in the middle of all these people because I realized, standing there with the crew, that one of them had to be the one who'd done it. I knew that it was time to tell Linc, but I didn't want to do that without telling Bailey my plans.

"Excuse me," I murmured, and I hurried off the set in the direction that Bailey had gone.

The door to Bailey's green room was closed. I turned the knob and found that it wasn't locked. I knocked and pushed the door inward. "Bailey?"

I don't know why it was called a green room at all because it wasn't green. In fact, it was completely devoid of color. The floor, walls, and furniture reminded me of the oatmeal that my mother used to make on cold winter days at the farm for my siblings and me after morning chores. I hate oatmeal, and she always got angry at me for not eating my portion. It was all I could do to choke down a few mouthfuls. I knew if I didn't at least do that, I would have nothing at all to eat until midday, and doing chores on a farm was hungry work. I didn't miss those days. There were pieces that I missed, the animals, the sunrises, the warm comforting air in my mother's kitchen, but not the oatmeal or the work or being told I couldn't have the life I wanted. I guess that's why I was here. I was still figuring out what kind of life I wanted. It had been so hard to walk away from my family all those months ago, but if I hadn't, I would have to walk away from the person I wanted to be or thought I could be.

Bailey was in the makeup chair wiping the makeup from her face. She showed me the cloth. It was covered with foundation. "The makeup artist certainly cakes it on. She's not going to be happy with me when she finds out she will have to start over, but I didn't know how else I would be able to get the sneezing powder off my skin."

"Are you all right?" I asked.

Dark eye makeup was smeared under both of her eyes, making her look like a raccoon. Bailey was a beautiful girl, but at the moment she was a bit of mess. She washed her face with a damp cloth, running the cloth beneath both of her eyes. "I think so. I don't know when I have had such a fit of sneezing in my life." Her makeup was all washed off, and she held a cool washcloth to the corner of her eye. "You said it was sneezing powder? Why would someone play such a prank? It doesn't make any sense."

"It's not just one prank."

She looked at me. She was no longer wearing any makeup, and I thought she was just as pretty without it. "What do you mean?"

"This is the third time that someone has played a prank or tampered with the production."

"What?" And then her expression cleared. "The explosion and then Jethro running off. You think someone here on the set of my show is making accidents happen on purpose?"

I nodded. "I'm afraid so."

"Tell me why."

And so I did.

When I finished telling Bailey all my suspicions, including the fact that I thought Maria might be the person behind all of it, she sat back in the makeup chair with a loud groan. Then she hopped out of the chair. "I'm not going to let someone mess with my show. I have to do something."

This was the exact reaction I'd expected from her, which was why it had taken me so long to share my suspicions with her.

"Maria is going to get an earful from me," Bailey said angrily.

"I just think it's Maria. I don't know for sure."

"There's only one way to find out and that's by asking her, and we need to tell Linc what's going on. He should know." She headed to the door, and then stopped. "It would be better if we approached her with some kind of evidence. Did you grab the sneezing powder? I don't want to smell it, but I would like to see it, and it's our only proof."

"Oh no," I said. "I should have thought of that. I'll get it." I ran out of her green room and back onto the set. Everything was quiet. I didn't know where everyone had gone. The only thing I knew for certain was that there was no sign of the black sneezing powder.

Chapter Eleven

Bailey wasn't going to like it when I reported back about the missing sneezing powder, but I knew that I'd seen it. I wasn't the only one either; Bailey and Todd had too. Todd. That's who I needed to find. He was the one who'd told me it was sneezing powder in the pretzel container. Why would he help clean it up if he knew that it represented some kind of sabotage against Bailey? Yet he and Maria would be the only ones who would have cleaned it up.

I left the set and went in the opposite direction from Bailey's green room. This other way led me down a hallway that opened up into other soundstages. Technically, I wasn't supposed to be there. Raymond had been very direct in saying that I shouldn't wander around the studio when I wasn't needed on the set because there were other people filming throughout the building and I might make noise that would reflect badly on him. Raymond seemed to be very concerned about everything that might reflect badly on him.

I crept down the poorly lit hallway. To my left I saw lights flashing, and there were murmurings coming from another set. It wasn't loud enough for me to hear the words, but I knew that it must have been some kind of cooking show because those were the only programs that taped at Gourmet Television. It smelled like the Mexican restaurant Bailey and Cass had taken me to on our first night in New York. My stomach rumbled just thinking about it, and I wished I'd grabbed a snack from the food table today before all the uproar.

I inched behind the director's chair just as the man cooking on the set added liquid to his saucepan, and a giant flame flew into his face.

I yelped.

"Cut!" the director yelled. "Who made that noise? The perfect take was ruined. Whoever did that better get off my set!"

I ducked and dashed to another corridor. When I felt like I was safely away, I looked back, half expecting to see the angry director behind me. Were all directors angry? I wondered if that was some sort of job requirement. The hallway I found myself in was dark, and that's when I realized I would never find Todd in this maze of passageways and sets. An even bigger problem was that the only way I knew how to get back to the set of *Bailey's Amish Sweets* was by going past the set with the angry director. I wasn't sure I was ready to risk being seen by him again. I inched forward in the corridor, wishing that I had a candle or lantern to light my way. I'd never thought I would need either of those in New York. Electric light wasn't in question here like it was back in my community in Harvest.

I inched forward and bumped the toe of my sneaker into a barrel. Why on earth would they need a barrel on a television set? The world of TV was peculiar.

When my toe hit the barrel, it made a scraping sound across the concrete floor.

"Did you hear that?" a hushed male voice asked.

I froze, thinking more and more that I should have stayed back in the green room with Bailey. She should be the one out here getting frightened and yelled at. She had more experience with such things than I did; that was for certain.

"I didn't hear anything. You can't ignore this like nothing happened. I know what you've been up to," another voice whispered back.

The second was higher and spoke more quickly. I guessed that it was a woman, but I couldn't be sure. If Bailey were with me, she would know. She had eavesdropped on more people than I had. I knew I would have to pay more attention the next time she told me that she was in the middle of an investigation. Clearly, I hadn't picked up as many sleuthing tips from her as I should have.

"I know I heard something. It could have been a mouse."

"There are no mice in Gourmet Television," the woman said.

"Perhaps," he said. "But there are plenty of rats."

"Are you speaking as one?" she said.

The man said something in a low voice that I couldn't hear, but the woman's voice rang out loud and clear. "And don't change the subject," she said. "You told me that I was next up for a show on this network, and now I'm hearing that I'm not because some Amish girl comes to town, and Linc falls all over himself to impress her. Do you know how hard I have worked to get where I am today? How many ridiculous things I had to do? And now you are telling me this girl, who didn't even want a show, gets it without earning it. No thank you. You owe me more than this."

"Everyone in this business has been pushed aside at one time or another because someone new came along. It is the nature of the game."

"Well, I don't accept that, and I'm going to change the rules of the game starting right now."

"What are you saying?" the man asked.

"I'm saying that you had better make it right or there will be consequences that will have a huge impact on your career, ones that you might never recover from. You might hate working for Gourmet Television now, but I can make it so you don't work for them or anyone else."

"Are you threatening me?"

"Consider it a warning and an encouragement to get what we both want. You need to know that I'm serious. I'm not going to let some girl from Amish country, you, or anyone else destroy my chances of getting exactly what I have earned, and what I've earned is a show of my very own. Ask anyone in this network and they will tell you that."

"You've put in the time, but that doesn't mean you have the natural talent that it takes to carry your own show. It's not something you can learn. You either have it or you don't."

"So you're saying that I don't."

"Honestly," the man said, "I don't care either way. I just want to wrap up this shoot and then I want the show to fail so that I can get on with my life."

"You're not going to be able to do that with me around. I will tell you that."

"I could destroy your career."

"Could you?" she demanded. "I doubt that after I tell the network what I know about you. Don't think it won't reach other networks and studios, ones that you would much rather work with. This is a small industry, or at least that's what you have always told me."

There was a clatter as if something had fallen to the floor, and I instinctively took a step forward. Had the man hit the woman? I shivered at the very thought.

"Be careful," the woman said. "You don't want anything else on the set to break. Haven't you told us all time and again that we are pressed for time on this shoot?"

"I'm leaving."

There was more scuffling, and then I heard the quick steps of someone walking toward me. They were coming my way. I ducked behind the giant barrel just as a woman walked past. By that time, my eyes had adjusted enough to the dim light to see that it was Maria.

When she had gone, presumably back to the set of Bailey's show, I hid behind the barrel for another two minutes just in case the man decided to follow her, but he never appeared. I stood up and smoothed out my skirt. Habitually, I placed my hand on my prayer cap to make sure it was still in place. It was. I glanced back in the direction Maria had gone.

I had been right all this time. Maria did have it out for Bailey, and I wouldn't be the least bit surprised if she wasn't the one behind all the problems on the set, but what man was she talking to? It seemed he knew something about Bailey's show too.

I started down the corridor and tripped over something, probably an electrical cord. There were so many of them snaking their way around the studio, through and around the set. Growing up in a home without electricity, I found the cords hard to get used to, and I tripped over them constantly. I never knew when they would pop up.

I bent to feel what the obstruction was. But it wasn't a cord. It was the empty pretzel container. I knew it had to be the same container that Bailey had had on the set. I didn't think that chef making Mexican food had been using pretzels in his flambé recipe.

To be sure, I sniffed the can and immediately sneezed. There must have been enough sneezing powder left on it to bother my nose.

Now I was even more convinced that Maria was the one behind the pranks. She was talking about the show, and now I'd found the container that had caused Bailey all that trouble right in the spot where she had been talking.

Footsteps came toward me while I stood in the hallway, but this time there was nowhere to hide. I tucked the can behind my back.

Todd pulled up short. "What are you doing back here? This area is only for employees."

I was about to tell him that I was off looking for him, but the words caught in my throat. I was still so overwhelmed by the conversation that I had overheard.

He flicked on a light, and suddenly the hallway was brightly lit. "Why are you standing here in the dark?" he asked.

I blinked.

Before I could answer, he asked, "What's that you are hiding behind your back?"

"I'm not hiding anything behind my back."

He grunted. "I thought Amish people don't lie. I can clearly tell you have something." He tried to peek around my side.

I pivoted my body so that he couldn't see the container.

He laughed. "It must be good, whatever it is." Then he dashed around me and grabbed the container from my hand before I knew what had happened. "You're going to have to be quicker than that if you want to keep something from me." He looked at the can. "Pretzels? Are you going to make those birds' nests for the show?"

"No, I mean, yes because it's part of Bailey's show, but those aren't new pretzels. They are the same ones from the set with the sneezing powder on them."

He handed the container back to me. "How did you get the container? I thought that it was thrown away. I've looked all over the set for this container," he said.

"Me too, and it's the evidence that I need to show that Maria is behind the pranks on the set."

"What do you mean? You really think it's her?"

I nodded. "I heard Maria talking to someone about Bailey in this very hallway just a moment ago, and when I come here to see where she was standing"—I pointed at the container in my hand—"I find this."

"All right. You need to settle down just a bit. What did Maria say?" He took the container from my hands.

"She said Bailey took her place, and whoever she was talking to was supposed to fix it or she would tell some secret about him."

"Who was she talking to?" Todd asked in a tense voice.

I frowned. He was no longer the friendly, jovial young man that I knew. His eyes narrowed just a tad, but it was enough for me to notice and to make me nervous.

"I—I don't know. That's why I came down here. I was hoping that I could get a look at him, but by the time I got here, he was gone. It was definitely a man, though, and I saw Maria. She walked right by me."

"Did she say anything to you when she walked by?" His voice was even sharper than before.

"She didn't see me. I was hiding," I said, and I could tell that Todd was trying hard not to laugh, which just made me more upset. This wasn't a laughing matter if Maria was trying to ruin Bailey's show. If the show failed, it would impact a lot of people, from the director all the way down to Todd.

I was just about to remind him about that when he asked, "Where were you hiding?"

"Behind a barrel. That's beside the point. The point is Maria has it in for Bailey, and we have to do something about it."

"We? We don't have to do anything."

I stared at him. "You're not going to help me?"

"Geez, don't give me those Amish puppy dog eyes, I can't withstand their power."

I folded my arms and waited, back on familiar turf with his teasing.

He sighed. "Yes, I will help you."

"*Gut.*"

Chapter Twelve

"Can you tell me more of what Maria said?" Todd asked.

I nodded. "She said something about being passed over so Bailey could have her show. Not those exact words, but that was the gist."

He touched his chin. "I'm not surprised that she said that. Maria is mad at the world. She thinks everyone owes her something."

"Was she supposed to have her own show? Did Bailey's show ruin it?"

"The way that she tells it, yes, but that doesn't make it true. I don't know if anyone believed that she was supposed to have her own baking show. She has been working at Gourmet Television for five years and is still a page. If she was any good, don't you think that she would have been promoted to something else by now?"

My brow wrinkled. "Baking show?"

He nodded. "She claimed that she was promised a cookie-baking show, but then when Linc came back from Ohio all fired up about Bailey and her Amish candies, Maria says she was told that there wasn't enough room on the network for two new shows about sweets. She believes Bailey was picked ahead of her because of the Amish angle. People enjoy thinking about simpler ways of doing things. That's very trendy right now." He rolled his eyes.

"Trendy?" I asked.

"In, hip, cool."

I just nodded as if I knew what he was talking about. I didn't. I held out my hand. "Give me that container. I want to take it back and give it to Bailey."

"No," he said.

My brow wrinkled even more.

"I'm not up to something," he said with a smile. "I thought the Amish are far more trusting than you seem to be."

"There is nothing in our faith that says we have to be trusting of people we do not know. Instead, we are always to be a little wary of the outside world."

"Well, you don't have to be wary of me, Charlotte. I would just like to carry the container because I don't want you to get any more sneezing powder on you. It's the gentlemanly thing to do."

I frowned. "I don't mind carrying it."

"And neither do I," he said. "Let's go back to the set. That other camera should be here by now." He walked around me and down the hallway.

Short of tackling him, I didn't know how I would be able to get the container from his hands, and I hadn't tackled anyone since I'd knocked down my older brother when I was eleven after he burned some of my sheet music back on the farm. My *daed* had not been pleased with me then. He still wasn't, to be honest.

I followed Todd down the hallway and walked past the show with the male chef. I held my breath as I walked by so I wouldn't make a noise. I didn't want that director to shout at me again. When we were safely past the Mexican chef, we arrived back on Bailey's set. Bailey was there along with everyone on the production team.

"There you are, Charlotte," Bailey said. "I was getting worried."

I noted that her makeup was all back in place. Clearly the makeup artist had gotten ahold of her. Her eyes were still slightly red from the sneezing powder, but it wasn't too noticeable.

"Where have you been?" Bailey asked.

I looked around the room at all the people there. Bailey, Cass, Linc, Raymond, Juliet, Jethro, Todd, Teven, and Maria all watched me. I licked my lips. "I've been solving a crime."

Juliet, who was holding an ice pack to Jethro's head, gasped.

The pig didn't seem to mind the ice pack. At least he didn't pull away from it as I would expect, but I supposed that he trusted Juliet implicitly. As far as pig life goes, Juliet gave him a good one. I didn't know of another pig on the planet that had an agent or flew on a private plane. However, knowing the odd ways of the *Englischers*, I would guess there were more.

"What has happened?" Juliet asked in her most dramatic voice.

I wasn't used to so many people waiting for me to say something important. It wasn't the Amish way for a young woman to command a room like this. A small part of me liked it. I scanned all the faces in the room. "Someone here has been tampering with the set with the intention of destroying the show."

"Listen, you Amish girl, I don't know who you think you are, but you can't come in here and make those kind of accusations," Raymond said. He rubbed his forehead. "How can this possibly get any worse?"

"No," Linc said. "I want to hear what she has to say because many odd things have been happening on this set. Don't think that I haven't noticed."

"Everyone has noticed," Bailey said. "But Charlotte was the first one to realize that these events might actually be intentional." She looked to me. "What did you learn, Charlotte?"

I swallowed hard. Now, they really were all staring at me. I couldn't lose my nerve at this point. I was glad that I was Amish at the moment because my long skirt hid the fact that my knees were knocking together from fear. I had never spoken out in such a public way before, and now I wondered if I really did know what was happening on the set of *Bailey's Amish Sweets*. What if I was wrong and I was about to accuse an innocent person?

Maria glared at me.

Then again, I was pretty sure I was right.

I took a deep breath. "Maria has been causing problems on the set."

"Excuse me?" Maria screeched and took a step toward me with her hands up.

Cass jumped in front of me as if she was going to protect me. Maria stopped. Cass was small but fierce. I wouldn't want her glaring at me like that either. "Let Charlotte say her piece. I know her. She wouldn't speak unless she is certain about what she has learned."

"Right," I whispered back.

I stepped around Cass, and now they were surrounding me in a circle. There were friendly faces there: Cass, Bailey, Juliet, and I supposed even Jethro, but I never felt so different, so Amish, in all my life. Who was I to stand up to this *Englischer*?

"If you have something to say, pilgrim, say it," Maria snapped.

"Who are you calling a pilgrim?" Bailey put her hands on her hips and glared at Maria.

"Don't get me started on you, chocolate girl," Maria scoffed. "You're the root of all the trouble here."

Bailey looked like she was about to say something very unkind, but Cass pushed up the sleeves on her black sweater. "You want to go? Because I'm ready."

Linc put his fingers in his mouth and whistled. "Stop. Everyone, stop right now." He turned to me. "Charlotte, the claims you are making are very inflammatory. Do you have proof to back any of this up? We can't believe that Maria did anything wrong just on your say-so." He glanced at Maria. "I want this discussion to be fair to all parties involved."

I nodded. "Three strange things happened on this set to halt production. The explosion, of course, was the scariest. Thank goodness no one was hurt. I believe Maria was very lucky that no one was hurt, or everything could have been so much worse."

Cass nodded. "If that had happened, we would be calling the police right now."

I shivered at the very thought, and then I took a breath to continue. I had to get everything I wanted to say out before I lost my nerve. "Then, it was Jethro getting loose in the park because he was scared by a loud horn, and finally there was Bailey's sneezing fit. I believe that all of these accidents were staged and planned by the same person. It wasn't until the sneezing powder incident that I was sure."

"What sneezing powder?" Linc asked.

"Why would anyone want to do that to poor Bailey?" Juliet set Jethro on the floor, and the pig settled back on his haunches. He cocked his head as if he was listening as closely to what I had to say as the rest of them.

I turned to Todd, who was on the very edge of the set with his hands in his pockets. "Todd, where's the pretzel container?"

He shrugged. "I don't know what you're talking about."

I stared at him for a long moment. "Yes, you do. The container that you took from me in the hallway."

"I didn't take any container from you." He was looking at the floor and refused to meet my eyes.

I swallowed hard. "You were with me right after I found it, and you took it from my hand. You said you would keep it safe."

Everyone in the room was staring at us at this point. Todd shrugged. "I don't know what she's talking about. It must be something lost in translation since she's Amish and all."

A painful pang hit me in the chest. Why was he acting this way? I thought he was my friend.

Bailey stepped forward with her fists on her hips. "If Charlotte said that you took the container, then you did. She doesn't lie."

I took a breath. "It doesn't matter. There was sneezing powder in the pretzel container that caused Bailey to sneeze, which scared Jethro, who then ran into the camera. Of course Maria couldn't have known when she put the sneezing powder in the can that the camera would break, but she at least knew that she would make Bailey look bad once again, and since this was the third time, maybe it would be just enough to get Bailey's show canceled and hers picked up."

"Charlotte, Maria doesn't have a show," Linc said.

"But she wants one," I replied. "Very badly, badly enough to ruin Bailey's."

"Everyone knows that she wants one," Raymond said. "Everyone working in TV wants their own show someday. It's one of the biggest reasons that people go into this business."

"You lying little..." Maria held out her arms as if she was about to grab me by the throat.

Cass stepped into her path. "You might what to rethink whatever you are about to do or say next."

"She doesn't know what she's talking about," Maria cried. "Yes, there is someone tampering with the set, but it wasn't me. It was Raymond!" She pointed at the director with a metallic fingernail.

The director's face turned the same impressive shade of red that it had earlier. I hoped he wouldn't pass out.

Chapter Thirteen

"You have a lot of nerve to throw accusations like that around, little girl. I could ruin you in this business," Raymond said with so much venom that it made me inch back.

The moment he said that last sentence, I knew that he had been the man who'd been arguing with Maria in the hallway, and I began to doubt myself. What if Maria was telling the truth?

"You were in the hallway with Maria," I said with far more courage than I felt. "You threatened her then just like you are now, and she told you that she would tell everyone your secret. *You* tampered with the set?"

Maria folded her arms and smiled. "That's exactly what happened, and I do have proof. He was the one who scared the pig at the park, by blowing a toy horn he had in his coat pocket. I saw him do it on purpose. It didn't take me much time after that to put two and two together, and he was the one behind the explosion as well. He wants to get out of this job just as much as I do. Isn't that right, Raymond? But your contract won't let you as long as you have a show on the network. The only way to get out of your contract is to make sure the show tanks before it even gets out of the gate."

Incredibly, his face turned even redder; it was closer to purple now. "Todd created the explosion."

Now everyone in the room swung in the direction of the male page.

Todd shook his head. "He's crazy. Raymond has finally lost his mind. I knew that it would happen eventually. He's complete nuts, driven crazy by filming too many antacid commercials."

"You would turn on me?" Raymond snarled and then looked at the rest of us. "It wasn't me! It was Todd!" He pointed at the young page. His whole body shook with anger.

"What is this, accuse-the-next-closest-person day?" Cass asked. She held up her hands as if in surrender. "Because I didn't do anything. I'm saying that now before anyone points the finger at me. I thought the world of cooking was crazy, but you TV people take the cake."

"You paid me to do it," Todd said to Raymond.

"I never told you to blow anything up. Someone might have been killed!" the director screeched.

Maria pointed at Raymond. "See! He confessed!"

"I just told the kid to make a disturbance to stop the filming. I never told him to blow anything up. I would never be so stupid. No one can follow directions anymore. I asked him to do one small favor, and he completely screwed it up."

Todd opened and closed his mouth. "I did what you told me to do."

"You did it wrong!" Raymond snapped. "And now you will probably go to prison for endangering lives."

Todd gasped, and then he spun on his heel and ran from the set. Jethro wandered away from Juliet's side at the same time and walked directly into the page's path. Todd was going too quickly to change his course and fell over the pig with a yelp.

Jethro gave a high-pitched squeal, and everyone froze.

Todd started to scramble to regain his feet, but Linc put a foot on his back, pinning him in place.

Juliet scooped up the pig. "Oh, are you hurt?" she cooed to Jethro. To the rest of us, she yelled, "Ice! I need more ice. I need more ice for Jethro."

The pig looked fine from what I could tell, and everyone else was staring at Todd lying spread-eagled on the floor with Linc's foot in the middle of his back.

"I want someone to tell me what is going on," Linc said, looking up from his foot.

"From what I gather," Bailey said, "Raymond asked Todd to play pranks on the set so that the show's production could be shut down, and he paid Todd. Isn't that right, Todd?"

Todd lifted his chin just far enough off the concrete floor to nod.

Bailey nodded too. "Todd took it a little too far by tampering with the knobs on the burner and by scoring the glass bowl in the double boiler, thereby causing the explosion. Raymond didn't want anything to happen that might hurt another person. However, he wanted whatever it was to be big enough to cancel the show because he wanted out of his contract with the network so he could do other things. At some point, Maria caught on to what was happening and wanted to blackmail Raymond into giving her a show of her own. She didn't stop the pranks because she wanted my show to be canceled too. Charlotte noticed her odd behavior and the fact that Maria was always around when something odd was going on and jumped to the conclusion that Maria must be the culprit." Bailey folded her arms and rocked back on her heels. "How's that for a summary?"

"That's just about right," Todd said from the floor. "Can I get up now? I promise that I won't run away."

Linc removed his foot.

Todd struggled to his feet. "I don't want to go to prison."

Linc glared at him. "We aren't calling the police. The network wouldn't want the bad publicity, but you will pay for the damages from the explosion out of your next paycheck."

"That would take my entire check."

"Probably more than that. But it seems to me more than fair." He paused. "And you are also fired." He pointed at Todd, Maria, and Raymond in turn. "You are all fired."

"You can't fire me!" Maria shouted. "I didn't do anything wrong."

"Yes, she did," Todd shouted. "She was the one who put the sneezing powder in the pretzel container. I never would have done that."

Maria glared at him. "No, that's right, you would just try to blow the entire set up!"

"You should have come forward when you knew something was amiss with Todd and Raymond instead of planning a prank of your own," Linc said to Maria. "You are fired like the other two, and I wouldn't use me for a reference if I were you."

"But I was supposed to get my own show! I was promised my own show," Maria cried.

"No one promised you anything," Linc countered, and he turned to Raymond. "And you have gotten what you wanted. You're free from your contract, but I believe by breaking it in such a way, your forfeit your pay. I wouldn't use me or anyone at Gourmet Television as a reference either."

"You can't do that!" Raymond bellowed.

"I can, and if you have read your contract, you know I'm right, which is why I think that you went to such great lengths to get out of it."

Raymond looked in every direction. "What choice did I have? I need to get out of this contract, and the only way to do that was for the show to fail." He wrinkled his nose. "Bailey was a no-name. No one would be surprised if she cracked under the pressure of TV. It's broken tougher people before."

Bailey put her hands on her hips. "I'm tougher than you think."

"She's not kidding," Juliet said as she held Jethro close to her chest. "Bailey has chased down killers."

"Why didn't you just ask to get out of your contract?" Bailey asked. "I'm sure there are a bunch of new directors who would like a chance to work for Gourmet Television."

"I did." He shook with anger. "But Linc and the network wanted to keep me locked in out of spite. They don't want me to leave the network and follow my passion. They are stifling me."

Linc folded his arms. "We're not stifling you anymore—I want you out of here in the next hour. If you don't leave on your own, I will have security escort you out. You have wasted the network's time and money. You'll never work in food television again."

"Good! Because that's not what I want to do! I'm better than your piddly little cooking shows. I have bigger dreams than watching someone bake all day long."

A security guard walked onto the set.

"Did you call him here?" Raymond asked Linc accusingly.

"Of course I did. I texted him to come up. I can't have you or your accomplices tampering with any more of my set." Linc turned to the guard. "Will you be so kind to usher Raymond and his accomplices out."

The guard reached for Todd's arm.

Todd jumped away from him. "I was just doing what I was told. I have to follow his orders. He's the director. What choice did I have?"

"And I'm the producer." Linc rose to his full height, which was still five inches or more shorter than Todd. "That means I outrank him and what I say goes. You should have come to me, but whatever money he bribed you with was just too enticing, wasn't it? You're all fired. I want you out of this building." He nodded at the guard.

I watched as the guard grabbed Todd by the arm and started to pull him toward the door. With his other hand he grabbed Raymond's arm. "Don't touch me. You have no right to touch me. I will go on my accord. I don't want to be here anyway." He laughed. "See? In the end I got my way and got out of my contract, so I'm really coming out the winner in all of this."

Todd stared at me as he walked by, but I couldn't meet his eyes. How could I have been so naïve and trusting of him? He was behind this all along. He had never wanted to help me. He had wanted to keep it all a secret.

"I'll show myself out," Maria said. "I don't need a guard to guide me to the door."

Linc nodded, and the guard led Todd and Raymond from the room.

Maria walked over to me and stopped. She studied me. "I was passed over so that Bailey could have this show, and it was hard for me. Television is a tough business. The network was looking for a new face to take it in a new direction, and Bailey is a beautiful and well-spoken young woman. She was a perfect fit. I could see that as well as anyone. I was jealous. I wanted my chance and felt that she stole it from me." She forced a laugh. "I guess everything backfired terribly since I have lost my job and have no chance of having my own show on Gourmet Television now." She looked like she was about to cry. "I'm sorry."

"You should apologize to Bailey, not to me."

"I plan to do that." She studied me. "Bailey is lucky, you know?"

"Because she got this show?" I asked.

She shook her head. "She's lucky to have a friend like you, who will fight so hard to protect her and look out for her."

I watched Bailey across the room. She was holding Jethro and speaking with Linc as if talking to the television producer while holding a pig was the most natural thing in the world to do. Jethro was still in the room, but I had no idea where Juliet had gone to. Both she and Cass were gone, probably hatching plans to make Jethro a star. I didn't think a few pranks would stop Juliet in her quest for pig fame.

Bailey smiled at me from across the room.

I turned back to Maria. "I'm lucky to have a friend like her. I was just repaying for a kindness she did for me some time back."

"I don't think she expected anything in return for that kindness she did." Maria glanced at Bailey. "She did it for you because she was your friend."

I nodded. "She is that."

Epilogue

There was just one week left of filming and then Bailey and I were flying back home to Ohio. I was looking forward to returning to my familiar life in Harvest. At least I was for the most part. I knew the time was coming for me to decide whether or not to join the Amish church or become an *Englischer.* I was over twenty and far too old to be straddling the fence for so long. I knew the bishop in Cousin Clara's district was eager for me to make up my mind. It would be the hardest choice I would ever have to make, but I couldn't avoid it forever.

Bailey and I would be flying home alone. Juliet and Jethro had already gone home weeks ago. Bailey and I were in Cass's tiny apartment kitchen making a pizza. Bailey was teaching me how to make a proper New York-style pizza.

"Guys! It's on!" Cass called from her living room.

I dropped the mushroom I was holding on the cutting board and ran with Bailey into the living room just in time to see Bailey's short Easter demo of making birds' nests come up on the screen.

"Easter candies don't have to be hard," the Bailey on the television said. "One of my favorite things to make this season is birds' nests. I used to make them with my grandfather when I would visit him in Amish country over Easter. It's a great project to introduce children to the craft of candy making."

I stared at myself on the screen and was impressed that I seemed calm as I stood with Jethro and handed Bailey the ingredients she needed. Jethro, too, behaved perfectly. This take that made live television was much different from the one when Bailey was accosted with sneezing powder.

Bailey held up a plate of the candy birds' nests. "And it's as easy as that. I hope you will tune into *Bailey's Amish Sweets* later this year. See you in the summer!"

The screen faded into a commercial.

Cass picked up the remote and turned off the television. "That was perfect, Bai. You nailed it just like I knew you would."

"I'm just glad it's almost over. I'm ready to go home."

"And see Hot Cop?" Cass asked.

Bailey rolled her eyes.

Cass cocked her head and looked at me. "You know, Charlotte, you were a natural on camera. You might have a future in show business. If you ever think about going that route, I could help you just like I have helped Bailey and Jethro. Look how far they've come. Jethro might even be the product mascot for a pet clothing line. Nothing is set in stone there. We are in negotiations." She studied me more closely. "I see a lot of potential for you, Charlotte. We could work the Amish angle. There's something there that resonates with people."

"Cass, no," Bailey said, shaking her head. "Leave Charlotte out of your agenting schemes."

"What schemes?" Cass asked innocently.

Bailey and I groaned.

Botched Butterscotch

Chapter One

I buzzed about the front room of Swissmen Sweets, the candy shop in Harvest, Ohio, that I ran with my Amish grandmother, Clara King. As I scurried about, I hit every flat surface that I could reach with a feather duster. I dusted the maple shelves that held the glass jars of jelly beans, lemon drops, licorice, and hard candy, all of which were made in this very shop. I stopped just short of dusting the shop cat, Nutmeg, a little orange striped feline who watched my feather duster with studied interest.

"Bailey," my grandmother said from behind the half-domed glass counter where we displayed our most enticing treats: molded chocolate creations, truffles, and fudge all had a place of honor behind the glass. At the moment, my grandmother was sliding a tray of butterscotch peanut bars into the case. "You must calm down, *kind*. You are making us all dizzy." After the tray was in place, she patted the prayer cap on the back of her head. "Your parents will be here any moment. The shop is as clean as it's ever been. There is nothing more you can do."

"Cousin Clara is right," said Charlotte Weaver, our young Amish shop assistant and my cousin. She put away the bottle of vinegar water she'd been using to clean the counter. "You are making me nervous."

"I know I'm wound a little tight. I just can't believe that Mom and Dad are actually coming to Harvest today. I thought they never would again." I stepped behind the counter and stowed the feather duster in the cabinet below the cash register with the other cleaning supplies. As I moved, my dangly silver earrings knocked against my cheeks. Being the only non-Amish person in Swissmen Sweets, I was also the only one wearing any type of jewelry. I have always been partial to dangly earrings.

I never thought my parents would return to Swissmen Sweets because my father ran away from Harvest when he was a young man. He left the Amish community and Ohio so that he could marry my mother. When I was a child, they came back once a year so my grandparents could see me, but once I was an adult my parents stopped those visits. I didn't think they had been in Ohio in over ten years, except for a very brief trip to attend my grandfather's funeral. My nerves were heightened by the fact that my parents did not approve of my decision to leave my job as a prestigious New York City chocolatier to move to Amish Country. I suspected in their eyes I'd gone backward, since I'd settled in the place they'd fled when they were young.

I straightened up and ran my damp palms over my jeans. *Maami* was right. I needed to get a grip. I calmed down just as the front door opened and my mother and father walked in. Dad looked like any other suburban New England father. He wore chinos, loafers, and a light blue Polo shirt—Polo with a big P—and his gray hair was combed back from his face. A pair of sunglasses sat in the breast pocket of his shirt. He was clean shaven. Looking at him, you would never know that he spent the first twenty years of his life in the Plain community.

My mother, on the other hand, had not grown up Amish. She was originally from Holmes County too, but from an English family in the county seat of Millersburg. She wore a long, flowered sundress and short-sleeved cardigan, and I thought the best evidence that she'd never been Amish was the flower tattoo on the inside of her right arm. It was something she got as a teenager when she wanted to assert herself, or so she'd told me when I wanted one as a child. Tattoos were forbidden in the Amish world, and I always suspected, having grown up in Holmes County, the tattoo was my mother's way of stating her Englishness.

My mother's parents passed away before I was born. They were farmers, and she didn't want that for herself or her husband. When she and my father fell in love, he left his Amish district and they ran away to New England. He went to college on a scholarship and got a corporate job, and my mother delved into her first love: painting. She sold her New England landscapes in gift shops around the region.

When I was old enough, my parents would leave me in Holmes County for the entire summer. This gave them time to travel and see the world without a child tagging along behind them. During those weeks and months when I was alone with my Amish grandparents, I fell in love with chocolate. I know people say all the time that they love chocolate, but I *really* did, and do to this day. At five I asked my grandfather to teach me the art of candy making, and I never looked back. However, I can't say my parents were pleased with my dream.

I refused to go to college and instead enrolled in culinary school with an emphasis on chocolate and desserts. It was my goal to be a world-renowned New York chocolatier, and I almost made it. I was days away from being promoted to head chocolatier at JP Chocolates, where I had been the protégé of owner Jean Pierre Ruge for six years—until I walked away from it all to move to Harvest and help my grandmother at Swissmen Sweets after my grandfather's death.

I knew it was the very last place on Earth my parents wanted me to land. Mom and Dad thought I had thrown away my career by leaving New York, but I felt differently. In New York, I was a workaholic. Everything about my life was related to my work, but in Harvest I could be a new person. I could have a life outside of candy that included friends, a boyfriend, and a bit of sleuthing too.

However, I wondered if my parents' opinion would change soon. In two months, my cable television show, Bailey's Amish Sweets, would air on Gourmet Television. I had been going back and forth between Harvest and New York City for months to shoot the show and publicize its debut. Maybe when my parents saw that I could succeed in both worlds, Harvest and New York City, they would believe that I'd made the right choice. Then again, there were no guarantees when it came to television.

"This place has not changed a bit," my mother, Susan King, said the moment she stepped into the shop. "I swear I just traveled back in time. Though I always feel like that when we come back." She shook her head. "I don't know why I expect Holmes County to change."

My father, Silas, was far less vocal than my mother. "It is nice to see the old shop."

Swissmen Sweets was more than just a shop to my father: it was his childhood home. He and my grandparents had lived in the apartment above the shop when he was a child. Charlotte and my grandmother lived there now.

I stepped out from behind the counter just in time for my mother to envelop me in a hug. "Bailey!" She smelled like roses and sunscreen, and it reminded me of childhood weekends along the shore. "I'm so glad we are finally here. I thought we would never make it. It's so easy to forget how out of the way Harvest is. It was cow after cow on the drive here. Isn't that true, Silas?"

My father smiled at my mother. "It's true. But we haven't really been away from Harvest long enough for you to forget about the cows, my dear. We were here last year."

There was a quiet moment when everyone realized this was when they'd come for *Daadi's* funeral.

"I suppose not," she said, passing over the unsaid words. "It's so nice to see you too, Clara."

My grandmother smiled and gave each of my parents a hug. "We are glad you came. It will be a very special weekend for us all." She turned to gesture to Charlotte. "And I don't think you have met our cousin, Charlotte."

Dad shook his head. "That's the thing about being Amish. There are cousins I never knew all over the county."

Charlotte blushed so red her face was almost the color of her hair.

Mom smoothed her dark hair, the same color as mine, over her shoulder. "I'm just so happy to spend Mother's Day weekend with my girl." She turned to me. "What do you have planned, Bailey?"

I frowned. I should have realized that my mother would want an agenda. Mom was what I would call a "super planner." Grocery lists were organized by the layout of the supermarket, and family vacations were run like military ops. She wasn't the free spirit her tattoo would suggest. "Well," I began. "Tomorrow there's a tea—"

Before I could finish my thought, the door opened again, and this time Juliet Brody and her polka-dotted potbellied pig Jethro tootled into the candy shop. Once Jethro was inside, he made a beeline for Nutmeg, and the cat and pig bumped noses.

Dad stared at the animals. "Do they know each other?"

"Oh yes," *Maami* said. "They know each other quite well."

"Jethro," Juliet said. "Don't be so rude. Come back here! We're here to meet Bailey's parents. You can visit with Nutmeg another time." She pulled lightly on the pink polka-dotted nylon leash tethered to Jethro's collar. The leash matched her skirt, which was also pink polka dot, and she'd paired it with a white sweater. To say that Juliet loved polka dots was a grave understatement. This was becoming more and more apparent to me as her wedding to Reverend Brook drew near. I was to be her maid of honor, and every swatch of cloth and piece of stationery I saw had polka dots on it.

The pig didn't budge at Juliet's tug. I wasn't the least bit surprised. Jethro was the most stubborn animal I had ever met, and I had a pet rabbit named Puff who ate my slippers. Jethro caused more trouble, and sixty percent of the time it was on purpose.

My mother put a hand on her chest. "You brought a pig into Swissmen Sweets?"

Juliet bent over and scooped Jethro up off the ground. "Of course I did. This is my comfort animal, Jethro. He goes everywhere I go. I can't imagine life without him; I need him with me. He keeps me calm, especially now that I'm trying to plan my wedding."

Mom wrinkled her nose. "But you're inside a candy shop." She paused. "With a pig. Is it sanitary to have a pig inside the candy shop? What if the health inspector decided to drop in?"

Juliet frowned. "The health inspector would understand. I have to have Jethro with me at all times. I have a note from my therapist, if you would like to see it."

"That's not necessary," Mom said, and peered down at Jethro as if he were a bug under a microscope.

The little pig looked up at her and cocked his head.

Mom gasped. "It's almost like he understands we're talking about him."

"He does," Juliet said. "You know pigs are very intelligent, on the same level as dolphins, some say."

I glanced down at Jethro. As much as I loved him, he was no dolphin.

The door opened again. This was the third time in ten minutes, and not a paying customer among them. Sheriff Deputy Aiden Brody stepped into Swissmen Sweets and scanned the room with his chocolate brown eyes like he always did when entering a building. Years of being a deputy had taught him to take everything in before letting his guard down even a little.

My heart gave a flutter when he made eye contact with me and smiled.

"Did someone call the police about the pig already?" my mother asked.

I thought it was best to ignore her question. "Mom, Dad, this is Aiden." I stopped short of saying "my boyfriend," although Aiden and I had been dating for several months. Instead, I said, "He's Juliet's son."

"So this is Aiden. Can I give you a hug?" My mother wrapped her arms around him before he could answer. Mom pulled back. "Bailey has told us a little bit about you, so we know that you're important to her. She's very closed-mouthed about her personal life. The last time she had a boyfriend, we didn't learn about him until we read it in the papers."

I felt my face redden. I didn't want to be reminded—or have Aiden be reminded—of my failed relationship with a celebrity pastry chef back in New York.

"He seems so much more stable than your last boyfriend. Not that I met the last one, but based on the articles," my mother said in a stage whisper, and I wondered what it would take for the floor to open up and swallow me. I was open to the possibility. It seemed a whole lot better than standing there, watching my mother assess Aiden's worth as my boyfriend.

Juliet clapped her hands. "Aiden, I just knew you would come over to meet Bailey's parents. Now that we are all together, we can start making plans." Juliet took my mother's hand. "I am so excited to finally discuss the wedding."

"Your wedding?" my mother asked, looking down at Juliet's firm grasp on her fingers.

"Oh no. I do love talking about my wedding—I would talk to you about it all day and night if you let me." She beamed. "But in this case, I'm speaking of the union of our two families."

"What's that?" my father asked.

I shot Aiden a panicked look.

"Mother," Aiden interrupted. "I think it would be much better for us to spend this weekend celebrating you mothers and all that you do for us. That's what Mother's Day is about."

Juliet patted his cheek. "You are the finest and kindest son." She dropped her hand and beamed at my parents. "He has always put my happiness first. That's why I need to think about his."

Dad folded his arms. "What is going on? What is this about a wedding?"

"Juliet is getting married on the weekend of July Fourth. It is going to be a great event. Aiden is best man, and I'm maid of honor. Jethro will be the ring bearer," I said, hoping that if I overwhelmed them with information about Juliet's wedding, they would forget any mention of another wedding—namely a wedding involving Aiden and me as groom and bride. We weren't even engaged.

"A pig as a ring bearer?" my mother asked in a tone that implied she had now heard everything.

"Yes, it will be such a special moment." Juliet wrapped her hands around Jethro's leash. "Reverend Brook was hesitant at first, but when I told him that Bailey would walk Jethro down the aisle, he was on board."

My mother stared at Juliet as if she had a unicorn horn in the middle of her forehead.

Juliet laughed. "But we should really stop talking about my wedding and speak about the wedding between—"

The candy shop door opened for a fourth time, and I was never so happy to have a conversation interrupted. Over the next three days I would have to do my very best to keep Juliet away from my mother, so that she didn't plant the idea of my nonexistent wedding in my parents' heads.

"You should start selling tickets to get in here," Charlotte whispered.

"No kidding," I muttered back.

The next person to walk through the door to Swissmen Sweets was none other than community leader and super organizer Margot Rawlings. Margot was a woman in her late sixties, with short curls on the top of her head and a walk that would instill fear into anyone trying to run away from her. There was just something about the way Margot marched that told you there was no real escape. You might slip away from her once, maybe twice, but if she had you in her sights, she would eventually track you down. I had never met anyone with more determination, and I'd lived most of my adult life in New York City.

"Bailey. Just the woman I wanted to talk to." Her tractor-beam gaze was locked and ready to pull me in. I had no idea what I was in for now.

Chapter Two

Margot folded her arms and took stock of the shop's front room. "Busy today."

"My parents are visiting from New England," I said.

Margot nodded at them. "It's nice to meet you both." Then she turned back to me, and I couldn't help but smile. No one distracted Margot from her mission.

"I'm glad to find you in the candy shop—you aren't always here." She laughed. "You seem to find a way to travel all over the village, and even the county, but since no one has been murdered, I should have known you would be here."

"Murdered? What's that?" my father yelped.

Margot went on as if he'd said nothing at all. "We must talk about tomorrow's event."

"Swissmen Sweets is more than ready, Margot. Were there any last-minute special requests?" I asked, hoping there weren't.

"I wanted to make sure you remembered what time to be at the church tomorrow for the Mother's Day Tea." She looked at her watch as if to make a point about timeliness.

I sighed. That was just like Margot. She made a house call when a simple text would have sufficed—but then again, I had never received a text from Margot. She much preferred her communications face-to-face so she could bully the other party into doing exactly what she wanted. Margot would not let her plans be disrupted by an easily ignored text message. Smart woman, I suppose.

"Yes," I said. "I'll be there at two thirty, just like you asked. Charlotte and I have already made most of the treats; they're in the kitchen."

"Good, good. The tea will start at three thirty, but I know some of the ladies will get there early because they will want a good spot." Margot shook her head.

"There's a Mother's Day tea?" my mother asked. "Bailey, why didn't you mention this before? Am I going to the tea? I am your mother."

"I was just about to tell you before everyone arrived. I got tickets for you, *Maami*, Charlotte, and me. I will be up and down, since I'll be serving."

"Pishposh," Margot said. "You act like all I want you to do is work and have no fun."

No comment.

"You can sit with your mother at the tea," Margot insisted. "This is what these events are about, bringing women together to help other women." She turned to my mother. "I'm very glad you will be there. It's all for a good cause."

My mother frowned. "What cause is that?"

Margot clicked her tongue. "Bailey, have you told your parents nothing at all about what happens in the village?"

"They just got here, so—"

"The tea is a fundraiser. Tickets are selling for thirty dollars each. I know that seems expensive, but all the money will go directly to help the women at Abigail's Farm."

"What is Abigail's Farm?" Dad asked.

Margot stood up a little taller. She loved to speak about her events. "It's a retreat for women who are struggling with drug or alcohol addiction. They go to the farm for rest and rehab, and they learn to farm while they're at it. Working with their hands and caring for animals can be a real godsend while they rebuild their lives. These women have already been through traditional drug addiction treatment. Abigail's Farm is a place they can go when they feel they need a little more time before restarting their lives. Many women with substance abuse problems come from families with a history of drug and alcohol addiction, or they've suffered some other form of abuse that made them turn to drugs and alcohol to cope. For these women, reentering the world can be frightening. Places like Abigail's Farm can ease them back in."

"It sounds like a great organization," my mother said.

Margot nodded. "It is. They do wonderful things. But the farm is struggling financially. The women attend at little cost, and the farm is not affiliated with any government agency that might subsidize it. We hope this tea will not only raise money for Abigail's Farm, but also raise

awareness. The farm needs to find bigger donors. At least that's what I
keep telling Polly Anne."

"Who is Polly Anne?" Dad asked.

"Polly Anne Lind is the kindest woman," Juliet said. "She's the person
behind Abigail's Farm. She really has a heart of gold, even after everything
she's been through. I admire all she's done. I know many ladies from the
church will be there to show their support. Reverend Brook reminded
them last Sunday. He's such a big-hearted man, and he wanted the ladies
to know that it was essential our church members show up, especially
since the event is being held in our building." She sighed happily as she
thought of her husband-to-be.

Margot nodded. "Polly Anne is a good person. However, she doesn't
have much business sense, and even a nonprofit such as Abigail's Farm must
run like a business. That's where I come in. I'm on the board, and I want
to see the farm flourish so that it can help as many women as possible."

Maami cocked her head. "You seem to be on the board of just about
everything in this village."

Margot nodded. "It does feel that way at times. I just run from meeting
to meeting. Right now, I am headed home to put my feet up for a bit. Juliet,
will my volunteers be able to get into the church tonight? We plan to be
there about seven. I want everything set up tonight to avoid confusion
in the morning."

"Of course," Juliet said. "I will be there to help too. Reverend Brook
is happy that our fellowship hall is being used for such a wonderful event.
This will be a memorable Mother's Day weekend, to be sure."

I didn't doubt that for a moment as I looked around, from Aiden to
his mother, my parents, *Maami*, Charlotte, and Margot. I felt like I was
in some kind of alternate universe, seeing them all in the same place
at the same time.

"And Bailey, everything is ready on your end?" Margot always double-
checked. She never left anything to chance.

I nodded. "We have the sweets covered. Do not worry about that."

Margot made a check mark on her clipboard. "Good, good. We have
the tea and finger sandwiches handled by the ladies at the church." She
looked at Juliet for confirmation.

Juliet nodded. "Yes, the ladies will put everything in the church
fridge this afternoon. They're working on the sandwiches and finger
foods as we speak."

Margot made another check mark on her clipboard. "Excellent. It seems that we are all set. What could possibly go wrong?"

I really hated that she'd said that. In my experience, something always went wrong, and terribly wrong at that.

Chapter Three

The next afternoon, I rolled the wagon that I had filled with candy and other sweets across the green. Charlotte asked me if I needed her help setting up, but I told her to stay back at Swissmen Sweets until it was time for her and *Maami* to come over for the event. She would be much more of a help there, to my grandmother. It was the day before Mother's Day, one of the busiest days of the year for our shop. Men and children always stumbled inside hoping to find a last-minute treat for their wives and mothers. For the last hour and a half of the day, our other assistant, Emily Keim, would manage the shop while *Maami*, Charlotte, and I were at the tea.

By the time I crossed the street with my wagon, I was exhausted. I had spent all morning wandering around the county with my parents so they could visit all of their favorite childhood haunts. I really didn't know why I had to go on that excursion, but my mother seemed bound and determined to cram in as much mother–daughter time as possible. Even though I would've preferred to take them to a nice breakfast or let them sleep late and relax a bit, I was glad to spend time with them. Besides, I shouldn't have been surprised by my mother's itinerary—she'd always been a woman on the go. Their flight back to Connecticut was very early Monday morning. As much as I loved my parents, I was already looking forward to it.

The one advantage of being with my parents all day was I had been able to keep them away from Juliet, who still seemed set on having a heart-to-heart with my mother about getting Aiden and I hitched as soon as possible. However, I knew that both of them would be at the tea, and since I would be busy with the desserts, there wasn't much I could do to keep them separated.

The square was quiet, which was unusual for a holiday weekend. There were a few families picnicking and a man walking his dog. Margot loved to host big events on the square around any and every holiday, no matter how minor. She had plans for Groundhog Day, and Harvest didn't have a groundhog mascot. But knowing Margot, she'd find one.

I imagined that Margot hadn't planned an event this Saturday because of the tea for Abigail's Farm at the church. I knew she had a busy summer lined up for the entire village and, by extension, for Swissmen Sweets and me. Even without Margot's plans I would have a full docket. This summer would bring the debut of my television program, and of course, Juliet's wedding. It would be a wonder if I had enough time to breathe over the next four months. I prayed the summer would be quiet, at least, in regard to murders. I knew Aiden wanted that as well.

The rubber wheels of my wagon bumped over the curb onto the church parking lot. Instead of going through the grand purple front door at the top of the church steps, I pulled my wagon around the side of the building to the back door. On this side of the church there was another small parking lot that overlooked a cemetery that, to be honest, was quite lovely in the spring afternoon light. Because of Mother's Day, many of the graves had been decorated with floral wreaths and fresh bouquets. It made me think of my grandfather's grave. I hadn't visited it since he died, but the Amish attitude toward death was different. Just like their lives, the graves of the Amish were simple and plain. They believed the person wasn't there. What was left behind when a person died was just a shell of who they were. The Amish believed they went on to their heavenly reward after death. If anyone deserved such a reward it was my grandfather, Jebidiah King.

An old brick held open the back door to the church. I knew that the members preparing for the Mother's Day tea would be in and out of the church throughout the day. I guessed that most of them had been there working for hours. The event would be lovely and perfect, I was sure. Juliet might be a little quirky, but she did a wonderful job of involving the church in the community, and of course Margot was a force to be reckoned with.

I rolled my wagon into the small utility room. As I did, a large man pushed his way through. "Excuse me," he muttered as he forced his way past me. I was taking such care not to dump my wagon that I never got a look at his face. Within seconds, he was gone. I only caught a glimpse of his back.

I shook my head and rolled the wagon out of the utility room, down a short hallway, and into the church kitchen. I loved this kitchen. I knew my grandmother would chastise me for envying it so much, but the church kitchen was enormous and had everything a cook could possibly want, from a massive conveyor belt dishwasher to a double convection oven. Even more enticing, it had counter space for days. Any chef, baker, or cook would tell you: counter space was where it was at in the kitchen.

At the moment, much of the counter space was taken up by the church ladies, who were filling crystal plates with finger sandwiches, cut vegetables, fresh fruit, and cookies.

"My goodness," I said with a smile. "Your spread is so amazing. I'm not sure you need treats from Swissmen Sweets."

One of the ladies laughed. "We always need treats from Swissmen Sweets. I hope you saw my children over there this week, buying my favorite fudge. I count on it every Mother's Day."

I had seen the woman's children. I smiled. "A chocolatier never gives up her secrets."

The ladies chuckled.

Margot bustled into the room. "Ah, Bailey, good. You're here. I thought I heard your voice. Come out into the fellowship hall, and I will show you what I need you to do."

Margot wore a floral dress with a crinoline underneath. I blinked. I had never seen Margot in anything other than slacks or jeans. This Mother's Day tea was a special event indeed! I was happy I'd chosen to wear a dress as well. My work uniform tended toward jeans and funky tops. I suppose that was because I was surrounded by plainness all the time. Sometimes I just wanted to be around bright colors.

I waved to the ladies and wheeled my wagon out of the kitchen and into the fellowship hall. The large room, which almost ran the entire length of the church, was half hardwood flooring and half industrial carpet. The hardwood was part of an abbreviated basketball court for the youth group. At the moment, the two basketball hoops were tethered to the ceiling. Because of the size of the event, twenty-five round tables had been set up across both halves of the space. Each table could seat eight people.

The tables were covered with linen cloths, and the church had broken out the good china and silverware for the event. Bouquets of hyacinths, tulips, and daffodils decorated every table. I guessed that they'd gotten them from Edy's Greenhouse, the best nursery in the village. The scene was lovely. It made me think of the English countryside and days gone by.

"I cannot believe we sold out of tickets," said a round woman with wispy blond hair and a blue sleeveless tea dress. "It's more than I could have ever expected. The community came out, just like you promised they would."

Margot patted her skirt and it bounced right back out. She frowned as if she'd just realized the poufy crinoline was a bad idea. I could not wait to tell my friend Cass, who lived in New York but visited me in Ohio as often as she could. She'd think Margot's dress was a hoot.

"Polly Anne," Margot said. "When I make a decision to sell out an event, I sell out the event." Case closed. I suppressed a smile. I supposed a comment like that would have sounded obnoxious in the wrong context, but Margot spoke the truth. She made things happen.

Margot turned to me with her pen poised over the clipboard. "Bailey, I'm glad you got here right on time." She made a check on her clipboard. Apparently, Bailey King's arrival was check mark worthy. "I'd like you to meet Polly Anne Lind from Abigail's Farm."

I let go of my wagon handle and shook Polly Anne's hand. "It's so nice to meet you. This is going to be a lovely event. Thank you for asking Swissmen Sweets to be part of it."

Polly Anne smiled and her green eyes shone as bright as a cat's. "Thank you for doing this. The pleasure is all mine." She held my right hand in both of her own. "I can't tell you how much it means to me that you would donate your sweets and time to this cause."

"It's an honor to be a part of it. I know your work has touched so many women." I gently pulled my hand away.

She blushed. "Thank you. As of this morning, the fiftieth woman to go through our program has left with a new lease on life. Her journey will have challenges—those who struggle with substance abuse always do—but she has a good chance for success now. I rest my heart in that. It's hard to fathom all the lives that have been impacted by Abigail's Farm. It does my soul good knowing the difference that it's made for so many women. Of those fifty, there's only one that we know of who went back to using. Sadly, even though it was just the one, I consider that a failure. My prayer is that they all stay clean and win their lives back for themselves and for their families."

"Forty-nine out of fifty is quite an accomplishment," I said. "You should be proud. Therapies work differently for different people. Maybe yours didn't help that one person, but I'm sure she got something out of it. Hopefully she will find the treatment that really works for her."

"From your mouth to God's ear," Polly Anne said just above a whisper. "That would be a real blessing. I like to believe that I make an impact on each woman who comes to the farm, no matter where her life may take her next."

"I'm sure you do," I said.

"Yes, yes," Margot agreed, clearly impatient to get down to the business of party prep. "Bailey, you will learn more about Abigail's Farm during

Polly Anne's presentation, and the two of you can chat during the tea. However, now we need to get ready. We only have fifty minutes until the women start to arrive." She waved her pen in the air as if it were a wand.

I straightened my shoulders. "Where would you like the sweets? I can set up anywhere."

Margot nodded, pleased by my response. After being drafted to participate in so many of these events, I had finally learned that the best way to deal with Margot was to do it her way. I could be a good soldier for a short amount of time. I only pushed back when I really had to. By and large, her ideas were on point, even if she was a bit on the bossy side. Okay, more than just a bit. I couldn't forget the nine-foot-tall chocolate toffee bunny that she'd had me create for Harvest's Easter Days festival.

Margot waved her wand again, the movement different this time, more as if Polly Anne and I were members of her orchestra. Perhaps she viewed everyone she bossed about in that light. I wouldn't be the least bit surprised. "I have three-tiered china plates ready for your sweets. There are two on every table. Eight women per table. You brought enough that each lady can have three pieces, correct?"

I nodded. "A little more than that, actually. It's always good to have extra. If they don't eat everything, I'm sure we will have volunteers to take the remainder home."

"All right, you had better get busy." Margot checked her watch. "Forty-five minutes and counting." She bustled off toward the kitchen. I hoped the church ladies were ready for the Margot tornado coming their way.

I took a breath and stared at the tables. I was going to have to work fast to get everything done in time.

"Can I help you?" Polly Anne asked.

I wasn't sure it was right to put the guest of honor to work, but I had twenty-five round tables to fill with sweets and not nearly enough time to do it. I had waited until the very last minute to bring the treats over. I knew the volunteers would be using the refrigerators for the finger sandwiches and other food. I didn't want my candies to be in their way. If I'd brought them over too early, the chocolate would have melted. Although the fellowship hall was air conditioned, I worried about the candies being out too long in a room full of people.

I smiled at Polly Anne. "If you don't mind, that would be great. I know Margot will be fit to be tied if I'm putting candies on the tables as the women arrive."

Polly Anne smiled. "When I asked Margot to help me with the tea, I never knew how organized she was. She's...intense."

I laughed. "She is, but she cares a lot about Harvest and the people in it. She's the person to see if you need to get stuff done, so you made the right choice when you chose her as general of this operation."

"I didn't know she was taking the general post, but I am glad I picked her. She's really taken the reins, and I know this tea would not have sold out if I were trying to do it alone." She smiled. "I moved to the farm from Columbus about two years ago, and I still don't know many people. I have been so consumed with getting Abigail's Farm off the ground, and then caring for the women who come to it, I haven't had time to make many friends outside of my next-door neighbors." She clapped her hands. "But enough about that—what would you have me do? This is perfect. It will keep me busy so that I don't fret over my speech. I have written and rewritten it four times. I don't want to rework it a fifth time. If I stand idly by, I might just do that."

"Thank you again." I removed a white bakery box from the wagon. "These are truffles. Be sure to set eight at each table. When you are done with those, I can give your another box of something else."

Polly Anne smiled. "Good. Keep me busy until the ladies arrive. Busy hands keep worries at bay—that's something I tell the women at my farm. I believe that's why the farm's rehabilitation model works so well. When you are busy caring for something else, you are able to hold back self-defeating thoughts. It's not foolproof, but it helps."

I could understand Polly Anne's philosophy. Whenever I was anxious about something, I wanted to take action, even if that action had nothing to do with the problem. I needed to move before I could settle down, and throwing myself into work was the easy answer. Since coming to Harvest, I'd had to reassess what work looked like for me. I didn't work at the candy shop on Sundays. For one, my grandmother didn't allow it. She was strict about keeping the Sabbath and wanted everyone at the shop to do the same. At first, I bristled at the idea. I believed I was wasting time when I could have been cleaning the candy shop or updating the website or anything, really. It was hard for a worker bee like me to take any time off. But even more than I wanted to work, I wanted to avoid upsetting my grandmother. So I took her rule to heart.

Sundays had become my days to rest and recharge, and I was surprised to find that I was getting the same amount of work done every week regardless. Maybe there was something to this whole resting thing. I wished that I had known about it sooner—I might have been happier in New York if I had.

Polly Anne got right to work, and I decided that I would be the one to divvy up the butterscotch peanut bars my grandmother had made. Each bar was cut into a one-by-one-inch square, an easy bite for a tea party. Removing the butterscotch bars, or any soft candy, such as fudge, from a box without cutting into it or leaving a thumbprint behind was an art form I'd mastered over the six years I worked for Jean Pierre at JP Chocolates. In fact, I had been so good at removing the candy, Jean Pierre would only let me pack the fudge if a bride requested some for her wedding. It was critical at fancy New York weddings that every last detail be perfect. Thumbprints on fudge would have ruined Jean Pierre's reputation.

I wondered how Juliet's wedding would go. Something was bound to go wrong, but I doubted that it would be much more than a snafu with her dress or someone running a little late to the ceremony. Her wedding planning lists were so thorough, I couldn't imagine her forgetting a single thing. In the wedding planning department, Juliet gave Margot a run for her money.

I placed all the butterscotch bars on a platter away from the three-tiered plates and set a little card beside it noting that the treat contained peanuts. Margot loved *Maami's* butterscotch peanut bars, but I was always careful where I positioned anything with peanuts because of possible allergies. With the butterscotch peanut bars in place, I moved on to fudge. I glanced across the room and saw Polly Anne still working on her first box of truffles.

I had two kinds of fudge with me. One was the standard chocolate, because a chocolatier can't go wrong there, and the other was butterscotch fudge. It was a new addition to the fudge offerings at Swissmen Sweets, one that Emily, our other shop assistant, suggested we put on our menu because of the popularity of the butterscotch peanut bars. I was so glad we did. The number of visitors who came into the shop nostalgic for the taste of butterscotch had been overwhelming.

As I moved around the tables with my container of fudge, I noticed a cardboard box by the podium with "Donation" printed on the side of it. The box had been covered with flowered wrapping paper. For some reason, it reminded me of the empty tissue boxes we would decorate for Valentine's Day in elementary school. We'd cut a slot in the top, wrap the boxes in shiny wrapping paper, and decorate them with so many heart stickers you could no longer see the pattern. Then we'd set our boxes on the corners of our desks and hope that our crushes would drop Valentines declaring their unfailing love inside. If they included a few Snickers with their love notes, all the better. In reality, we girls filled each other's boxes, and then we would eat the candy together and commiserate that boys were stupid anyway.

Polly Anne walked over. "What next?"

"You're fast," I said. "You can put out the mini cheesecakes. That's the next container in the wagon."

She nodded and got to work.

I placed the last piece of fudge and went back to the wagon for the lemon bars. It was a new dessert for me, but I knew there was an off chance that someone wouldn't like chocolate or butterscotch. Of course, as a chocolatier, I couldn't understand anyone not liking chocolate. Chocolate was one of the five major food groups—or at least it would have been if I had been in charge of making the chart.

My grandmother's tiny cheesecakes were the size of mini-cupcakes, each in its own foil wrapper. Some of them were topped with Amish-canned cherries, the others with Amish-canned blueberries. I hoped there would be a cherry one left over for me, because my grandmother's mini cheesecakes were my favorite treat—aside from chocolate.

I was at the round table closest to the kitchen, starting to place the lemon bars, when I heard a voice.

"I can't do it right now," Polly Anne said. She was on the other side of the fellowship hall, at the main doorway that led into the church. She spoke so loudly her voice carried across the room.

"You promised," a faceless voice shouted even more loudly than Polly Anne. The unseen speaker was on the other side of the double doors.

"No." Polly Anne's voice was sharp, and I blinked at the harsh sound. Could this be the same woman who had volunteered to help me put out the candies? Whose life's work was to help women suffering from substance abuse get back on their feet? I shook my head and went back to work. Whatever argument she was having, it was none of my business. That's not to say my natural nosiness wasn't cued up. Aiden would have shaken his head. He believed I stuck my nose in where it didn't belong. This time, I was staying out of it—or so I thought.

Chapter Four

Since Polly Anne was preoccupied, I put the last few cheesecakes on the tables and stepped back. I was quite pleased with how the display had turned out. My family's candy and sweets looked lovely on the delicate, three-tiered china plates that Margot had found.

Because Swissmen Sweets was an Amish shop, our candies were rarely displayed in such a fancy way. Out of respect to my grandmother, we kept the shop the same way it had been since she and my grandfather first opened its doors. Well, for the most part. I had made some hidden changes, including adding a website, Wi-Fi, and an online order business. *Maami* had been reluctant to make these changes at first, but with my television show hitting cable in a few weeks, they were definitely needed if we wanted to take advantage of the exposure Bailey's Amish Sweets would bring us. The Amish were strict in their beliefs and their adherence to the rules set forth by their bishops, but they were also practical businessmen and women. Many of them ran *very* successful businesses.

I finished putting everything out and looked for Polly Anne. She was no longer by the doorway at the other end of the fellowship hall. In fact, I didn't see her in the large room at all.

Juliet floated into the room through the door attached to the church. "The women are arriving. I have them waiting in the hallway. Everyone is so excited, and it appears that everyone on the guest list came!" She adjusted Jethro in her arms. "I'm absolutely tickled by the turnout."

Margot popped out of the kitchen like a jack-in-the-box. "Clean up anything that shouldn't be seen and let them in."

As quickly as I could, I tucked all the bakery boxes and plastic containers back into the wagon and stored it in the church kitchen. Then I returned to the fellowship hall and stood by the kitchen door.

Across the large room, Juliet and Margot met the guests at the door. Juliet greeted each woman with her endearing smile and Margot, all business, checked their names off the list attached to her clipboard. I was relieved that she did not insist on asking for their IDs, although I wouldn't have been the least bit surprised if she had. Polly Anne was nowhere in sight. After Margot checked each person's name off the list, Juliet collected the money in the flower-papered box I had seen earlier. She thanked every person who paid her for a ticket. While I watched them, I wondered about the argument Polly Anne had had with the person on the other side of the very same door where Juliet and Margot stood now, and then I tried to put it out of my mind. I reminded myself that it was none of my business.

Cheerful chatter filled the space as the women took their seats. It took some time for the ladies to settle, and I was happy to hear their gleeful comments about all the desserts on the tables.

I was also happy to see that my mother, *Maami*, and Charlotte had come together for the tea. It had taken a bit of convincing on my part to get *Maami* to attend, but Charlotte had been no problem at all. My young Amish cousin looked around the room with awe. I could see why. This was not an Amish get-together, not by a long shot. The three of them sat at a table to the right of the podium where Polly Anne would give her speech. There was an empty seat between them that I knew was for me. A woman with a walker sat at that table as well. Her hair was set in curls and she had a bright smile when Charlotte helped her with her chair.

When the last woman checked in, Juliet walked over to me. "Everything looks gorgeous." She hugged me. "It's amazing how supportive this community is of meaningful causes, and each other. My, it's enough to bring a tear to your eye."

I hugged her back before I let go.

"Oh good, Linda is sitting with your family," Juliet said. "That's perfect."

"Linda?" I asked.

"Linda Benson. She's the lady with the walker. She's just about the sweetest soul you could ever meet. She's not been doing well, so I'm a little surprised to see her. She's getting treatment for bone cancer. It's very serious."

"I'm so sorry to hear that," I whispered.

Juliet nodded sadly. "She and her husband come to our church when she's feeling up to it. She and Polly Anne are close friends and neighbors.

I'm sure she wants to support Abigail's Farm. I know it will be hard for Polly Anne when they move away."

"Move away?" I asked.

"The Bensons plan to sell their farm so Linda can be closer to the treatments she needs. There are limitations in Holmes County when it comes to medical care. I believe they are moving to Cleveland to be closer to the large hospitals."

I nodded.

Margot appeared at my side, put her hands on her hips, and scanned the room. With her poufy, crinoline-filled skirt, she looked like a turn-of-the-twentieth-century schoolmarm about to give her class a severe talking-to. "We need to get this show on the road. Have either of you seen Polly Anne?"

I bit my lip. What was I to say? That the last time I had seen her she was arguing with someone in the hallway? Thankfully, I was spared from making that choice when Polly Anne appeared over Margot's left shoulder.

Polly Anne smoothed her dress. "I'm right here," she said. "I just stepped away for a moment to compose myself. I'm nervous about the speech. Performance jitters."

I noted that she didn't look as put together as she had before. Her bangs were matted to her forehead and she appeared to be out of breath.

Margot didn't seem to take notice of Polly Anne's appearance, or if she did, she didn't care. She had a timetable for the tea, and by God she had a plan to stick to. "Good, good. Bailey, Juliet, take your seats, and Polly Anne and I will begin the program. Chop, chop!"

As Juliet and I walked to our seats she whispered to me, "Did Margot actually say chop, chop?"

I nodded and made a beeline for my seat, just in case the chopping pertained to removing my head from the rest of my body.

I smiled at the ladies at my table and said hello to my mother and grandmother. Linda leaned across the table and shook my hand. "Thank you so much for being here. Polly Anne told me about Swissmen Sweets' donation. It was so kind. I was just telling your grandmother so. You don't know how much this means to Polly Anne."

"It was our pleasure," I said and sat in the empty chair next to my mother.

"My, Bailey, you didn't tell me that this event would be so well done," Mom said. "I would almost think I was back in New England."

A lady across the table from us snorted, and I blushed. I didn't respond because Margot was at the microphone. "Ladies, thank you so much for being here today as part of this celebration and fundraiser for Abigail's Farm. It is so heartwarming to see so many women here this Mother's

Day weekend to support such a wonderful cause. Please enjoy your tea and treats during the presentation. Now, it's my pleasure to introduce you to Polly Anne Lind. Polly Anne is the founder of Abigail's Farm, and she will tell you more about what the farm is all about."

Polly Anne went up to the microphone. "Thank you, Margot, not only for the kind introduction but for putting this event together. I would also like to thank the church, all of the volunteers, and Swissmen Sweets for their time and food donations. Believe me when I say that you would not be eating half as well if I were today's chef." She chuckled. "Many of the women who come through Abigail's Farm would much rather cook for themselves than have me do it."

There was polite laughter, and Polly Anne took a breath.

"The donation you made today makes it possible for Abigail's Farm to continue operating. For those of you who may not know, the farm started eight years ago when my daughter Abigail succumbed to heroin addiction. I was in such a dark place after she died. I was frustrated that all the treatments we'd tried didn't work. I felt there had to have been something she could have done after rehab to ease her into her new life. I thought she would have done better if she had been eased back into society instead of thrown back into it, and I thought I could do something about that, if not for Abigail, for another woman in her shoes.

"I knew I had to do something to help other addicts, parents, and family members from suffering the same fate. Abigail was a bright and beautiful girl, but she made a bad choice. For her, after her first hit of drugs, it was almost impossible to turn back. She was in and out of traditional rehab a number of times. What if she'd had an opportunity to get away from her world and go to a new place, a place where all she had to think about was one or two tasks? Where all she had to work on was getting clean. Everything else would be taken care of. At the same time, my uncle died and left me this farm in the middle of Holmes County. I was living in Columbus when Abigail died. Everyone told me to sell the farm, to take a vacation, to run away from my memories and my life. I wasn't going to do that. I took the farm as a sign that I could help other women like my daughter. That's where the idea of Abigail's Farm came from, and it took me five years to get it off the ground."

Tears sprang to my eyes as I heard Polly Anne's story. I glanced around the table, and then the room. There were tears in all our eyes.

"And I couldn't keep the farm open if it wasn't for donations from women like you." Polly Anne leaned over the podium. "Even if you never see the farm with your own eyes, you are the backbone that is holding it up. It's true that the farm was free to me, but there are so many expenses to run it: taxes on the land, food for the women and for the animals that they care for. They pay a nominal fee to come to Abigail's Farm, and some of that is covered by their insurance, but I want to keep the cost low for them. I can only do that with your help." Polly Anne began to list what the ten thousand dollars the tea had raised would go to, including food and clothes for the women, tools and animal feed for the farm, and general repairs around the property.

Out of the corner of my eye, I saw a middle-aged Amish woman at the doorway to the kitchen. She had her arms crossed over her chest, glaring at Polly Anne for all she was worth. I frowned. I didn't think she was a member of my grandmother's district. I thought I had at least seen all the women in *Maami's* district by now, but there was only one way to be sure. "*Maami*, do you know who that Amish woman is there, in the doorway?" I whispered in her ear.

She looked up from the lemon bar she was cutting into precise, bite-sized pieces. My grandmother was a pro at cutting things in proportion. She never had to measure. She could just tell by one long look how to make uniform pieces of fudge, lemon bars, or any other kind of candy. I, on the other hand, had to get out my ruler. I was too afraid to make a bad cut going just by instinct.

Maami looked in the direction of the doorway. "What woman?" she whispered back.

I spun around, but the Amish woman was gone. I shook my head. I knew I hadn't imagined her. The only Amish women at the tea that day were my grandmother and Charlotte, and I'd bought their tickets. The Amish usually gave to charity without expecting anything in return, so having good food to eat while making a donation didn't make sense to them. I knew it confused my grandmother, but I was very happy see her at the tea regardless.

"She must have left," I whispered back.

"Now, I thank you for your time," Polly Anne said, coming to the end of her speech. "You don't know what this day has meant to me and for Abigail's Farm. Just today we have raised over ten thousand dollars. This is not only from ticket sales, but also from kind donations by you, the community. This money will sustain the farm for months to come, but if you find it in your heart to contribute more, you can tuck it in the box here." She gestured to the back of the room, where the box that reminded me of an elementary school Valentine mailbox sat on a table next to the main doors. "Now please enjoy the rest of your tea. I'm happy to float

around and answer any questions you might have about Abigail's Farm."
She stepped back from the microphone, and Margot took her place.

"Don't be shy," Margot said. "If you have money to spare, do it. A lot
of these women in recovery have children. They want to go home to them.
Won't you make that possible?"

Women talked and laughed as the event went on, and I noticed women
walking up to the box and tucking bills inside. I wouldn't have been
the least bit surprised if Abigail's Farm raised another thousand dollars
that afternoon.

"What a lovely event. I'm so glad that the church was able to host it,"
Juliet said. Aiden's mother still had her just-engaged glow as she floated
over to where I sat in between my mother and grandmother. Juliet clapped
her hands. "Oh my, aren't the three of you as pretty as a picture." She
waved her cell phone.

My grandmother looked as if she were about to say something, but
Juliet held up her hand. "Do not worry, Clara. I know better than to take
any photos of you."

Maami smiled. "My bishop will be most relieved." The Amish did not
take photographs of people or put faces on anything, even dolls, because
it went against the biblical teaching of not making graven images, or at
least the Amish interpretation of that verse.

"I'm glad everything went so well," I told Juliet. "It's been nice for
me to be here with my grandmother, mother, and Charlotte, and to see so
many ladies enjoying our treats."

"Yes," my mother agreed. "And Juliet, I would like to talk more about
what we were discussing earlier. I believe you're right: a little bit of
encouragement would move the situation along nicely."

I narrowed my eyes. "Encouragement of what?"

My mother patted my cheek. "Don't you worry. You just focus on
those candies."

"I think that's a great idea," Juliet began. "In fact—"

Whatever Juliet was going to add was drowned out by a wail, and then
a voice rang out clearly: "The money is gone!"

Chapter Five

Juliet left our table and ran to the front of the room. Jethro's pig ears flopped up and down as she hurried to the podium. I jumped out of my seat too.

My mother grabbed my hand. "Bailey, what are you doing?"

I stared at her hand on my wrist. "I'm going to see if I can help."

"Why? Whatever happened has nothing to do with you. Why get yourself involved?" She shook her head. "Sit down and let someone else handle it."

I removed my hand from my mother's grasp. "If I can offer help, I will." I went toward the front of the room.

At the podium, Margot stood next to Polly Anne, who looked like she would cry at any moment.

"This is so horrible. I don't know how much longer I'll be able to keep the farm running if we don't get that money. Who would do such a thing?" Polly Anne asked.

"Maybe someone put it somewhere for safekeeping," Juliet suggested, holding Jethro close to her chest. The little pig's eyes bulged slightly.

Margot shook her head. "If none of *us* did, there was no one else to do it."

"Are you really sure that the money is gone?" I asked. "All of it?"

Margot picked up the cardboard box where Polly Anne had dropped it and opened the lid. It was empty. I'd been hoping in vain that the thief had missed something.

"If the donations were checks, they would have been made out to the farm, right?" I asked. "Whoever took them can't cash them."

Margot shook her head again "Most of the donations were in cash, so there's no way to trace the stolen money. I'm sure whoever took it will toss the checks and pocket the rest."

I frowned, knowing that Margot was likely right.

"Someone in this room has to have taken the money," Polly Anne said as she clenched her fists at her sides. "I thought the ladies here today cared about what Abigail's Farm was doing for other women. I'm sorry to find I was wrong."

Juliet bristled. "Now, let's not jump to conclusions. Most of these women go to my church, and I can vouch for them as fine, upstanding ladies."

Margot snorted at that. "Like a fine, upstanding lady never did anything wrong? Don't be naive, Juliet."

"I would like to think that none of these women would steal, but it has to be someone in this room. No one else had access," Polly Anne said, then she let out a breath. "Even so, I'm sorry. I shouldn't have thrown out an accusation like that. It takes just one dishonest person to spoil everything. I'm sorry, Juliet. You and your church have been so kind to my organization. I wouldn't ever want to say something that would upset you."

I swallowed hard and glanced around. There was a very good chance a woman in this room had stolen the money. But every seat was filled, so it wasn't as if one of the women had crept away—did that mean someone was sitting on ten thousand dollars while sipping her tea and nibbling on butterscotch peanut bars? Or that someone from outside the event had slipped in with no one the wiser? I pondered this as I glanced back at Polly Anne. She was probably the only person who could've kept her eyes on the box, because she had been at the podium with a view of the whole room. Granted, she'd been glancing at each table, making eye contact with the attendees and occasionally glancing down at her notes. But surely she must have seen something.

Behind us, the women murmured as they watched our little conference play out beside the podium.

"Someone call the police. There has been a theft," said a woman holding a tiny baby at the nearest table.

"How can we be sure? Maybe the money was just misplaced," the lady next to her suggested.

"It wasn't misplaced," Polly Anne said to the two women. "The box holding the money is still here, and it's clear that there is nothing in it. Someone took the money." She showed them the box in a way that reminded me of a street magician performing some kind of trick, but this was a different sleight of the hand. It wasn't intended to amuse and delight. It was intended to steal.

"I didn't think that a cardboard box was an appropriate container for all that cash, but it wasn't my place to say," another voice tsked.

I glanced over at the elderly woman who'd said this. I wished she had made such a suggestion, or at least that someone had guarded the box at all times.

To some extent this theft was due to naivete. The kind of small-town thinking that said it was safe to keep your doors unlocked, to leave the keys in your car, to leave ten thousand dollars sitting unattended in a church fellowship hall. I should have known better, because I had learned after living in this small town for the last year that bad things happened here—just like they did every other place on earth.

Someone must have called the sheriff's department, because five minutes later Deputy Little, a tall, thin deputy who was no older than twenty-three, walked into the room. He scanned the fellowship hall nervously. I suspected he was looking for another man to back him up, but he wasn't going to find much male support in the middle of a Mother's Day tea in the church basement.

Charlotte, who sat at the table next to *Maami,* straightened up when she saw Deputy Little, and I tried not to read too much into it.

The young deputy swallowed when he realized he was on his own. He gathered his courage by clearing his throat and shaking out his hands like an Olympic diver about to take the big plunge. Despite the seriousness of the situation, his physical reaction made me smile. "I heard a report of robbery," Deputy Little said loudly.

"Where's Aiden?" Juliet asked. "I would think if there was a crime committed at his church, where his mother and his beloved—" She pointed to me, and I could feel my cheeks turn red. I didn't think anyone would want to be pointed out as the "beloved."

"I would think, if that was the situation," Juliet went on, "that he would at least show up to investigate the case."

Deputy Little's bravado melted away in the face of his idol's mother. "Deputy Brody is out on another call, and dispatch sent me since I was in the area. Please know that Deputy Brody cares very much about every case in this county. And the rest of the department is tied up with a bad accident, so I'm afraid it will only be me investigating the case at this time."

Margot groaned.

He cleared his throat again. "You can be sure, Ms. Brody, that I will be taking this case very seriously and I will do my best to bring it to a resolution quickly." He looked around the room. "Now, can anyone tell me what has been stolen?"

Polly Anne held up her hand. "The money. The money that was raised to keep Abigail's Farm in operation. If we don't get it back, we will have to close. I can't bear the idea of telling the women at the farm. They would be devastated."

Deputy Little frowned. "How much money are we talking about?"

When Polly Anne told Deputy Little the amount, he whistled. "And most of it was cash?" He sounded concerned, doubtful that there was any hope of seeing that money again. I think we all knew it would be difficult to recover that much money in cash. It was virtually untraceable.

"We will do the best we can to get those donations back," Deputy Little said.

Women began to leave the tea, as it was clear that the proceedings had come to a grinding halt with the disappearance of the money. Nobody wanted to become embroiled in a police investigation, and I couldn't say I blamed them.

Deputy Little watched them rise from their seats with alarm. "Please, ladies, do not leave just yet."

Three women scowled at him and kept walking. His shoulders drooped even more. He was a law enforcement officer, after all, and he deserved respect.

I decided to speak up. "Please, ladies, can you wait one moment for Deputy Little to take a look at the crime scene?"

There was a murmur through the hundred-some ladies who were still in the fellowship hall, but I was gratified to see that nobody else left.

Deputy Little nodded at me, and I took it as acknowledgment that I had been of help. It wasn't much, but at least I'd been able to do something.

He cleared his throat. "I'm going to have to ask you ladies to think back before the money was found missing. It would be very helpful if you could try to recall anything at all, no matter how small or inconsequential it might seem. I will be coming around to each table to ask if you remember anything out of the ordinary. Time is of the essence in cases like this."

"Who was the last person to see the money in the box?" Deputy Little asked.

"That would be me," Margot said. "I checked just before Polly Anne gave her speech, because I wanted to rally the ladies to donate even more than the cost of their tickets."

"Where was the box at that time?" the deputy asked.

Margot pressed her lips together and pointed to the back of the room at the registration table by the door.

Deputy Little frowned when he saw how far away the box had been from the podium. I bet he and I were thinking the same thing: Leaving the box on the registration table had been a very bad idea. With all of the women focusing forward, their eyes glued to Polly Anne, someone must've snuck in and absconded with the cash. They could have taken it without ever being seen.

"And all the money was there when you checked the box?" Deputy Little asked.

"As far as I could tell," Margot said. "I didn't count it, but there was a lot in there."

Deputy Little looked at the box as if he were trying to commit the shape, width, and depth of it to memory.

"You can keep it," Juliet said. "It's just an old printer paper box that I covered with wrapping paper. It's not worth anything, and I can always make another."

"I suggest that next time you have an event that collects this much money you do a little better than cardboard," Margot said and sighed. "I knew I should have taken over the collection box, but I can't do everything. A leader has to delegate somewhere." She sighed again.

"How was I to know that someone would steal the money?" Juliet asked. "This is a ladies' tea."

"How were you to know that someone *wasn't* going to steal the money?" Margot countered.

"I wasn't the one who left it in the back of the room," Juliet countered.

Margot narrowed her eyes.

I sighed. This argument could go on for hours.

Deputy Little took the box. "I will take it with me and see if we can get a print off of it. The techs will surely try. Who all touched the box?"

Juliet, Margot, and Polly Anne raised their hands.

"I touched it too. It sat crookedly on the table, and I had to fix it. I can't stand anything out of place," an elderly woman at the table next to the podium said.

"I'm not sure how conclusive this will be. I might need to fingerprint those of you who touched the box, just for comparison's sake."

"You will not fingerprint me, young man. And if you have a problem with that, you can take it up with my son." The elderly woman paused and looked around the room. "The sheriff."

Deputy Little looked as if he might just lose his supper when he heard who the woman was. I was willing to bet he didn't want his first solo case to involve the sheriff's mother.

The sheriff's mother rose from her seat. "And now, I'm going home." She grabbed the last two pieces of fudge from the service dish on her table, wrapped them in a napkin, and tucked them into her purse. With that, she bustled out of the fellowship hall.

Deputy Little didn't make a single move to stop her. His Adam's apple bobbed up and down. "If anyone has anything odd to report, I would love to hear it."

No one said a thing.

"Deputy Little," I said. "Can I talk to you for a minute?"

He looked at me with relief, since getting information from the other women wasn't going well. Deputy Little followed me away from the crowd and the podium. "Did you see something, Bailey?"

"Maybe," I said, doing my best to keep my voice low. "There was an Amish woman here earlier, and it struck me as odd."

"Your grandmother and Charlotte are here," he said.

I couldn't help but notice that his voice went up an octave at the mention of Charlotte. I really hoped I wasn't reading too much into his reaction.

"Yes, but that's because I bought them both tickets. They are the only Amish here. This really isn't an Amish event."

"I guess you're right," he said. "Who was the Amish woman you saw? What was her name?"

I shook my head. "I don't know. I asked my grandmother who she was, but by the time *Maami* looked at where she was standing in the kitchen doorway, she was gone."

"Do you think she would take the money?" Deputy Little asked.

I pressed my lips together and thought. There was nothing to indicate that she would steal, but I did have the gut feeling that something was off about her. "I don't know. She wasn't anywhere near the box when I saw her, and she wasn't here very long. The only reason I mentioned it was because this is a very English tea, and her presence seemed odd."

He nodded. "I will make a note of it and ask the other witnesses if they saw her." He lowered his voice. "I can't let anything go wrong on this case. It's very important to me. Deputy Brody wants me to work this one on my own."

My eyebrows went up.

He licked his lip. "It will be the first case I have conducted completely solo. I mean, other than a traffic stop. Deputy Brody told me this was my chance to show the sheriff what I can do. If it goes well, I have a chance at a promotion. Do you think the sheriff's mother will turn in a bad report about me?"

"You let her leave," I said. "There's no reason for her to say anything to the sheriff about you." In my head, I thought if the sheriff's mother was anything like her son, she wouldn't need much of a reason to speak ill of someone.

"Would you like a little bit of help from me?" I offered.

"I don't think that's what Deputy Brody meant when he said he wanted me to take this case alone."

"You know that I know Aiden well, and I'm certain what he meant was no other help from the department. Help from me doesn't count, and I can look for the Amish woman." I smiled and tried to look as helpful as possible.

"Well, I suppose you do have more access to Amish women than I do." He blushed. "I only mean that you know more of them, and they will talk to you. I know the Amish are not fond of law enforcement."

"You're right about that."

He pressed his lips together as he thought it over.

"It will be our little secret, Deputy," I said. "Don't worry about it at all. Aiden never has to know."

The beads of sweat that gathered on his forehead said he was worried, and I was kidding myself. Of course Aiden would find out. He always did, but if I could find the Amish woman before that, all the better.

After my conversation with Deputy Little, the young deputy moved around the fellowship hall and spoke with each of the women. After he'd spoken to them, the women were free to go. *Maami* and Charlotte went back to Swissmen Sweets to help Emily shut up the store. The ladies from the church began to clean up the tables one by one. It was sad that such a wonderful event had ended on such a low note. Polly Anne was surely shaken up by it, as she sat next to her friend Linda, who was patting her hand. "The police will find the money. Don't you worry about it."

Polly Anne nodded dumbly. By the look of it, shock had set in. I wanted to ask Linda how she was so certain, but Juliet beat me to it. "You don't worry about it at all. My Aiden will get to the bottom of this, and he has Bailey to help. No crime goes unsolved with the two of them on the case." She looked at me. "Bailey will find out what happened to the money."

I pointed at my chest with my brow up way past my hairline. "Me?"

Juliet nodded. "Of course, it's what you do. You find the bad guy."

Jethro, who was in her arms, grunted as if he agreed with that assessment.

"Bailey, what on earth have you been up to since you moved to Harvest?" my mother wanted to know. "Why does Juliet think you can find out who stole the money? You make candy."

"You didn't know that Bailey solves murders?" Juliet asked, as if this were a fact everyone on the planet was aware of.

"What?" My mother shouted almost as loudly as Polly Anne had when she'd discovered the money was missing.

I jumped out of my seat. "I'm going to help the ladies clean up." I hurried into the church kitchen. Maybe I was a coward, but a conversation about murder wasn't something I wanted to have with my mother right then, if ever.

Chapter Six

I realized after I left the church that I'd forgotten to tell Deputy Little about the argument Polly Anne had had with whoever was in the hallway right before the tea began. I frowned. Would it make a difference? I knew Polly Anne hadn't stolen the money; the money was for her farm. Then again, why was I making that assumption? I knew nothing about her except what I'd gleaned in those few hours before and during the tea. Maybe, just maybe, she'd stolen the money for her own use. Maybe she did want the farm to close, so she could take the money and run instead of being stuck with the farm. I imagined it was hard work, and emotional work at that. The women who came under her care arrived with a lot of baggage and problems. After some time, maybe Polly Anne had realized that it was too much for her to handle, or it reminded her too much of her daughter.

Then I thought about the heartfelt speech she'd given. I couldn't imagine her abandoning a cause that she'd created in honor of her daughter. Perhaps I was giving her too much benefit of the doubt, but I couldn't see her being that sneaky. At the same time, I couldn't rule it out completely.

"Bailey, can I talk to you a minute?"

I turned around and saw my mother marching across the parking lot toward me. "Mom, I thought you went back to your hotel."

My parents were staying at one of the large Amish hotels on Route 39. It was just a short drive from Harvest and had all the amenities they needed, but at the same time it wasn't like the places my parents usually vacationed, with spas and private chefs. But it was the best I could do in Holmes County, and it was better than their staying in my little rental house. I had a two bedroom, but only one double bed and a lumpy loveseat, on which it was terribly uncomfortable to sleep. I knew this from firsthand experience.

"I was just about to leave, but I wanted to talk to you. What is all this I'm hearing about murders and you helping the police?"

"There have been a few." I gave her a very condensed version of the crimes I'd solved and how Amish people had disclosed vital details to me.

"But you're not Amish," she said.

I frowned. "I know that, but *Maami* is."

"So Clara condones this?" Mom folded her arms. "I wouldn't have expected that from her. Doesn't she know the risks you are taking?"

I frowned. "I don't think *Maami* is encouraging me to do this. I'm an adult. She knows I only want to help."

"Help Aiden?" my mother asked. "He's a sheriff's deputy. He should be able to handle himself."

I nodded at her. "He can, and he does an excellent job, but because of my connection to the Amish, he can resolve cases much more quickly with my help."

"What does Aiden think of this? Does he approve of your helping?"

Despite myself, I made a face.

She nodded. "See? He doesn't like it. Aiden seems like a wonderful young man. Do you really want to put that relationship in jeopardy?"

I stared at her.

"Susan, Bailey," Juliet called as she hurried down the front steps of the church. "I'm so glad I caught you. I wanted to invite both of you and Bailey's father to my home for a Mother's Day brunch after church tomorrow. Of course, Charlotte and Clara are welcome too."

"That's very kind of you, Juliet," I said. "They might be able to come. I don't think they have church tomorrow." The Amish met formally for church every other Sunday. The off Sunday was meant to be a family day of devotions and prayers at home.

"Wonderful!" Juliet clapped her hands. "And it will give us all time to visit as a family."

This sounded like a very bad idea.

My mother accepted Juliet's invitation on her and my father's behalf, and then said she was going back to the hotel to relax. My father was there. I guessed that he had spent the day working out in the hotel gym. My father was a fitness fanatic. I could safely say that trait had not rubbed off on me.

I said goodbye to Mom and Juliet and tried not to worry about the fact that they continued to chat after I reached the square. I sensed some plotting going on, and I knew it had to do with Aiden and me.

I put my mother and Juliet out of my head. If they wanted to scheme, that was up to them. I was more worried about the missing money.

My phone rang in my pocket. I looked at the screen. It was a number I didn't recognize, but it had a Holmes County area code. Usually I let calls like that go to voicemail because they were thinly veiled telemarketers, but this time something told me to answer. "Hello?"

"Hello, is this Bailey?"

"Yes," I said slowly. I was ready to hang up before the person on the other end could try to sell me an extended warranty on my car.

"Bailey, this is Polly Anne from Abigail's Farm." Her voice was breathless.

"Oh," I said, surprised. "Hello, Polly Anne."

"I hope it's okay that Juliet gave me your number."

"Yes, it's fine. Is everything all right?" I paused. "I mean, I know that everything is not all right, but did something else happen?"

"No, but many of the women at the tea said that you could help me find the money. I was wondering if you'd be willing. I just don't know what will happen to the farm without those funds." She sounded as if she would burst into tears at any moment.

"Do you know anyone who would have a reason to take the money from you?" I asked. "Does anyone have a grudge against the farm?"

She gasped. "You think this was an act of sabotage against Abigail's Farm and not a random act of thievery?"

"I don't know, but your farm is the best place to start." What I didn't tell her was if it was a random act, it would be near impossible to find out who'd taken the money. We'd have much better luck finding out who'd done this if they had some kind of connection to Abigail's Farm. I supposed the other angle I could look at was the church.

Polly Anne didn't speak for a long while. "Polly Anne, are you still there?" I asked.

"Yes, I'm still here. I do know one person who would want the farm to close. I hate to even mention it. I don't want to get anyone in trouble."

"But you want the money back?" I said.

"Yes, of course I want the money back. I need it to run the farm. The women here need it."

"Who is this person?" I asked.

She was quiet for a moment. "I think it would be easier to explain if you came to the farm and saw for yourself."

I bit the inside of my lip. "When would you like me to come?"

"Now, if you could."

I thought about this for a minute. No one needed me at the moment. My parents had gone to their hotel for the evening. Swissmen Sweets was closed. Aiden was working on a case. "I can come now," I said.

"Oh, would you?" She let out a breath as if she had been holding it for a very long time. "That would be a great relief. I think if you saw what we do here you'd see why getting this money back is so important."

I asked for the address and told her I would be there as quickly as I could. I wasn't sure how Deputy Little would feel about my going to Abigail's Farm, but I had told him that I would help with the Amish angle on this case, and that's what I meant to do.

Chapter Seven

The drive from my little rental house in Harvest to Abigail's Farm took longer than I anticipated. The farm was off the main county highway, along a gravel road tucked in a valley between a set of rolling hills. As my car bumped along the road, I kept a lookout for a sign that might tell me I was going the right way, but there were none, not even the standard Amish buggy sign found on every road in the county. A white frame house that sat back from the road came into view. Freshly plowed fields surrounded it on three sides. The electrical line leading to the house told me it was an English home, but I knew it wasn't Abigail's Farm, because Polly Anne had told me to look for a giant gray barn. She said I couldn't miss it.

I passed the white house and drove another half mile before I saw the barn off in the distance. She was right. It was hard to miss, and I was relieved to have spotted it. I was beginning to wonder if my GPS had led me astray. It had been known to happen in Holmes County, where directions were usually given by locals, in relation to where an oak had been struck by lightning or where an old schoolhouse once stood.

If I needed more confirmation that I was in the right place, Polly Anne stood in the middle of the yard. I turned into her driveway and got out. There was a modest sign along the road that read "Abigail's Farm," but the sign gave no indication that the farm had anything to do with women struggling with addiction.

The front of the house was a massive garden. Petunias, rhododendron, hydrangeas, and tulips were all in bloom as early spring flowers gave way to late spring flowers. There was a young woman in a large-brimmed sun hat weeding the garden. She had headphones in her ears and appeared perfectly content with her task.

Polly Anne nodded at the woman. "She's one of our current residents. She loves gardening. I've encouraged her to look for work at a greenhouse after she leaves the farm. I offered to write a recommendation." Tears sprang to her eyes. "I just can't believe I won't be able to help more women like her after what happened today."

"We don't know that for sure. We could find the money," I said, and patted her shoulder.

"To find the money would be some kind of miracle." She sniffed.

I silently agreed with her. "On the phone, you wouldn't tell me who might want to hurt you or the farm."

She swallowed. "It's my neighbor."

"Your neighbor?" The only neighbor I'd heard of was Linda, the woman with a walker at this afternoon's tea. Could Linda have stolen the money? I frowned. I didn't think so. She had been sitting at my table, and she never got up. I realized that no one sitting at my table had ever gotten up. Did that mean they were all in the clear?

She nodded. "My Amish neighbor."

As soon as she said that, I thought of the Amish woman I had seen at the tea, the one who had been shooting daggers at Polly Anne during her speech. "I passed another farm on the way here, but it looked English to me."

"Oh." She shook her head. "That's the Benson farm. You met my friend Linda at the tea today. The Bensons are perfect neighbors. I have no problem with them at all. The neighbors that I mean are the Mast family. They are south of Abigail's Farm. If you passed the Benson home, you came from the north."

"I don't think I know that family," I said. I couldn't remember my grandmother mentioning anyone with the last name of Mast in her church district.

"They're farmers," she said. "The father is Samson Mast, and he has been upset with Abigail's Farm from the very start." She glanced behind her to make sure the woman working in the garden couldn't hear. "He's made it no secret that he doesn't want a refuge like this so close to his property. He believes it's bad for his children to live near Abigail's Farm." She put her hands on her hips. "I told him that he might as well move, because the farm isn't going anywhere."

It sounded to me as if Samson Mast was a viable suspect indeed. There was another person I needed to ask about too. "Right before the tea began, I saw you having a heated discussion with someone in the hallway outside of the fellowship hall. Who was the person you were speaking to?"

"I don't know what that has to do with any of this," she said.

I cocked my head, surprised at her sharp tone. "It might have a lot to do with it, since the money was stolen less than two hours after that."

She pressed her lips together and then took a breath. "If you must know, it was one of the women here. I had given her a ride into the village. She said she wanted to do a little bit of shopping and just wanted to see Harvest while I was at the tea. Every once in a while, the women can leave the farm. They have to. If they don't, how will they feel comfortable rejoining the rest of society? Anyway, when she asked if she could come with me to the village, I agreed."

"You brought her to the village," I said. "Why wasn't she at the tea?"

Polly Anne frowned at the ground. "I didn't want her at the tea. I thought she would be a distraction."

I frowned. "Polly Anne, how could she have been a distraction?"

Polly Anne tugged on the cuffs of her dress. "She wanted to speak at the tea, and I told her no. I needed the presentation to stay on message, and I was afraid that message might be garbled if she spoke. She has a hard time staying on the same subject. I couldn't let her ramble in front of that group. She might have dissuaded them from donating more."

I disagreed. "I would think it would be even more inspiring to meet one of the women the farm helped."

Polly Anne shook her head as if I couldn't possibly understand.

"I'm going to need to speak to her," I said.

"Why?" She acted surprised.

I rocked back on my heels, glad that I'd had the good sense to change out of my party dress and heels into more practical jeans and tennis shoes. "Because she was at the scene of the crime, and if the two of you were at odds, it gives her a motive."

"She doesn't have a motive. She wanted to speak in front of the group. She thought if she shared her story, it would move the women to give more. We disagreed on that, but I don't think she would take the money from Abigail's Farm if her intention was to raise money for it."

"She might have been upset enough with you to steal money in retaliation," I said.

Polly Anne scowled. "She wouldn't do that."

"If you're so sure, let me talk to her."

Polly Anne hesitated. "Fine, follow me, but I am telling you: it's the Amish, not the women here, who are responsible for what happened."

As I followed her across the yard, I wondered how many times the Amish in Holmes County were blamed for something that went wrong and how many times they were innocent of those accusations.

Polly Anne led me around the side of the house, which was purple. That's right; the color of the house was purple. I supposed a better way to describe the color was lavender. She must have noticed me staring at it because she said, "I know the color isn't what you normally see in Amish Country. That's why I picked it. I wanted to show that Abigail's Farm was something different."

She had certainly accomplished that. I had never seen a lavender house in Amish Country. Around the back of the place, there were rows and rows of plants covered with burlap and tethered in place with twine. A painfully thin woman with blond hair in a high ponytail raked between the rows of burlap.

"Jenna," Polly Anne called. "I have someone I would like you to meet."

Jenna turned around and smiled. When she saw me, her face fell, and she looked at Polly Anne with questioning eyes.

"Jenna, this is Bailey King. She was one of the women who helped out with today's tea," Polly Anne said.

Jenna nodded. "It's nice to meet you." She glanced at Polly Anne. "I wasn't invited to the tea."

"But you were there," I said.

Her brow knitted together. "Just for a few minutes before it started."

"I told Bailey as much." Polly Anne held her hands in front of her waist.

"Did I do something wrong?" Jenna asked. There was real worry in her voice. I guessed after what she'd gone through in her recovery, she might have real fears about being asked to leave Abigail's Farm before she was ready.

I was quick to set her at ease. "No, I'm just trying to talk to people who were at the tea, before, during, and after. Did you see anything strange while you were there?" I asked.

"No, why do you ask?" Jenna was clearly confused.

I looked at Polly Anne, and she gave a slight nod. I swallowed. "Money was stolen from the donation box."

She jumped back from me. "I didn't steal it! Is that what you came here to ask me? If I took the money? I didn't!"

"No," I said, even though that wasn't the complete truth. I did want to know if she'd taken the money. "But you might have seen something that will lead us to the person who did take it."

She brushed her bangs away from her eyes. "I wasn't there long enough to see anything. I was only there to share my story about Abigail's Farm. Polly Anne said that she didn't need or want me to do that, so I left. I waited in the village gazebo on the square until she was ready to drive back here.

I don't have a car, so it wasn't like I could leave the village. It was a nice spring day. I didn't mind the wait, and by the time Polly Anne was done at the tea, I had cooled down." She turned to Polly Anne. "I know I tend to ramble, and that was the reason you didn't want me to speak. I understand." "I'm glad, Jenna. If your feelings were hurt, I apologize," Polly Anne said. Jenna nodded.

I felt my shoulders droop just a little. It seemed to me my conversation with Jenna hadn't turned up any information at all, but maybe that wasn't a bad thing. Marking off leads when they went nowhere was part of the investigation process. I smiled to myself, thinking how much Aiden would hate the idea that I had an "investigation process." I motioned to the burlap rows. "What's under there?"

"Oh, lavender," Jenna said excitedly.

"Lavender?" I asked. "You can grow lavender in Holmes County? I would have thought there would be too much rain." I remembered reading somewhere that it grew in an arid climate.

"That's true," Polly Anne said. "But with the right treatment to the soil and drainage, it grows very well here. These plants are still covered from the winter. Our Ohio winters are too harsh to leave the plants uncovered when it drops below freezing."

Jenna nodded. "It's my job today to check the plants and make sure they are still happy under the burlap. I'm also spreading straw with a rake to keep the weeds down between the rows. When summer hits, weeds will definitely be encroaching on our plants, and we can't have that. We won't uncover the lavender plants until the final threat of frost has passed. That doesn't happen in Ohio until the middle of May. I think in another week, we can take it off."

Polly Anne nodded. "I think so too. Spring weather is so unpredictable in Ohio. It's better to be safe than sorry."

Jenna cleared her throat. "I hope that money is found, because what I would have said if I had spoken at the tea was that this place has helped me a lot. It's given me time to focus on caring for something, the plants and the farm animals. When I was using, all I cared about was myself and where I could get my next fix. I destroyed a lot of friendships and relationships that way. It got to the point that getting high was all I cared about. Rehab helped. It got me off the drug. I got counseling, but it didn't make me care about anything outside of myself the way Abigail's Farm has."

Tears came to my eyes. It was a moving testimony, and one that I wished Polly Anne had let her share at the tea. I thought it would have moved the women to open their pocketbooks a little bit more, but if they had, I supposed that money would have been stolen too.

"I hope what happened with that money won't impact the farm," Jenna said. "I know everyone must be upset that it's missing, or stolen, but Abigail's Farm is going to be okay, isn't it?"

I glanced at Polly Anne, and her face was stoic. "Not to worry. Abigail's Farm will be fine."

Jenna's shoulders sagged in relief, and she went back to raking. Then she stopped. "I do remember something about the tea; well, it wasn't really about the tea because it happened while I sat in the gazebo waiting for you."

"What was it?" Polly Anne asked.

"That Amish man who's always coming to the farm and yelling at you, Polly Anne, he was there," Jenna said.

Polly Anne gasped. "Samson Mast was at the tea?"

"I don't think he was at the tea, but he was at the church. He drove up in his buggy. I recognized him right away because he has stomped over here so many times when I have been checking the lavender plants."

"Did he go inside the church?" I asked.

She shook her head. "Not that I saw. A woman got out of the buggy and went inside. I thought maybe she was going to the tea." She frowned. "It didn't seem like a very Amish thing to do, but I didn't grow up around the Amish. I don't really know."

"Was the woman in the church for a long time?" I asked.

She thought about this for a minute. "She wasn't in there as long as Polly Anne, and she came out at least forty minutes before most of the other women did. I could tell when the event ended because the women were coming out of the church in groups. The Amish woman left the church before that, and she and Samson left the village in the buggy as soon as she got into it. I remember thinking that they looked like they were in some kind of hurry."

I shared a look with Polly Anne. It was very possible we had found the person who'd taken the money. It must have—it could have—been that Amish woman. If she was with Samson, who hated Abigail's Farm, it wasn't too great a stretch to think that they were the ones behind the robbery.

"You've never seen the woman before?" I asked.

"I may have. I just don't know. I was too far away to see her face, because a bonnet covered most of it," Jenna said as she began raking again.

There was only one way to find out, and that meant a trip to Samson's farm.

Chapter Eight

It took some doing, but I was able to convince Polly Anne not to go with me to the Mast farm. If Samson really didn't like her so much that he would steal money from her farm, he wouldn't want to see her.

Before I left, I called Deputy Little.

"This is Little."

"Hi Deputy, it's Bailey. I've been doing some poking around on the Amish angle." I tried to keep my voice cheerful.

He sucked in a breath. "The more I think about this, Bailey, the more I think Deputy Brody would not like it."

"Oh," I said. "I know he wouldn't like it, but I'm giving you a heads up on what I've learned." I told him about Jenna and Samson Mast. "I'm on my way to the Mast farm right now. Hopefully we will have this case wrapped up by the end of the weekend."

Deputy Little groaned. "I can be there in thirty minutes. You should wait until I get there."

"I think it's good of you to offer, Little, but the Mast family won't talk to me about Abigail's Farm with you there. As soon as they see your department vehicle, they will clam up."

"I see your point," he said. "But please be careful. If anything happens to you on this case, Deputy Brody will never forgive me." He sounded terrified of the possibility.

"What could possibly happen, Deputy Little? It's not like I'm chasing a killer. Though I've done that a time or two, and everything has come out just fine."

Deputy Little groaned.

I ended the call and made the short drive down the gravel road to the Mast farm. While the farmhouse on Polly Anne's property was lavender, the house on the Mast farm was twice the size and plain white. Even the front door and the shutters were white. There was no color in the house at all, but that wasn't to say there was no color on their land. In front of the large home, there was a flower bed overflowing with white, yellow, orange, and even pink spring daffodils.

I parked my car halfway down the driveway and straightened my shoulders. I really didn't know how this conversation would go, but I had planned a script in my head. I guessed that was the best I could do.

I walked up to the house and knocked on the front door. There was no answer. I was surprised. In fact, I was even more surprised that no one had come out of the house to greet me. I couldn't remember the last time I had to knock on an Amish door. It seemed to me, any time I visited an Amish family, they had the door open even before I reached the porch.

Maybe they weren't home. I frowned. I could leave, of course. That's what Deputy Little would want me to do. I knew he was an emotional wreck knowing that I was at the Mast farm without him, but he should consider himself lucky that I'd told him at all.

Instead of leaving, I decided to walk around the side of the house to the barn out back. It was possible that the family was working in the barn and simply hadn't heard my car pull up.

I had just gone around the side of the house when I heard a high-pitched keening sound coming from behind me. I didn't even have time to turn around before what felt like a boulder hit me in the back of the legs. I toppled forward and fell onto the grass. The back of my knees were sore where I'd been hit, and my right elbow hurt from landing on it. As quickly as I could, I rolled onto my back and came face to face with a large pig snout.

I did what any other normal person would do: I screamed, and the pig screamed back.

"What is happening?" a deep male voice with a thick Pennsylvania Dutch accent wanted to know.

I shimmied back on my elbows, and the giant pig that had knocked me down looked at me curiously. I spent a fair of amount of time with Jethro the pig; probably even more time than I wanted to. It seemed that any time Juliet needed a pig sitter, I was her girl. So I understood pigs a little, but Jethro was the size of a toaster. The large pink pig standing in front of me was the size of a VW Bug. Okay, that was an exaggeration, but she was definitely motor scooter size. It was no surprise that I went down when she hit me in the back of the knees.

I stumbled to my feet and took four giant steps back from the pig. I broke eye contact with the enormous animal and found an Amish farmer standing nearby with a pitchfork in his hand—I should explain that the business end of the pitchfork was pointed away from me, but it wasn't any less concerning.

"Layla won't hurt you," the Amish man said.

I stared at him. "She hit me in the back of the knees and knocked me to the ground."

"The children have taught her to play tag. She thought you were playing a game," he said, as if it made perfect sense to play tag with a giant pig.

I eyed the pig. Likely story about the game playing. I wasn't buying it. I had a strong suspicion that the sow had wanted to take me out.

Layla sat on her hind quarters in the grass. I had a feeling that she wanted to have a staring competition, but she would have to find someone else for her fun and games. I had stolen money to find. I turned to the Amish man, taking a good look at him for the first time. He was short and stocky, but it was clear that he was in shape from hours of working outside. I guessed that running from Layla during a game of tag would keep anyone in top physical condition. "Are you Samson Mast?" I asked.

He frowned at me. "I am. Why do you want to know?"

"I just came from Abigail's Farm, and—"

He shook the pitchfork in the air. "*Nee, nee,* I will not talk to any of the drug-addicted women from that place. I knew that your kind would slip over onto my property. I just knew it." He shook his finger at me. "I need you to get off my land. I don't want you near my children."

I frowned at him. "First of all, the women at Abigail's Farm are in recovery. Second of all, I don't live there. I'm Bailey King from Swissmen Sweets."

"Are you related to Jebidiah King?" he asked.

"Yes, he was my grandfather. I now work at the candy shop with my grandmother, Clara."

He folded his arms. "I see. I knew that Jebidiah had a son who left the Amish. I take it you are that son's daughter."

"I am," I said. "And I'm here to talk to you about the Mother's Day tea at the church on the square earlier this afternoon."

He scowled at me. "What do I know of it? I'm not *Englisch.* I have no reason to go to that church."

"You were spotted outside the church, sitting in your buggy."

I thought he would deny it, but he went on to say, "What difference does that make? Is there an *Englisch* law that says I can't park there?"

I shook my head. "No, but some money was taken. I'm here to find out what you might know about that."

"What?" he cried. "You are here because you think I stole money from a church?"

Layla the pig appeared to take offense too, because she stood up and walked over to her owner in a move of solidarity. If Layla was anything like Jethro, she would be very loyal to her owner. I knew how much Jethro cared about Juliet.

"I'm not saying you took the money, but since you were there, you might know something or have seen something."

"I didn't see a thing," he snapped.

"You might not have, since you never left the buggy." I took a breath. "But there was a woman there with you. She went into the church. Maybe she saw something that can help us find the money." I paused, wondering if I should say more. I decided to do it. "The money was for Abigail's Farm. Since you have a contentious relationship with your neighbor, and you were near the church when the money was stolen, I thought I should pay you a visit."

"A candy maker?" he asked. "A candy maker is paying me a visit to ask about missing money? Has the *Englisch* world completely lost its mind?" Before I could say anything, he went on. "I do not like the women who moved in next door. I don't like them so close to my home and my children."

"They are trying to rebuild their lives," I said.

Layla walked over to me and pressed her cold snout in my hand. I pulled my hand back and patted her between the ears. It seemed that one of them had warmed up to me. I looked down at the pig, and she smiled. Maybe this was why I did so well with Jethro. Perhaps I had an untapped gift of pig taming. I supposed it was good I had left New York City for Holmes County all those months ago. It certainly wasn't a gift I would get much use of in Manhattan.

"That is well and good, but they can try somewhere else. They don't need to do it here in Harvest."

"Without the stolen money, Abigail's Farm will have to close," I said with my hand on Layla's head.

"They can go to another place for help. They do not need to bring their troubles here. I have children. I must think of them first." He paused. "They should have thought about their children and families before they became addicted to drugs."

I frowned. That didn't sound like Amish compassion to me, and I knew a lot about it. My grandmother was the most compassionate woman I had ever met.

I frowned, and was about to argue with him some more when a woman came around the side of the house. She spoke Pennsylvania Dutch, but as soon as she saw me she stopped talking. Our eyes locked for a moment, and I was certain it was the same woman I had seen standing in the doorway to the church's kitchen.

"Amelia, what is it?" Samson asked.

"Rusty Benson called the shed phone. He plans to stop by later."

"I don't have anything to say to the Bensons," Samson said. "They picked their side."

Their side of what? I wondered.

Amelia nodded and turned to go, but I wasn't going to let her get away from me. "Amelia, you were at the tea earlier today."

She turned and looked at me. "Do I know you?"

I told her who I was, and she shook her head.

"Some money went missing from the tea. You were there. Did you see anything out of the ordinary?"

Amelia shook her head and began to walk away.

"You seemed to be upset with Polly Anne when she was speaking," I called after her. "I saw you there, in the doorway to the kitchen."

I noted that her shoulder twitched ever so slightly as she continued to walk away. She didn't get far though, because just then Deputy Little came around the side of the house.

Samson glared at me. "You called the sheriff's department. You think I took the money!"

"I don't know if you took the money," I said. "But the sheriff's department has a duty to try to find it."

"Maybe they do, but why are you here, candy maker?"

I frowned. I didn't think telling him that Polly Anne had asked me to help her was going to win me any praise from Samson Mast.

"Mr. Mast," Deputy Little said in his most official voice. "Can I ask you a few questions about the tea party?" He glanced at Amelia. "I would love to ask you both a few questions."

"My wife knows nothing. I will answer your questions, and then I will ask you to leave. Your being here upsets the simple life we live. You are not welcome here." He looked at me when he said that. I didn't think I would be coming back to visit my new friend Layla any time soon, but truth be told, Jethro was more than enough pig for me.

Samson answered the deputy's questions, but he said over and over again that his wife didn't know anything. I disagreed. I had a feeling Amelia Mast knew exactly who had taken the money, but as far as I could tell, there was no way to get her to talk.

Chapter Nine

Samson didn't tell Deputy Little anything he hadn't already told me, and the deputy and I walked back to our respective cars.

He removed his ball cap. "I don't know. I think the money might be gone by now. Anyone in the church could have taken it, and I don't have enough information for a warrant to search the Mast home."

"I don't think a warrant is a good idea anyway. It would just create more animosity between the Amish and law enforcement." I didn't add that I thought Sheriff Jackson would enjoy the idea of searching an Amish home. I wasn't sure enough that the Mast family was behind the theft to put them through a stressful police search.

Deputy Little scratched the top of his head. "I suppose you're right." He sighed. "Maybe it was too much to hope that I would be able to solve this case. The sheriff wants me to table it if I don't have any good leads by Monday morning. Unfortunately, we have to do that sometimes when a case goes cold. There are other cases that the sheriff and Deputy Brody want me to pay attention to. I can't spend time spinning my wheels trying to find this money, money that by now may already be spent."

I thought about Jenna and women like her who needed Abigail's Farm to get back on their feet. "We will find a strong lead," I said. "I'll make sure of it."

He opened the door to his department SUV. "Deputy Brody said that you were stubborn. He told me that you wouldn't give up. I guess he was right."

"I'm choosing to take that as a compliment." I smiled.

I was walking over to my own car when a just-washed pickup truck pulled into the Masts' driveway. The driver of the pickup saw that I was about to leave, so he pulled his pickup into the front yard.

Deputy Little nodded at me that it was time to leave, and I frowned.

An English man got out of the car. He was large, well over six feet tall and broad through the shoulders, with steel gray hair and an impressive gray mustache. He wore jeans, a flannel shirt, and a giant silver belt buckle. He looked familiar, but I didn't know from where. It was possible that I had seen him around the village, or that he'd come into Swissmen Sweets a time or two.

Samson Mast came around the house and waved at the man. I noted that Layla the pig came around too. The English man glanced at me and then walked over to Samson. Without speaking, the two men went into the house together and the screen door slammed closed after them. I wished I were a fly on the wall in that house at the moment. Was I right in thinking that they were there to talk about the robbery?

Layla didn't go into the house. Instead she settled down behind the bed of daffodils like she was tucking herself in for a nice long nap. I smiled at the sight of her nose sticking out among the stalks.

Deputy Little and I left in our separate cars. I didn't feel up to giving Polly Anne a full report, so I texted her when I got back to Harvest that Samson said he wasn't involved. I decided not to share my suspicions about Amelia. I told her that Deputy Little and I were doing our very best to find the money, but secretly I thought along the same lines as Deputy Little. It might just be too late for any hope of getting that money back.

* * * *

The next day was Mother's Day, and I met my parents outside Juliet's church. Since leaving the Amish faith, my father hadn't been a regular churchgoer, but my mother went from time to time back in Connecticut. Juliet had invited her to the service, and knowing my mom, she felt it was impolite to refuse.

After the services, *Maami* and Charlotte would join us at Juliet's house for a Mother's Day brunch.

I beat my parents to the church, but instead of going inside I waited out in the church yard and watched the English population of Harvest walk into the large white building with the purple door.

A minivan parked in the handicapped spot in front of the church, and the large man I had seen at the Mast farm the evening before got out. He hurried around the side of the van and opened the back door. He removed a walker, set it up on the pavement, and then opened the passenger door too.

He carefully helped Linda Benson out of the van. I blinked. The man I had seen at the Mast farm had to be Linda's husband, and then I remembered Amelia telling Samson that Rusty Benson had planned to stop by. I should have made the connection before.

I was debating going over and talking to them when something hit me in my calves. I was wearing heels and stumbled forward. Happily, I didn't fall completely to the ground. I spun around and found Jethro looking up at me. "You too, Jethro?" I asked. I really didn't know what it was with pigs wanting to take me out recently. I'd stopped eating bacon and pork when I made Jethro's acquaintance.

"Bailey, dear," Juliet called. "Jethro was so eager to greet you that I had to set him on the ground and let him run." She rested a hand on her cheek. "I love to see how much he loves you. He already views you as his sister."

"Sister?" I squeaked.

"Oh yes," Juliet said. "I see Jethro as my piggy son, and when you marry Aiden, you will be his sister of sorts."

Jethro wiggled his curly tail. I frowned. I wasn't sure whether it was love, or if he just liked to mess with me. And I didn't know how I felt about the whole swine sibling situation either.

"Bailey," my mother said. She and my father walked across the lawn. My mother wore three-inch high heels and clung to my father's arm to keep her footing.

Juliet smiled at them. "I'm so very happy that you all were able to come to the service today. Mother's Day is such a special day. Aiden should be here shortly. I'm just tickled to be here with my family and my family-to-be."

I suppressed a groan. I doubted Juliet was going to let up as long as my parents were in town.

When I looked back at the minivan, the Bensons were gone. I frowned. I expected I would see them in church. There was something about seeing them that put me ill at ease. I didn't know what it was. It was apparent that Rusty doted on his wife and took good care of her.

"We should go in," Juliet said. "The service starts in five minutes, and Reverend Brook does not approve when parishioners walk in late."

We went in and sat in what I had come to think of as Juliet's pew. It was six pews from the front on the right side. It was in the middle of the sanctuary, and from that spot we could see most of the room. I wondered if that's why she'd picked it. I sat on the end of the pew, expecting Aiden to come in any time.

Juliet was on my right, and Jethro was on her lap. If anyone thought it was odd that there was a pig in the church, no one said anything. I suspected that, aside from my parents, the parishioners were all used to it. Jethro was a constant fixture around the church, and he would become even more so when Juliet and Reverend Brook got married. He would be the top pig in the church—if not in all of Harvest. I hoped the fame would not go to his head.

Aiden didn't show up at the beginning of the service and my phone vibrated in my hand. It was a text message from him. *Got called into the station. Will try to get away by brunch.* I sighed, and beside me, Juliet sighed too. I guessed she'd received the same text. I knew it was harder for her to deal with since it was Mother's Day. I knew she wanted her son to be with her at church, but Aiden was the best deputy in the department, so he was the one who was called away most. He had to support other deputies, like Deputy Little, who might need help on a case.

Linda and Rusty Benson sat on the other side of the aisle two rows in front of us. I knew that I was supposed to be listening to the service, but instead my eyes were boring into the back of Rusty Benson's head. I knew I had seen him before, I was just trying to place him. I didn't understand why I couldn't remember. He was a big, imposing guy and would be difficult to forget.

The organist began to play the second hymn, and the congregation stood up. I did too, holding my hymnal, but my mind was not anywhere near the words in front of me: it was on Rusty Benson. I knew the memory was there, I just had to worm it out. We were on the last verse of the song. Juliet, who was also in the church choir, was giving it her all, and then it hit me. I gasped as I realized where I had seen him before. He was the man I had bumped into when I'd entered the building on the way to set up tea. I recognized him from the back. That meant he could have been in or near the church around the time of the robbery.

When the song was over and we sat back down, I fidgeted in my seat like I had when I was a child. I was dying to question Rusty about the tea. My mother reached across Juliet's lap and placed a hand on my knee, just like she used to when I was young. I felt my face grow red.

After the sermon, we stood again for the last hymn, and during the singing Rusty whispered something to his wife. She nodded, and then he walked out the side door of the sanctuary in the middle of the song. I knew this was my chance. I leaned over to Juliet and whispered, "Jethro looks like he needs to go out. I can take him."

She beamed at me. "That's so very thoughtful of you, Bailey. You are going to make the most considerate wife."

It took all my power not to grimace at that statement. I scooped up the pig, tucked him under my arm, and hurried out of the church. When I went out the sanctuary doors, I found the church's purple front door wide open. Through those doors, I spotted Rusty pacing on the front lawn. It looked to me like something was weighing on him pretty heavily.

I nodded to the pig. "You're my cover, okay, so try to keep it together." I set Jethro on the ground.

The little bacon bundle smiled up at me. It was almost as if we had done undercover work together before, which, come to think of it, we had. He started nosing around the bushes near the church's foundation as if he were looking for a good spot. Jethro was a very clean pig. Somehow Juliet had been able to train him to go to the bathroom outside like a dog.

Rusty frowned at us and kept pacing.

I left Jethro to his own devices and walked over to Rusty Benson. "You must be Linda Benson's husband. Rusty, is it?"

He gave me the side eye. "It is. What's it to you?"

I felt my eyebrows go up. It seemed to me that Mr. Benson was as grumpy as his wife was kind and nurturing. "I met her yesterday at the tea." I paused. "Didn't I see you there?"

He snorted. "I'm not going to any ladies' tea."

"That's odd, because I know I saw you there. You were leaving just as I was coming in, through the back door?"

He frowned. "Maybe I was there at the beginning, to drop Linda off. She needs help getting into the building. It's my job to take care of her." He glared at me as if he were challenging me to dispute that.

I wouldn't even try. It was clear that Rusty loved his wife very deeply.

He scowled at me. "What is it you want?"

"I'm sure Linda told you about the missing money," I said.

"So what if she did?" His cheeks immediately turned red. People started coming out of the church and down the steps. "Now, if you will excuse me, I have to see to my wife," Rusty said.

As he turned away, another idea hit me. "You've been having trouble selling your farm, haven't you, Rusty?"

He turned to face me very slowly, like spooky-movie slow. I wouldn't have been surprised to find him wearing a clown mask when he turned around. Thankfully, he wasn't. "What did you say?"

"You have been having trouble selling your farm. Linda told me. She said you were worried about money because of her medical expenses."

"That farm is worth a million dollars! I have three hundred acres, and it's been well cared for. It's some of the most fertile ground in the entire county. Ask anyone and they will tell you the same thing!"

Polly Anne helped Linda around the side of the church. With her walker, she couldn't come down the front steps like the other members of the congregation. Linda's round face was red. "Rusty, dear, what has gotten into you? I could hear you yelling from the other side of the church. And where did you go? Polly Anne was kind enough to help me out, but I was worried about you. I thought something happened. You are always at my side."

Tears sprang to Rusty's eyes. "I will always be at your side. I would do anything for you, Linda. Do you understand that? I would do anything."

And anything could include stealing money from a farm that was trying to help struggling women get back on their feet, I realized.

"Rusty," I asked quietly. "Did you steal the money so Abigail's Farm would close?"

Polly Anne and Linda gasped. "He would never!" Linda exclaimed, and then she studied her husband's face. "Rusty, you didn't, did you? You wouldn't!"

His face crumpled like a child's.

"I have the money. It's right there in the minivan. I was planning to put it back. I was going to hide it in the church kitchen and be done with it. I knew it was wrong the moment I took it." Tears were in his eyes. "All I could think about was what the Realtor said to me when I had the farm appraised last week. She said that it dropped in value by a third because of the proximity to Abigail's Farm. Young farmers with families wouldn't want their children close to a place like that."

Linda gasped. "But we believe in the mission of Abigail's Farm. We've even donated to it, and I gave extra money at the tea."

"I know." He hung his head. "But it's one of those situations where I care about you more than those women. You are my wife. My duty is to you first, and I have to do everything within my power to make your life easy. I wish I could take away your pain and suffering. I swear I would take it upon myself if I could." He looked up. "But I can't. The only thing I can do is make sure you have the very best care and the very best life possible. That takes money. Money I have in the farm, but can't use because it was devalued by those women."

Deputy Little walked over to us. Aiden was a few steps behind him, but I could see he was pulling back to let the younger deputy take the lead. Aiden locked eyes with me for just a second. "What's happening here?" Deputy Little asked in his most official voice.

No one answered.

Deputy Little looked at me, and after a beat, I gave him a quick summary. He nodded at Rusty. "You did this?"

Rusty nodded. "I snuck back into the church and grabbed the money while everyone was watching Polly Anne's speech."

Deputy Little removed the handcuffs from his belt. "Sir, I'm going to have to take you in for robbery." He took a step forward.

Polly Anne jumped between him and Rusty. "No, don't arrest him." She held up her hands in the universal stop sign. "Please, don't arrest him. If he gives the money back, we will say that's the end of it." She turned to Rusty. "I know what you're going through. I know what it's like to love someone so much that you would do anything to help them." She choked on her words. "You would do anything to keep them alive. That's what I would have done for Abigail if I could have. If money could have saved her, I would have stolen it too."

Deputy Little looked back at Aiden for permission. Aiden gave a slight nod, and Deputy Little put the handcuffs back on his belt. "Where's the money?"

"It's in my minivan," Rusty said. He hurried over to the van, opened the passenger side door and reached under the seat. He came up with a plastic storage bag filled with bills. He walked back to us and handed it to Polly Anne. "It's all there. You can count it. I didn't take one penny."

Polly Anne held the money to her chest. "Thank you, Rusty. Thank you for returning this. You don't know what it means to the women at Abigail's Farm, and to me."

Tears gathered in Rusty's eyes. "I think I do."

Linda wiped away tears. "Polly Anne, I am so sorry. Rusty never should have done that."

Polly Anne put a hand on her friend's shoulder. "Please don't be. All is forgiven. You are a lucky woman to have a man love you so well." She took a breath. "Now, I just have to go to the Mast family and apologize for accusing them. I feel awful about that."

"We will go with you," Rusty said. "The Mast family needs to hear what happened from all of us."

"I think that's a good idea," Polly Anne said, and then she turned to me. "Thank you, Bailey."

I smiled. "Thank Deputy Little," I said. "It was his case."

Deputy Little blinked, as if surprised I would say that.

"Great job, Deputy Little." I clapped him on the shoulder. He blushed, and Aiden winked at me. I think he knew how the case had really been solved.

Epilogue

"My goodness," Juliet said while we sat around the table at Mother's Day brunch in the little bungalow she rented just a few blocks from Swissmen Sweets. "That was quite a morning."

Everyone at the table, *Maami*, my parents, Charlotte, Reverend Brook, Juliet, Aiden, and I—and, oh, Jethro, who was on Juliet's lap—agreed. It had been quite a morning, but the money from the tea fundraiser was back in Polly Anne's hands where it belonged.

"I don't remember life in Holmes County being this dramatic," my mother said. "When I arrived Friday morning, I thought nothing had changed. Clearly, I was wrong."

"I thought the same," my father said. "But I'm glad that everything ended happily."

"We all are," *Maami* said. "We will have to pray for Abigail's Farm, and for Linda and Rusty as they travel the difficult road ahead."

No one said anything, but we all knew that she was thinking of my grandfather. I suspected we were all thinking about him.

My mother cleared her throat. "Thank you for the brunch, Juliet. It looks lovely."

And it was. Juliet, who was a great cook, had gone all out. She served omelets, hash browns, fresh fruit, muffins, bagels, yogurt, coffee cake, and turkey bacon. There was never any real bacon in Juliet's home, not with Jethro at the head of the table.

"It was my pleasure. I'm just so happy that our families can spend this time together and really get to know each other. It's important that we build a strong bond for Aiden and Bailey," Juliet said.

I suppressed the sigh that rose in my chest.

"What will happen to the man who stole the money?" my father asked, and I was grateful to him for changing the subject.

"Nothing," Aiden answered. "Polly Anne decided not to press charges. There are other crimes we could have charged him with; he did waste a lot of the department's time, but considering the situation with his wife, we decided to let it go."

"That was the right thing to do," *Maami* said.

"I let Deputy Little make the call. He did an admirable job solving this case. It gives me hope that he will be able to take on bigger cases alone in the future. I need more reliable deputies who can do that. Holmes County cannot say that we are isolated from urban problems any longer."

"We can see that," my mother said. "We used to worry about Bailey living in the city, but it seems to me there are problems everywhere."

Aiden nodded. "There are, but there are good people too, and that's what keeps me hopeful about the future."

"We are hopeful for the future too," Juliet said with a sigh. "Someday, we will all be a family, and that's something to hope for. I know I do."

"I do too," my mother agreed.

I shook my head, but when I looked up I found Aiden smiling at me. At that moment, the tiny flame of hope I had buried deep in my heart sparked a little bit brighter.

Candy Cane Crime

Chapter One

The soles of my black sneakers slipped and slid along the icy sidewalk, but I didn't slow down. I was just in too much of a rush to reach Swissmen Sweets to tell my cousins the news I had just heard. The cold wind blew dime-sized snowflakes against my bare cheeks. The scarf that I wore to protect myself from the blustery weather was no use. I felt it whipping behind my large, black bonnet in a gray curtain, and my legs caught in my thick skirts. It was no matter; I had to tell Cousins Clara and Bailey before Margot Rawlings did. They needed to be warned.

I ran across the village square and across Main Street. There was no traffic today. The weather was too poor. Amish farmers and merchants knew not to go out in weather like this, and even the *Englisch* schools had closed for the day due to the heavy snow. Perhaps half the village would be closed, but I knew that bad weather was not going to keep Margot away. If she was on a mission, that woman would stomp through a hurricane to reach her goal. Bailey said it was her most admirable—and terrifying—quality.

When I made it across the street, I grabbed the door handle to Swissmen Sweets, the Amish candy shop where I worked and also lived, and pulled hard. The wind fought me as I struggled with the door, but finally, I opened it wide enough to stumble inside, surrounded by a cloud of snow.

The candy shop fell silent as I regained my balance just inside the door. Everyone in the front room stared at me openmouthed, including Margot Rawlings, who had beaten me there. The woman had to be some sort of *Englisch* magician to pull off such an feat. I had been told she was at the Harvest Market almost a half mile away. I should have been able to reach the shop first because I had been only across the square delivering candy to Juliet Brook, the pastor's wife. And yet, there Margot stood, staring at me with her appraising dark eyes, her signature short curls covering the top of her head. She wore jeans and a thick sweater under an open winter coat. Her coat was still on, so I knew she didn't plan to stay long. It would be just long enough to announce her decree and leave. Her clipboard was in hand, so I knew she meant business. Poor Bailey.

I suspected that Margot had already told Bailey what she wanted her to do from the pained expression on my cousin's face. Bailey wore jeans, a fitted, purple flannel shirt, and dangly silver earrings. Her long brown hair was pulled back into a ponytail, and her blue eyes were worried. I would not have expected anything less after a face-to-face with Margot and her massive to-do list.

"Charlotte," Cousin Clara, Bailey's grandmother, said. "Come in from the cold and take off your cloak before the snow on it melts and you are soaked through."

Bailey sat across from where Margot stood, at a small round table at the front of the shop. We had the tables there so that customers could chat and taste our candies without the pressure of making a quick decision.

"I'm too late," I said.

Cousin Clara shook out my damp cloak with her wrinkled hands and hung it on the coat tree in the corner of the front room. She held out her hand and said. "Give me your bonnet as well. It needs to dry out, too."

I did what I was told. "I got here as quickly as I could," I whispered to Cousin Clara.

She added the bonnet to the coat tree as well. "Why were you in a rush to come home?"

"I had just heard that Margot was heading this way with a job for Bailey. I wanted to beat her to warn you both!" I glanced back at the table where Bailey and Margot spoke. Bailey was shaking her head "no" and Margot was nodding hers "yes."

"I'm too late."

"Oh, Charlotte, no one can beat Margot Rawlings when she is on a mission," Cousin Clara said in a low voice, so that Margot wouldn't overhear. "Other than the bishop's wife, Ruth Yoder, Margot is the most determined woman I've ever known. If the two of them joined together, none of us would have any peace. It's for the best the pair of them are rarely in agreement."

I had to agree with her there. Ruth Yoder scared me even more than Margot, but that had more to do with her being the bishop's wife and the fact that I was twenty-two years old and still not baptized into the Amish church—something Ruth Yoder did *not* approve of. She made no secret of what she thought, too.

"You are the obvious choice," Margot was telling Bailey at the table. There was a large cardboard box in the middle of the table between them, and she pushed it in Bailey's direction. "You've already made all the candy canes in this box. I'm not asking you to make more. You can always get others from Harvest Market. I don't think people will even know the difference between the ones made by Swissmen Sweets and the store-bought ones."

Bailey frowned and pushed the box back across the tabletop. "I know it makes sense for Swissmen Sweets to handle that Candy Cane Exchange. We are the only candy shop in the village. We were happy to make the candy canes for it. Charlotte did a great job with them. However, I thought we agreed that's where Swissmen Sweet's involvement would end."

"I don't remember saying that was the end of it for Swissmen Sweets," Margot said.

Bailey sighed. "I know why you thought of us first, and I am so grateful, Margot, that you think of our shop when problems arise."

I glanced at Cousin Clara and she smiled at me. I think we were both surprised that Bailey had been able to say that with a straight face.

"But," Bailey went on, "as much as I would like to help, Margot, I just can't. Because of *Bailey's Amish Sweets,* the candy orders this Christmas are three times what they were last year. We're working around the clock to finish everything on time. To make matters worse, I have to go to New York tomorrow morning to do more promotion for the show. That leaves my grandmother, Charlotte, and Emily with all the work. You can see why I wouldn't want this to fall on their plates, too, can't you?"

Margot folded her arms and didn't comment.

"We just can't take it on." Bailey pushed the box a little closer to Margot, and then Margot put her hand on the other side and pushed back. The cardboard creased as they pushed from the two opposite sides. If they pushed any harder, the candy canes inside would be crushed.

"What's the project? I made the candy canes, but I didn't know what they were for exactly," I said. Juliet had told me about the candy exchange when I was at the church, but I hoped that I could distract them both by asking. It would also keep the candy canes from being pulverized.

Margot eyed me and then removed her hand from the box. Bailey did the same.

"We're raising money for new costumes for the annual Christmas pageant on the square," Margot said. "We've had the same wardrobe for the last ten years, and the shepherds are starting to look threadbare. It's a disgrace! I know they were poor workhands on the hills of Bethlehem, but they can't have translucent robes. There are children in our audience."

Bailey made a face and brushed her long ponytail over her shoulder. As she did, the Christmas tree–shaped earring dangling from her ear swung back and forth. Unlike Cousin Clara and me, Bailey was not Amish and never had been. Her father, Cousin Clara's son, had left the Amish faith as a young man and married an *Englisch* woman, Bailey's mother. Over a year ago, Bailey moved to Harvest to help out with the candy shop after Clara's husband, Jebidiah, died. Since then, the business had grown by leaps and bounds, thanks to Bailey's guidance and her experience as a chocolatier in New York City. Bailey had turned the shop into more than a profitable brick-and-mortar store. Now it was also an online business and the basis for a television show, *Bailey's Amish Sweets*, which she filmed in New York City. It was all very exciting to watch, and I had even been able to go with her to New York for filming and the premiere. It was a thrill indeed, and I couldn't wait to go back. There was so much to see and explore in the big city.

"That sounds bad," I said in a sympathetic tone.

"It is bad!" Margot said and patted her short curls. It was a habit she had when she was especially worked up, and Margot was surely worked up now. "And there is no money left in the village budget to deal with it. As you know, the village Christmas pageant is one of the biggest events for Harvest. Every year it brings in tourists and visitors from as far away as Columbus and Cleveland, and even from out-of-state. People want this small village pageantry, and we have to put on the best show we can." She took a breath. "We can't do that without appropriate costumes. All I am asking is for Swissmen Sweets to manage the Candy Cane Exchange." She frowned at Bailey. "Goodness, it's not like last year, when I asked you to play Mother Mary."

Bailey shivered. She had played Mother Mary last year under extreme protest. Margot wouldn't take "no" for an answer then either.

"Thankfully," Margot went on, "there is a lady at the church who is about to pop with a baby and she's perfect for the part. I just hope she can keep from having the child for another week. That would put such a damper on everything. A pillow under a woman's costume is not like the real thing," she complained.

I glanced at Bailey, who looked as if she was in actual physical pain at Margot's words.

"Margot," Bailey said. "I want to help. I really do, but I just can't this year. We already had to hire extra seasonal staff just to get us through the orders we know we have."

"What do you want Bailey to do?" I asked.

Bailey gave me a look, as if I wasn't helping. I guessed I wasn't, but I was curious how Margot planned to raise money with candy canes. She always seemed to come up with ideas to save the day.

"Well, I have had the perfect idea, just as I always do," she added with a sniff.

Bailey snorted and then covered the sound with a cough. "I'm sorry. Allergies. I was sweeping the floor when you came in. I must have kicked up some dust."

There was never any dust in the shop—Clara and I cleaned at the start of each day and after each closing—and Bailey didn't have allergies.

"You kicked up some dust?" Margot narrowed her eyes at Bailey. "Yes, well, you might want to be more careful when you sweep, then."

I didn't know much about the *Englisch* ways, but I did know that in a town as small as Harvest, we did not want to be on the wrong side of a community leader like Margot. So I asked, "About that idea?"

Margot turned her attention back to me. "To answer your question, the idea I had was a Candy Cane Exchange. For one dollar, a person can have a candy cane delivered with a personal message to someone else in the village. The candy canes that Swissmen Sweets so kindly made are in this box." She scooted the box on the table closer to Bailey. Bailey didn't bother to push it back this time. There was a new look of resignation on her face. "We appreciate your donation of the candy canes, but I need more than that. I need someone to attach the notes to the canes and prepare them for the Christmas Eve delivery. The church youth group will deliver the canes." She eyed Bailey again. "So all in all, it's not that much work. You already did the hard part by making the candy, and I've already told Harvest Market that you might need more candy canes from them."

Bailey sighed. "I understand that, Margot, but…"

"Could someone from the church take this over?" I asked.

"No, they can't," Margot cried, as if it was the most ridiculous question she had ever heard. "You know how busy the church is during this season, and because it is Juliet Brook's first Christmas as the pastor's wife, she's doubling her efforts to get more out of her volunteers. I can't ask them to do anything else. The members are at their wits' end as it is."

Bailey raised her brow. I thought she must be thinking what I was thinking. If Margot thought the volunteers at the church were overworked, it really must be bad. I wondered what Juliet was having them do.

"Well, there has to be someone else in the village who can do this," Bailey said. "You don't have to have candy-making training to attach notes to candy canes."

Margot pressed her lips together and glared at Bailey. I could tell by the set of her jaw that she had come to the end of her rope. It took a long while for Bailey to tell someone else "no." She was, in general, very easygoing and agreeable, but it seemed this time Margot had pushed her too far, or her heavy workload had. I knew Bailey was struggling to complete everything she had already committed to by the end of the year. Maybe Margot's request was the very last straw. I had to do something to help and put an end to their argument.

"I—I could help," I heard myself say.

Behind Margot, Bailey waved her arms, shook her head, and mouthed *no!* over and over again, but I forged on. "I think it's a fun idea, and I think it would be nice for the pageant to have new costumes. There is no reason the shepherds should march around the square threadbare. You're right. That would not look professional."

Margot clapped her hands. "Finally, someone in this room is listening to some sense!" She stood, picked up the box from the table, and dropped it into my arms. I stumbled under its weight. I hadn't been prepared for how heavy it was.

"Very good." Margot slapped a white piece of paper on top of the box under my nose. "These are the instructions as to how you collect the notes and everything else you need to do." She headed toward the door and opened it, bringing in the wailing wind and a gust of cold air. Before she went out, she said, "Don't let the village down, Charlotte. Everyone is counting on you. It's up to you to save Christmas!" With that, she was gone into the whiteness.

Chapter Two

After the door banged closed, Bailey groaned. "Charlotte, are you sure you want to take this on? You're as busy as the rest of us. I want you to be able to enjoy Christmas, not be stuck working all the time. This will be one more thing you'll have to deal with. And Christmas is just ten days away."

"*Danki* for worrying about me, Bailey," I said. "I know that, but I think it will be fun, and the pageant costumes *are* looking a little shabby. I remember when you played Mary last year. I know it wasn't your fault, but you looked a little frayed around the edges."

"That could have been because I was dealing with my ex-boyfriend and trying to find a killer at the same time." She sighed. Dealing with killers was something that Bailey coped with on a surprisingly regular basis for a candymaker.

"You made a lovely Mary," Cousin Clara said in her encouraging way. "I'm surprised you don't want to do it again."

"I don't," Bailey said. "My Mother Mary days are far behind me."

"What's done is done," Cousin Clara said. "And I think it was very kind of Charlotte to volunteer to help. We all have to do our part for the village." She smiled at me. "And I think it will be very nice for Charlotte to have a project all her own for once. You do so much for us and the shop, Charlotte. You should have your own interests."

Bailey nodded. "True, and we should be able to get caught up on orders today…at least until more come in. I can't see anyone—other than Margot—braving this weather to come to the shop to order candy face-to-face, but I expect some business online." Her face paled a bit as she said this last part, as if the thought of looking at her computer was scary.

"We will get it all done, Bailey. Don't worry so much."

Bailey sighed. "I know. We always get it done, but I hate having to go to New York this close to the holiday. I feel like I'm leaving all of you in the lurch."

Her grandmother shook her head. "You may feel that way, but none of us do. Let's get to work. Busy hands always put your mind at ease."

Bailey smiled. "You know me so well, Maami."

"That I do." Cousin Clara turned to me and patted my arm. "Charlotte, why don't you read over those instructions while Bailey and I get back to filling the orders? Then you can come to the kitchen and give us a hand."

I nodded, set the box back on the tabletop, and sat down. Bailey and Cousin Clara went into the kitchen. I picked up the piece of typed paper from the box. Across the top, it said, "Instructions for Candy Cane Exchange Coordinator."

Coordinator? I had never been in charge of or asked to coordinate anything in my whole life. I suddenly felt better about taking this on. I would prove to Bailey and Cousin Clara that I was ready for more responsibility. Feeling very official, I sat up straighter in my seat and began to read.

"Here is all you need to know about the Candy Cane Exchange. You will not need to deliver the candy canes because the church youth group will do that on Christmas Eve."

I nodded to the paper because Margot had already told me as much.

"Step one—Collect candy cane notes. The notes will be found in the wooden box that is sitting on the post next to the gazebo on the square. You cannot miss it! The post is shaped like a candy cane."

I frowned. I hadn't seen a candy cane–shaped post either time I'd crossed the square that day, but then again, the snow had been so thick, I could barely see two feet in front of me. I shrugged and continued to read.

"Amish and English villagers can drop their money and notes in the box at their convenience, so check it often. Money and notes could be inside the box at any time.

"Step two—Keep track of the money. There is an envelope in the box and a log. This is very important! Make sure everyone pays. We will not deliver candy canes for free. This is not a charity! This is a fundraiser, for goodness' sake. If someone has not included payment with their note, set the note aside."

I looked in the box and saw a large manila envelope along the side. I pulled it out. Inside the envelope was the log. Each line asked for the name of the person giving the candy cane, the name and address of the person receiving the candy cane, whether the candy was paid for, and the date the order was received. It seemed simple enough. I went back to the directions.

"Step three—Adhere each note to a candy cane with ribbon—or some other way. I trust you can figure out something festive. Remember: This is supposed to be a special treat for the person receiving the cane, so make it look nice!"

I shook my head. Margot's forceful tone came through loud and clear in her instructions, that was for sure. I kept reading.

"Step four—Deliver the candy canes to the church by Christmas Eve morning. The high school students will distribute them throughout the day. We need the canes and their notes there by eight a.m. sharp."

The instructions went on. "The exchange will commence on Christmas Eve, so the box on the square will be there for ten days. This gives all the villagers ample time to write their notes and pay. If you have any questions, give me a call, but I trust that you will not need further instructions."

The page ended with Margot's name and phone number.

I wrinkled my nose. I wouldn't be asking Margot for further instructions. I had a feeling she would view that as some sort of failure on my part.

Despite the forceful directions, I was excited I had offered to do this. How much fun would it to be to be partly responsible for villagers getting a candy cane and a sweet note from a loved one? I pressed the printed page against my chest. How much more wonderful and romantic would it be if couples in the village used the candy canes to profess their love for another! I sighed at that very idea.

I had to check the box right away to see if there were any messages there already. I couldn't wait. There could be a love note waiting, and I was the protector of that note until I gave it to the youth group to deliver. It was a lot of responsibility, and I chose to take it very seriously.

I glanced in the direction of the kitchen. Bailey would tell me I was crazy to go out in this weather to check the box, but I couldn't wait. I had to know if there were any notes in it. I would just run to the square and back, and then I would go into the kitchen and help with the long list of Christmas orders. It wouldn't take me more than five minutes to check the box and come back.

I grabbed my bonnet and cloak, both of which were still freezing cold from being outside. I put them on and opened the front door into the wind, which was so strong that it almost pushed the door closed on me. I forced it back open and slipped outside. As soon as I was on the sidewalk, I knew it was ridiculous for me to want to check the box this afternoon. Who would come out in this weather to deliver a note? Even so, I was too overcome with the need to know to turn back.

I slipped the hood of my cloak over my large bonnet and ducked my head as I crossed Main Street against the wind. When I reached the square, I looked in all directions for the box that Margot's instructions described, but all I could see was whiteness and a few pine trees that were large enough to stand out against the snowy blur.

I turned in the direction of the gazebo on the square by instinct, not by sight. I decided that it was the most central place on the green and therefore the most likely place for the box to be.

The gazebo, which was also white, came into view. Its paint color didn't help my sense of direction, but the set of red and green twinkle lights wrapped around its posts gave me a point of reference. I was five feet from it when I walked straight into a wooden pole that seemed to come out of nowhere. I bounced off the pole and fell into the snow. When I looked up, I saw that I had found the candy cane box.

I struggled to my feet and dusted off what snow I could from my skirts and cloak. I knew by now that I would be gone from the shop much longer than the initial five minutes that I'd set for myself. Bailey would be wondering why it was taking me so long to read the instructions. She might even be worried that the Candy Cane Exchange was too much for me to handle.

After I dusted myself off as best I could, I looked at the box. It was a giant candy cane made out of wood and painted in red and white stripes, just like the piece of candy. There was a green bow also made out of wood right under the hook, and a hinged wooden box made up the center of the bow. I lifted the latch that held the lid in place and put my hand inside. To my surprise, I felt paper. There was already a note in the box! In fact, there were a lot of them. I felt elated. I knew that these notes weren't for me, but it was still an exciting discovery. Margot, for all her bossiness, does have *gut* ideas. I guessed the Candy Cane Exchange would be just the thing to raise the money she needed for the pageant costumes.

I gathered up all the notes and hoped that the money for each one was included. I hadn't thought about it until that moment, but it would be no fun to chase down someone who hadn't paid. I tucked all the notes under my cloak and hurried back to Swissmen Sweets.

I had just closed the front door to the shop and removed my bonnet and cloak when Bailey's head popped out from the kitchen. "Charlotte, are you still reading those directions?"

"I'm just about done. I'll meet you back there in a minute."

She nodded and disappeared into the kitchen again. I didn't think she noticed the snow on my skirts. She was far too stressed over the influx of

Christmas orders. Swissmen Sweets had never had a season like this before, and we were all overwhelmed with the amount of work that had to be done. But before I went into the kitchen, I had to take just one peek at the notes. The first one I read said, "To Sarah—Much love this Christmas. Love, Grandma and Grandpa."

Wasn't that sweet? I opened another one. Just one more, I promised myself; then I would get right to work on my job of making candy. I could work on the Candy Cane Exchange that night after Cousin Clara went to bed.

I gasped when I saw that the next candy cane note was addressed to me, "Charlotte Weaver at Swissmen Sweets." I blushed as I looked at the note, which I was supposed to attach to my very own candy cane. I opened it, wondering if the candy cane was from a friend or maybe a member of my family. Since I had left my conservative home district, I had heard little from my siblings and parents. I knew that I had made the right decision, but I'd be lying if I didn't admit that I missed them and wished they would at least speak to me from time to time.

I unfolded the note and a dollar bill fell out. I scooped up the bill, tucked it back in the envelope, and read the note. "To the sweetest girl in the village. May your Christmas be half as sweet as you. Love, your secret admirer."

I stared at the note and reread it three times. My *secret admirer*? I had a secret admirer. Who on earth could it be? I wondered if it was a mistake, but when I read the envelope again, it clearly said "Charlotte Weaver at Swissmen Sweets." Well, I was the only Charlotte Weaver who lived above the candy shop. That was for sure.

Bailey's head appeared in the kitchen doorway again. "Charlotte, we have work to do." She sounded just a touch impatient, and because Bailey was one of the most patient people I'd ever known, I guessed she had been waiting for me to come into the kitchen for quite some time. I couldn't put it off any longer.

"I'm so sorry, Bailey," I said. "I'm coming now. I will only work on these when the shop is closed."

She nodded and ducked back into the kitchen.

I tucked the letters into the box with the candy canes, but the one addressed to me, the secret admirer letter, I folded and tucked in my apron pocket instead. My heart thundered against my chest the entire time.

Chapter Three

The next morning, you would never have known how awful the weather had been the day before if it had not been for the snow. I peeked out of my small bedroom window over the candy shop. All of Harvest was blanketed in white. I could see that even though it was still dark outside because the twinkle lights glowed on the square across Main Street, and the gas lampposts that marched up and down the road were still lit.

It was four in the morning. Early, but this was the time I got up every day to start making candies for the shop. This was normal for me. But this wasn't a normal day at all. I had a secret admirer! Even though I had barely slept, I wasn't tired. I felt like I could run all day.

I had read the note from my secret admirer so many times during the night that I had put a crease in the paper. Also, because I hadn't been able to sleep, I'd prepared all thirty-one candy canes for delivery. Thankfully, I'd also collected thirty-two dollars for the costumes. Thirty-two counting the dollar from my secret admirer, of course.

I wanted the candy canes to feel special to the people who would receive them. I rooted through my sewing kit and extra fabric from various projects over the years, and came up with some red-and-green flannel. I had used it to make Bailey a scarf last Christmas. I had bought too much of the flannel that I needed for the scarf. There would be plenty to make ties for the candy canes. I punched holes in the notes, taking care not to punch through any of the words. Then, I cut the flannel into narrow strips that were just big enough to wrap around a candy cane twice, go through the hole in the note, and tie into a tiny bow.

In the dimness of my lantern light, I stared at the candy canes and notes that I had lined up on top of the quilt on my bed. I couldn't wait to go to the candy cane box later today to see if more notes had arrived.

Outside of my bedroom door, I heard Cousin Clara going down the steps, and I knew that was my cue to get ready for the day. There was much to do in the shop, and I knew we would have many customers who would have come the day before but had been snowed in. It would likely be twice as busy today.

When I made it downstairs ten minutes later, I was surprised to see Bailey and Emily Keim already working in the kitchen. Bailey usually came to work around seven. She lived in a little rental house a few blocks away, and Emily, the other shop assistant, lived miles away on her husband's Christmas tree farm. Typically, she arrived about the same time as Bailey.

"The farm has been so busy this season," Emily said to Bailey. "I'm so glad that you let me come to work early, so that I can be home to help at the farm in the afternoon. It seems that everyone in the county wants a live tree this year." She smiled her sweet smile. "We aren't complaining, of course. *Gut* business makes up for lean times."

"That is right," Cousin Clara agreed.

"And we are more than happy to have you come in early," Bailey said as she rubbed the back of her neck. "There is so much to do."

"Bailey, everything will get done. Don't you worry about that," Cousin Clara told her granddaughter.

"Christmas is so stressful," Bailey said.

Cousin Clara shook her head. "It's not meant to be. Christmas has been too commercialized, in my opinion. It should be the happy celebration of Christ's birth. Whether we complete the Christmas orders on time or not will not change the reason for the season."

Bailey smiled at her grandmother. "I know that, and with all your help, I'm sure we will finish everything in time. I only wish I didn't have to go to New York in a few hours. I hate to leave you to manage everything alone."

"We will be fine," Cousin Clara assured her. "Now, let's all get back to work so you have less anxiety about what remains to be done."

As I expected, the morning at the candy shop was busy. Even though it was a Wednesday, the shop hummed with customers. Most wanted to place more Christmas orders or just pop in for a piece of fudge and marvel at the amount of snow that had fallen.

Ruth Yoder, the bishop's wife, was one of the latter. She bit into the piece of vanilla fudge I had given her. After swallowing, she said, "We will have a white Christmas this year. That's for sure and certain." She wrinkled her nose. "I bet Margot Rawlings is over the moon about that. She will have snow for her Christmas parade and pageant. It means nothing to her that there was no snow in Bethlehem."

"I think the tourists will like it, too," I said.

She eyed me. "That may be so, but the Christmas parade is not the point of Christmas. I have heard that she has this ridiculous idea about a Candy Cane Exchange, too. Shouldn't the birth of our Savior be enough of a gift for us? Now, we must give each other notes tied to peppermint sticks?" She sniffed.

"Charlotte is the one in charge of the Candy Cane Exchange," Emily said.

I frowned at her. Why would she go and tell the bishop's wife that? I was already on her bad side because I wasn't baptized into the Amish church yet. In Ruth Yoder's mind, twenty-two was far too old not to have come to a decision on that topic.

"What is an Amish girl doing involved in that?" Ruth wanted to know. "If Margot wants to do this *Englisch* Candy Cane Exchange, that's up to her, but she should not involve a young woman from my district."

"Pish, Ruth," Cousin Clara said as she boxed up an order of mocha truffles. "It's not your district, and there is nothing in the *Ordnung* against Charlotte volunteering to help the village. In fact, service to others is something we are asked to do."

"Service for a *gut* cause," Ruth muttered. "Are costumes for an *Englisch* pageant that? I have my doubts."

Cousin Clara shook her head.

Ruth leaned across the domed glass counter and stared at me. "Just be careful when you are reading those notes. *Englischers* are not like us, and you might be shocked by what they say."

"There won't be anything rude on a candy cane note," Cousin Clara said. "Goodness, Ruth, your opinion of the *Englisch* grows worse by the day."

"My opinion of the *Englisch* hasn't changed in the least. I have always looked at them with suspicion."

Cousin Clara shook her head again and went off to help the next customer in line.

Ruth pointed at me. "Remember what I said. You might be surprised by what you find in that box." With that, she bustled out of the shop with the remains of her vanilla fudge tucked into her shopping basket.

What Ruth Yoder didn't know was that I had already been surprised by what I'd found in the candy cane box, very surprised indeed.

It wasn't until later that afternoon that I was able to steal away and check the receptacle again. With the *gut* turn in the weather, I was expecting even more notes in the box, so this time I had the *gut* sense to bring a shopping basket with me.

I had seen the snow from my bedroom window and from the front window of the shop, but those views were nothing compared to seeing it in person. Everything covered with snow sparkled under the white sunlight. The gazebo reminded me of a bright, white wedding cake under its frosting of snow, and the big, white church across the square looked like a painting I had seen for sale in the shops in Berlin. It was breathtaking.

"You seem to be enthralled by all you see around you," a gravelly voice said.

I turned to see Uriah Schrock standing on the sidewalk behind me. At his back, the walk was shoveled clear. Ahead of him there was what seemed like miles of white, unbroken snow. Uriah was an older Amish man with a long, white beard, the head groundskeeper of the square. It was a job that Margot had talked the village into creating when it became clear that there would be some sort of event every week on the square as long as Margot was in charge of planning the village social calendar. Uriah, who was in Harvest on an extended stay from Indiana, had held the job for quite a few months now. There were whispers in the community that he wasn't moving back home to Indiana because he was sweet on the local matchmaker, Millie Fisher. I didn't know what to make of those rumors.

Millie, a sixtysomething, no-nonsense type of Amish woman, didn't strike me as the sort who would entertain such feelings. She had been a widow for over twenty years and never seemed to want to marry for a second time. She had once even told me that she'd found her match when she was a child, and had been blessed to have him as long as she did. She claimed it would be selfish to look for a second one. That was something else I was unsure of; I had a feeling that Millie might be trying to talk herself into believing it, too.

"It's beautiful," I admitted. "It makes me wish that I was a child again, so I could fall into the snow and make snow angels like I did as a girl."

He leaned his snow shovel against his shoulder and pushed his black stocking hat back above his eyebrows. "If you fell down and did that, I wouldn't tell tales on you. I wish that I could do the same. But if I did, I might not be able to get up again without a little help, and my pride would not have that. A snow like this is a lot of work, but it does make the whole world sparkle."

I looked around in the late-afternoon light and saw that he had used the perfect word. Sparkle. That was just what was happening all around me. It was as if a billion little twinkling stars were trapped in the snow.

"Are you just out for a stroll to enjoy this pretty day?" Uriah asked.

I shook my head and puffed out my chest proudly. I knew that wasn't the way Amish women were supposed to be, but I wasn't baptized... yet. "I'm in charge of the Candy Cane Exchange and I'm going to the box to collect the notes that were delivered today."

He nodded. "That seems to be a very important job."

"Oh, it is," I agreed. "Every candy cane is one dollar, and we're raising money for new Christmas pageant costumes."

"Then you will be very happy. I have been on the square for two hours now, shoveling away, and I can vouch that the box has been busy. I think every person who came on the square today dropped an envelope in there, and they are coming from all over to do it. Why, there have been people who stopped by today to order a candy cane note that I have never seen here in all my time caring for the square."

I smiled. "I'm glad it's so popular. Margot will be pleased. Maybe there will even be enough money left over that she can apply the funds to another village project, too."

"With Margot at the helm, I don't doubt there will be. She has been pushing these candy canes in the *Englisch* papers and the Amish ones. I don't think there is a single person in the village who hasn't heard of the Candy Cane Exchange."

I nodded. That sounded like Margot. I was glad that she didn't expect me to do the advertising. I wouldn't know where to start. I had the easy part of the exchange: Check the box and put the notes on the candy canes for Christmas Eve delivery. Simple. It would be even simpler if I wasn't constantly daydreaming about who my secret admirer might be.

I was about to make my way to the candy cane box when I saw something burrowing through the snow. "What is that?"

Uriah lifted his shovel as if to protect me. "Step back."

Whatever it was ran straight for the candy cane box. It bounced off the post and squealed. That was when I saw its black-and-white head pop out of the snow. Jethro.

Chapter Four

"Oh dear!" Juliet Brook cried as she came running across the snow-covered square in pursuit of her beloved pig. "Is he hurt?" Even though there was over two feet of snow on the square, Juliet was dressed for Sunday church. She wore a blue, polka-dotted coat over a tea dress and black-and-white, polka-dotted puddle boots that matched her black-and-white, polka-dotted, potbellied pig perfectly. Juliet really loved polka dots.... I mean she adored them almost as much as she loved her pig. No one in Harvest would doubt that Juliet loved her pig. Most believed that if she ever had to choose between her new husband, Reverend Brook, and Jethro, the pig would win, hooves down.

Jethro lay on his side and stared up into the sky as if he was wondering how on earth he'd got there. Juliet took Jethro everywhere she went—and I do mean *everywhere,* even on airplanes—so the little pig had that same bewildered expression a lot.

"Is he all right? Should I call the EMTs?" she asked in a tearful voice.

Uriah stuck his shovel in the snow. "Call the EMTs for a pig?"

Juliet straightened. Uriah was almost a foot taller than she, but you wouldn't know it by the way she acted. "My son is the second-ranking officer in the sheriff's department. All the deputies and the EMTs who work out of the same building know how precious Jethro is, not only to me, but to the entire county."

Jethro wiggled and rolled over. He shook a bit of snow from the top of his head as he stood up.

"Look," I said, hoping to hold off an argument. "He's getting up. He's fine!"

"Oh, thank goodness!" Juliet said, seemingly having forgotten her irritation at Uriah. She scooped up the pig, who was covered from head to tail in snow, and held him to her chest. "My poor boy. You have to be more careful." She looked at us. "Jethro just loves the snow. He loses his head any time there is a big snow. He just wants to barrel through it like a bowling ball."

Calling Jethro a bowling ball was the most accurate description I'd ever heard Juliet make of her pig.

"And he's such a smart pig, too," Juliet went on. "He knew where I was going. I'm sure he just got so excited about coming to the candy cane box, he forged ahead." She kissed the pig on the top of his head. "Jethro is so supportive of everything I do."

Uriah looked as if he wanted to make a comment about pigs and support, but I jumped in, not only to stop him, but because I was happy to hear she was making her way to the box.

"You have a note to send with a candy cane?" I asked excitedly. I wouldn't be the least bit surprised if the note was for her husband, Reverend Brook. Everyone knew that she was head over heels in love with him. And he loved her just as much. It was a real-life love story, like one of the ones I had read in the books I snuck from the library when I was younger. My father didn't like me reading romances, so he never knew.

"Yes, I do. Margot tells me that you are the one handling the Candy Cane Exchange. I don't think she could have picked a better person."

I nodded. "I am."

"I'm so very glad. I know that she wanted Bailey to do it, but that sweet girl is stretched thin." She tapped her chin with the forefinger of her gloved hand. "Maybe that is why Aiden hasn't asked her to marry him yet. She's under too much stress." She frowned. "I hope that's not the case. I was one of the people who encouraged her to do her television show. I would hate to be partly responsible for the delay of their happily ever after." Her brow wrinkled in concern.

"I don't think it's that at all," I said, knowing nothing of the kind. I only wanted to protect Bailey from Juliet's telling her to give up the show to marry Aiden. I knew Bailey well enough to know such advice would have the opposite effect. Telling her to give up her career was not the way to go... ever. I don't think anyone should be asked to choose between the things they love.

Juliet's brow wrinkled, and I had a feeling that now she had that idea in her head, it would be difficult to remove it again. I wondered if I should warn Bailey or wait and see if Juliet actually brought up the topic with her.

"Well, since you are here," Juliet said, "I don't have to put the notes in the box. I can just hand them to you?"

"Of course." I held up my basket. "I was just making my way to collect today's notes. You can put them right in here."

"Jethro," she crooned. "I'm going to put you down for a moment. Don't you go running off in the snow again, you rascally piggy, you." She shook her finger at him, and then she removed her tote bag from her arm and opened it. She reached in and held up a huge stack of notes.

I stared at the massive pile. "Those are all from you?" I squeaked. At the same time, I thought I was going to need a lot more candy canes than the box Margot had given me if this kept up.

"Goodness, no. There are two or three in here from me, yes, but on Sunday we did a collection of notes at the church." She shook her head. "I know that was three days ago, but I just now found a moment to bring them over." She eyed the candy cane box. "I'm quite glad I ran into you. Now that I see the size of the box, I can tell they all couldn't have fit inside there. That would be a shame indeed. I would hate for a single person to miss out on getting their candy cane, and the village needs the money for the costumes, too!"

"You're going to need more candy canes," Uriah told me, and went back to shoveling the sidewalk behind us.

"I don't know when I'll have time to make them." I glanced back at Swissmen Sweets.

"You shouldn't have to make them. If you do need more candy canes, don't worry about that—just go to the market and tell the owner," Juliet said.

"Margot said I could do that," I said.

"And you can. The owner is a member of our church, and he will know how important this is for the community. You know that the church is very involved in the Christmas pageant. We have to be because it involves Jesus and everything."

I nodded dumbly as she dropped the notes into my basket. It felt heavy already, and I hadn't yet checked the box.

"Bernard Lapp has been stopping by the box quite often with notes. I thought I saw him twice today. If he comes by again, I will tell him about your need for more candy canes."

I nodded. Bernard was a young Amish man from my district who worked at Harvest Market, and he was very friendly. There were times, even, that I thought he was sweet on me. My jaw dropped. What if Bernard was my secret admirer?

"Are you all right, Charlotte?" Juliet asked. "You appear to be a bit overwhelmed."

I shook my head. "I'm okay. I—I just remembered something I forgot to do at Swissmen Sweets. I'm sure Cousin Clara has found it by now and corrected it." I hated to lie, and I knew I shouldn't. But I couldn't tell her about my secret admirer. I couldn't tell anyone.

Jethro shook his head, as if he was still a little stunned by his run-in with the post.

Juliet studied his face. "He's so overcome by the snow. I should take him to Swissmen Sweets to visit with Bailey. She always seems to be able to calm him down." She sighed. "I just wish that she and my son would make it official. It's very tiring waiting for the wedding."

"But they aren't even engaged," Uriah said from the sidewalk.

She eyed him. "That's a technicality. Everyone knows that they are getting married. Why are they putting it off? It makes no sense to me."

"They both work quite a lot," I said, coming to Bailey's defense.

"Work is not as important as love. My goodness, I feel like this generation has everything backward." She scratched Jethro between the ears, and the little pig closed his eyes in bliss. "Wouldn't a Christmas engagement be just the thing?" Juliet asked. "Engaged at Christmas. Married in June. It's like a fairy tale."

I understood what she meant. I wanted Bailey to marry Aiden just as much as Juliet did. The two of them were perfect for each other, and they had been a couple for well over a year. People in the village were beginning to wonder what the delay was. Most of them chalked it up to Bailey's being from New York City. "They do marriage differently in the city," they whispered to one another when Bailey couldn't hear. I hoped she never did. It would only upset her, and out of loyalty to Bailey, I said none of this to Juliet.

"Oh, there's Millie! She will be one to talk to about this." She waved to a petite woman who was just stepping out of the Sunbeam Café. The café was just on the other side of the church. The yellow building was impossible to miss.

Juliet waved to Millie and gestured to her to join us on the square. "She will be the one to ask about Aiden and Bailey," Juliet said as she continued to wave.

It was clear that Millie understood her gesture because instead of walking to her waiting buggy horse tethered to the hitching post in front of the café, she started walking in our direction.

Next to me, Uriah cleared his throat and tugged at the end of his winter coat. I could be wrong, but he looked nervous. It seemed to me that I was right about the groundskeeper's having a crush on the village matchmaker.

Jethro wiggled out of Juliet's arms and ran to meet Millie. She paused for a moment to pat the little pig on the head before continuing on her way. Jethro, who wasn't as tall as the snow was deep, followed her, barreling through the snow just as he had when he'd first startled Uriah and me by the candy cane box.

When Millie finally reached us, she said, "My, this snow is high. It comes over my boots. It will be nice to put up my feet in front of my potbellied stove when I arrive home. I think a hot cup of tea is in order as well." She smiled at us each in turn, and then her smile faded. "Is something wrong? The three of you are staring at me with so much concentration, it's more than a little unnerving."

"Nothing is wrong," Uriah said.

It was clear to me that he wanted to put Millie at ease.

Millie smiled at him, and Uriah's wrinkled face lit up as if he had won some sort of prize.

"There is something wrong," Juliet said. "Bailey and Aiden still are not officially engaged."

Millie sighed. "I should have known it was something like this. Juliet, worrying over when Aiden and Bailey will decide to marry will not make it happen any sooner. I know it is hard for you to hear this, but their choice has very little to do with your personal timeline."

Juliet bent over and scooped up Jethro, who appeared to be a little bit out of breath after his second run through the snow. She dusted off the snowflakes from his snout and his back with her gloved hand. "I was afraid you would say that."

"You were afraid I would say it because you have heard me say it before." Millie loosened the ribbon of her black bonnet, and I could see just the edge of her white hair peeking out. She was a small woman, so the bonnet hid much of her face when she was looking away from me.

"Maybe I should just go to Swissmen Sweets right now and ask Bailey what's going on," Juliet said. "It's best to go to the source, is it not?"

"Bailey is in New York today," I said.

"Oh, that's right," Juliet said with a frown. "She goes there quite a lot. Maybe that is the problem."

"I would think if you spoke to anyone, it would be your son," I said, feeling brave enough for the first time to voice my opinion. "He is the one who would be proposing, right?"

Juliet's brows knit together as she thought about this.

"It would be my advice not to speak with either one of them," Uriah said. "To let them write their own fairy tale any way they want the story to go. I think everyone would be much happier if they minded their own lives instead of the lives of others."

Millie nodded. "I could not agree more, Uriah." She smiled at him. He blushed and looked away.

Millie didn't seem to notice his reaction as she went on to say, "It's my job as the village matchmaker to help people find their matches, but what they do and their relationships after the match is made is completely up to them." She patted Juliet's arm. "Do not worry. I know that their time will come, but we must remember that it's their time, not ours, that matters most."

Juliet wrinkled her nose as if she didn't like the sound of that in the least. She sniffed. "I'm not trying to tell them what to do."

Uriah, Millie, and I shared a look.

"Well, I hope for all your sakes that's true," Millie said. "Now, if you will excuse me, there is a warm stove and a cup of tea calling my name back home. Not to mention I am way behind on my current quilting project. Ruth Yoder will have my head if I don't do my part of the piecing for the quilt our circle is making by tonight's meeting." She smiled at each of us in turn, even Jethro. "Merry Christmas." With that, she turned and trudged back through the snow to her waiting horse and buggy.

"Merry Christmas," Uriah said just under his breath. I thought I was the only one close enough to hear him.

"I suppose I can wait to broach the subject with Bailey until after Christmas," Juliet said. "She has seemed to be overworked as of late." She shook her head. "In any case, I need to get back to the church. As you can imagine, there is much to do to prepare for Christmas—both in the congregation and the village." She hoisted Jethro up higher in her arms and smiled at me. "I know you will do an excellent job with the Candy Cane Exchange, Charlotte. The teens in the church youth group are looking forward to delivering the candy canes as well."

"I'm glad they are doing that part. It would take me forever to complete deliveries on my own in a buggy," I said.

Juliet smiled.

As she walked back in the direction of the church, I flipped through the envelopes she had given me. There were at least fifty. Halfway through the stack, I came across an envelope addressed to me. It was in the same hand as the previous note. I recognized it because I had read and reread the first note so many times. What the note said and the slant of the handwriting were burned into my mind.

"Are you all right, Charlotte?" Uriah asked.

I blinked at him. I had been so consumed with seeing my name in the stack of notes, I hadn't realized he was still standing there. "I—I'm fine."

He frowned as if he wasn't sure whether he believed me, but then he nodded and returned to his task of clearing the walk of snow.

When his back was to me, I took a deep breath as I continued to stare at the envelope addressed to me. Was my secret admirer not Bernard Lapp but an *Englischer* who belonged to Juliet's church?

That changed everything.

Chapter Five

I had to get to the bottom of this mystery. My first question was, were all the notes from Juliet's church from *Englisch* members?

If they were, well, to be honest, I didn't know what I would do. I'd never imagined that the person sending me notes was *Englisch*. I didn't know what the *Englisch* courting methods were, but I would have guessed that they were a little more straightforward than the Amish ones. I did know that the men didn't talk to the woman's father before the couple went on their first buggy ride together. In the Amish world, at least in my old district, that's what would have to happen.

I wrinkled my brow. Since I'd left my own district, my father had had no interest in me any longer as his daughter. I wondered who a young suitor would have to talk to before courting me. Would it be Cousin Clara? She was the eldest relative I still communicated with. Just thinking that made my heart sink. Not because I didn't love Cousin Clara and trust her judgment on such things, but because there was so much of my life my family was missing and vice versa.

I knew this was why so many young Amish people—even though they were conflicted—went back to their home districts. Because if they left, they left everything they knew and loved behind. It was a hard choice, a hard sacrifice to make. But many Amish youths *had* to be away from their family to become their own person. I did, too. In many ways, it was torture, but I remembered how much worse I'd felt in the stifling life I'd led. I shook the cobwebs from my mind. I had made the right choice. I knew it all the way down to the soles of my black snow boots.

As much as I wanted to know about the notes from Juliet's church, I had to return to the shop, and I wouldn't have time to try to get answers until the shop closed for the night. I feared the clock would move very slowly today.

Hours later, after we closed and locked the door—on what was indeed the *longest* day I'd ever worked at the shop—Cousin Clara held on to the counter. "Oh my, it has been a busy few weeks. I think I'll go to bed early. It seems like a *gut* night to curl up with a book and a mug of hot cocoa. I don't want anything else. Do you mind getting your own supper, Charlotte?" she asked. "I'm just too tired to eat."

I frowned. "You should have something to eat." I knew that Bailey would expect me to make sure Cousin Clara was feeling well while she was away.

She nodded. "I will have some toast and jam. That sounds fine to me and the perfect complement to the hot cocoa."

My brow wrinkled. I knew Bailey worried about her grandmother growing overtired. "Don't worry about me at all, Cousin Clara. I think I will go for a walk in the snow. I will find something to eat." I smiled at her. "There's always fudge."

She laughed and then made her way to the steps that led upstairs to our apartment. Nutmeg, the shop's orange cat, followed her up the stairs.

After I heard her reach the top step, I changed into my boots and put on my cloak and bonnet. I had to find out more about my secret admirer, and I hadn't even read the second note yet. I hadn't wanted to do it when anyone was around to watch me. The shop had been nonstop all day, but we had finally gotten caught up with the online orders. I knew that more would come in overnight, but it was nice to feel we could catch our breath, even if it was only temporarily.

When I stepped out onto the sidewalk, I removed the second note from the pocket of my cloak pocket and opened it.

"To Charlotte, Wishing you the very best Christmas. Your secret admirer."

I stared at the note. There was nothing romantic about it. Someone could wish a friend Merry Christmas. Perhaps I had been mistaken in thinking that a suitor was involved. Maybe the note was just from a friend. Maybe it was even Bailey. I frowned. Was I disappointed by that possibility? I decided I would walk over to the church and ask Juliet about the notes she'd collected from the church. Maybe then I would able to narrow down who the secret admirer might be.

"If you think any harder, steam will start coming out of your ears," a disgruntled voice said to me in Pennsylvania Dutch.

I looked up from my note and saw Abel Esh leaning against the brick wall of Esh Family Pretzels. I should have known it was him by the grumpy tone. Abel was always in a foul mood. He was tall and lean and had the same cornstalk blond hair as his younger sister Emily. He would have been handsome if he were a kinder man. His disposition was what made him unattractive.

I quickly folded up the note and shoved it back into my pocket. I most definitely didn't want the rudest man in the district to see it.

"What do you have there?" Abel asked as he pushed himself off the wall. The way he moved reminded me of Nutmeg when he had an insect in his sights and was about to pounce on it. It was not a comfortable feeling being the insect in this case.

With his long legs Abel reached me in two strides. I wanted to step back and retreat from him, but because I knew that was the reaction he wanted, I held my ground. Abel liked to bully and intimidate others. I wasn't going to let him do that to me.

He studied me. "Are you going to answer the question?"

"To you? *Nee.*"

He laughed. "I can see that you have been around the *Englisch* too long. You're behaving like an obstinate *Englisch* woman. You should answer when a man speaks to you. I'm sure that my baby sister is much the same since the King family got their claws into her."

I glared at him. I knew that he was referring to Emily Keim. Emily hadn't been married for quite a year, but before her marriage she had been practically the indentured servant of her older sister Esther, and of Abel. She did everything in the family pretzel shop and had even been made to sleep in the shop on a cot to make pretzels all night long. When she married, she left that life behind and came to work for Swissmen Sweets. Her brother and sister never forgave her for it, or forgave Bailey and Cousin Clara for "stealing" Emily away from them. Bailey didn't steal Emily; Emily ran to Swissmen Sweets to escape her oppressive siblings' demands.

"I'm not going to talk to you about Emily." I lifted my chin.

He smiled. "There is no need to. The truth is I don't care what she's up to. She made her choice to turn her back on her family, and that's the end of it. I have no use for a person who would do that." He paused. "I think you made a similar decision about your family."

I scowled at him. My relationship with my family was none of his business.

But inwardly, I winced. In many ways, leaving my district wasn't that much different from Emily leaving her family. In her case, it might even be harder, because she saw her brother and sister often as their shop was the one right next to Swissmen Sweets. It must have been difficult when they refused to talk to or even look at her. At least my family was miles away, and I rarely ran into them.

I started to walk to the street, but Abel jumped into my path. I had been right in comparing him to Nutmeg when the cat was on the hunt. "Where are you going so soon? I haven't even had the chance to talk to you."

I narrowed my eyes at him. "And why would you want to talk to me?"

He folded his arms. "I heard that you were the one collecting the notes for the Candy Cane Exchange." He peered down at me. "Did you find anything interesting?"

I swallowed. "Interesting?"

"*Ya*, I'm sure that some people would use the candy canes to share how they feel about those they admire." He gave me a cold smile.

I felt sick when he said "admire." Could it be that Abel was the one sending me notes? And was it just to taunt me? I knew he was an unhappy man, but could he be that unkind?

"It's not my place to read the notes," I said in a haughty tone. "I only attach them to the candy canes and confirm that the address is correct so that the church youth group can make the deliveries on Christmas Eve."

"But if any were addressed to you, you would have to read them, wouldn't you?" He leaned closer to me. "You wouldn't wait until Christmas Eve? That would just be silly when you have the note already in your hot little hand."

I stepped around him. "I really don't have anything else to say to you."

He grabbed me by the arm and pulled me back.

"What is going on here?" a strong male voice asked. Deputy Luke Little walked up the sidewalk from the corner of Main and Apple Streets, and he glared at Abel's hand on my arm.

"Nothing at all, Deputy," Abel said and dropped my arm. "I was just offering some assistance to Charlotte here. She was about to trip, and I didn't want her to fall into the snow."

"I wasn't going to trip," I said. "And you know that."

Abel shrugged. "There is no honor in helping an ungrateful *Englisch* lover," he said in our language.

I gasped at his insult, and he smiled his oily smile, having finally gotten the reaction from me that he'd wanted. I scowled back. I knew that he'd spoken in Pennsylvania Dutch so Deputy Little wouldn't understand.

"Abel, don't you have somewhere you have to be?" the deputy asked.

Abel frowned at Deputy Little. "I am where I'm supposed to be. This is my family's pretzel shop, is it not?" He pointed a thumb back at the store.

As he did, the front curtains moved. I wouldn't be the least bit surprised if his sister Esther had been watching us the entire time.

"Well, I suggest you go inside," the deputy said, as if it wasn't a suggestion at all but more like an order.

Abel paused and seemed to measure in his head how far he could push the deputy before he got into any real trouble. He relaxed his posture. He must have come to the conclusion that it wasn't worth pushing Deputy Little to the brink today. That didn't mean he wouldn't try on another day.

Abel smiled at me. "Have a Merry Christmas, Charlotte. And I hope you find something special in the candy canes." This time he spoke in *Englisch*, so that Deputy Little would understand every word. I didn't think that was by accident.

He walked over to the pretzel shop and went inside. The curtain in the window moved again. Esther *had* been watching.

"Are you all right?" Deputy Little asked as he studied my face.

I smiled at him. "I'm fine. Abel is just being Abel. If he was not rude, I think we all would be shocked."

The deputy was a lean man just a couple of inches taller than I. He used to wear his hair long and style it with a part down the middle, but he had recently cut it short. I liked the new look. It made him appear more grown up and official. It must not be easy for Deputy Little to be the youngest member of the sheriff's department.

Deputy Little frowned at the pretzel shop. "I know Abel's up to something illegal. We have been trying to find out what it is for months. I smell something rotten with that guy."

"Could it be that he's not doing anything illegal, but is just a mean person?" I asked.

He smiled down at me. "I like how you give everyone the benefit of the doubt."

I smiled back. "I don't know if calling someone *just a mean person* is giving them the benefit of the doubt."

"It is in my book." He studied my face. "Are you sure you're all right? I saw him grab your arm. He didn't hurt you, did he?"

I touched my arm under my cloak, where Abel had grabbed it. In truth, that spot was a tad sore, and I might have a bruise there later, but I wasn't going to tell Deputy Little that. If I did, he might arrest Abel, and, even though they were estranged, that would be upsetting to Emily. Emily had been through enough over the last few years. I wouldn't be responsible for making things more difficult for her.

"I'm relieved," he said. "When he put his hand on your arm like that, all I could see was red."

"Thank you for the concern, Deputy." I stepped to the edge of the street.

"Are you leaving?" he asked.

"Just out for a walk. The snow is beautiful, isn't it?"

"It is," he agreed, and pulled a navy-blue stocking cap out of the pocket of his heavy coat. He put on the hat and pulled it down over his ears. "Hard to believe that terrible weather could leave something so beautiful behind. We had a lot of accidents the night of the storm, and all the deputies were out on the roads into the wee hours of the morning. Thankfully, no one was hurt."

I looked up at him. "It must be hard being a deputy and out all hours of the night in the cold. I know Bailey worries about Aiden even if she doesn't talk about it much."

"It's not an easy job, but it's rewarding. Sometimes I think it's harder on the people who are waiting at home than on those of us on the force. In my case, I don't have anyone to worry." His face turned bright red when he said that. "Anyway, I'm glad that I happened by and was able to provide you with a little bit of help when you needed it."

"And I thank you for it. I think I will check the candy cane box before my walk. I just can't help it. Every time I come outside, I want to see if another note is there."

"You look in the box for the notes?" he asked.

"It's my job," I said proudly.

"You're the one who is collecting the notes for the Candy Cane Exchange?" His eyes went wide. "I thought it was supposed to be Bailey."

I cocked my head. "Margot wanted Bailey to do it, but with all her television show commitments and the shop being so busy, she doesn't have the time."

"Oh." His brows knit together.

I frowned. "Do you think I'm not up to it? It's not exactly a hard assignment. It's just time-consuming."

He waved his hand. "No, no, nothing like that. Of course you can do it. I think you can do anything."

My brows went way up when he said that.

He cleared his throat. "I mean, candy-related. You can do anything candy-related. I don't really know what else you can do except play the organ. You're good at that, too," he rambled on.

"Are you asking about the candy canes because you want to send a candy cane note?" I said. "You can just hand it to me and save yourself the trouble of putting it in the box."

"No! I mean, no, I don't have any notes to place in the box. I don't write notes."

"Ohh-kay," I said, and realized that I sounded just like Bailey when she thought someone was fibbing to her. "I had better get to it." I crossed the street; it wasn't until I was on the other side and making my way to the wooden post shaped like a candy cane that I realized Deputy Little was following me.

I looked over my shoulder. "Is there something wrong, Deputy?"

He waved his hand. "Oh no, everything is fine. I just—I just was curious about the notes myself."

"I can't let you read any of the notes," I said. "Unless there is one addressed to you."

"Oh, I have no interest in the notes." He cleared his throat. "I mean, I think that it's a very good way to raise money for the village, and I could see why people would want to do it." He forced a laugh. "But who would I send a note to? I don't have anyone special in my life. My life is about the job."

I frowned. I wasn't sure why he was trying so hard to convince me that he didn't want to take part in the Candy Cane Exchange. It wasn't as if I cared whether he participated or not. I wished he would just let me go about my business. I didn't think that I could talk to Juliet about the Candy Cane Exchange with the young deputy hanging around. Although I didn't think he would follow me to the church.

I opened the lid of the box and was pleased to see there were ten more notes on the bottom. With Deputy Little looking on, I quickly flipped through the stack of notes, but this time there wasn't one from my secret admirer.

"You look like you are disappointed by something."

I blinked at him and tucked the notes in the pocket of my cloak. "I'm just preoccupied with everything that has to be done before Christmas. You know how busy this season is."

He frowned, as if I hadn't given him the answer he wanted. "I do know. I'll increase my rounds on the square to keep an eye on the box. It would be very easy for someone to reach in there and steal the money."

"Do you think someone in Harvest would really do that?"

"People steal things everywhere. Unfortunately. And it's much more likely to happen when the word gets out how lucrative this fundraiser has been for the village. It never hurts to keep a close eye on things."

"*Nee*, I suppose it doesn't. It was nice to see you, Deputy," I said, hoping that he would get the hint that I was ready to leave the square.

Deputy Little nodded. "It was nice to see you, too. Are you headed back to the candy shop?"

I shook my head. "I was on my way to the church. I wanted to chat with Juliet."

"I can walk you there. My cruiser is parked in the church parking lot."

I smiled at him. "That would be nice."

He smiled back at me with a strange look on his face. My stomach did a little flip. What was I doing, smiling at Deputy Little? He was a kind man, of course, but *Englisch*. Nothing was going to change the fact that he was *Englisch*.

Chapter Six

Deputy Little didn't say anything more to me as we walked to the church. When we reached the parking lot, he said goodbye. I watched as his cruiser drove away. Something odd was going on in this village, and I was determined to find out what it was.

I shook my head and skipped up the church steps. As I did, I tried not to think about the dead body Bailey had found on those very steps during the summer. Bailey had stumbled across a number of dead bodies in her time in Harvest. She was sort of a magnet for them.

During the day, the church was unlocked so members and people from the community could come and go as they pleased. After some violent events in the village, some of the church members had clamored for the church door to be locked on every day other than Sunday, but Reverend Brook refused. He believed that a church should always be open to the community. I didn't know how long the minister would be able to keep this policy as murder was becoming more and more common on Harvest's quiet streets.

I pushed open the purple door of the church, and it thudded shut behind me. It sounded like the gong on the organ. I made my way into the sanctuary and let out a breath as I looked down the aisle at the huge instrument. A feeling of peace washed over me. The church was dressed for Christmas. There was greenery at the end of every pew, and seven-foot-tall Christmas trees, which I was certain were from the Keim Christmas tree farm, stood on either side of the massive organ tucked back in the narthex.

The organist was a kind man who let me practice as much as I wanted on his beautiful instrument. I wished that I had time to play now, but with Bailey on her way to New York, I knew that I had to get some rest after I left the church. Tomorrow would be another busy day in the shop.

The door behind the pulpit opened and Reverend Brook stepped out. "Oh!" he said in his mild way. The only way I had ever seen the minister react to anything was mildly.

"Hello, Reverend Brook. I'm sorry if I startled you." I lowered my bonnet and let it hang behind me from its black ribbons around my neck.

He put his hand on his chest. "I didn't know anyone was in here." He relaxed his shoulders. "I was just working on my sermon. When I do, I lose track of time and sometimes even where I am. I'm deep in edits right now. It's very important to me to get the message right every Sunday for my flock."

I nodded. "I know that Juliet is very proud of you for that."

He blushed at the mention of his wife. I thought at times that Reverend Brook couldn't believe his good fortune in marrying Juliet.

"What are you doing here, Charlotte?" Reverend Brook asked. "Have you come to practice? I'm sure the organist wouldn't mind if you did. He wants the instrument to be played. You can go right ahead."

He was a short man with a bald head, but a compassionate smile. There never seemed to be much that got the reverend worked up. He was the complete opposite of Juliet, who was worked up most of the time. Bailey said they were a perfect example of how opposites attract.

"I wish I had time to, but I should get back to the shop." I sighed and stared forlornly at the keys. I hadn't had time to practice in weeks because of the busy Christmas season at Swissmen Sweets. I promised myself that as soon as things settled down at the candy shop, I would return to the organ bench. However, I didn't know when they would settle down. It seemed that Bailey's television show only gave us more and more business every week. I don't think anyone, including Bailey, had guessed how successful *Bailey's Amish Sweets* would be.

I smiled at the reverend. "I would love to sit down and play for a bit, but there is so much going on at the shop."

"Oh, I have heard from Juliet that business is brisk. A blessing and a curse, I would guess."

I nodded. "Very much so."

His brows knit together. "Is there something I can help you with?"

As he said this, the door behind him opened and Jethro sauntered out. He held his curly tail high in the air.

"Can I speak to Juliet?" I asked.

"Oh, Juliet isn't here. Jethro is with me this evening. My wife had a late hair appointment, and after Jethro knocked over the waxing station last week, he was banned from the salon."

I wrinkled my nose at the image of hot wax all over the floor. "Was anyone hurt?"

He shook his head. "Jethro could have gotten burned, but he can move when he wants to. He got out of the way in time."

Thank goodness for that. Jethro could be a bit of a troublemaker, but I didn't think anyone in the village wanted to see him hurt. He was a mascot of sorts for Harvest. No one would deny that.

Reverend Brook studied my face with his compassionate pastor expression. That's what Bailey called it, at least. "Is there some way I could be of service?"

I thought about it for a moment. "Maybe you can. I don't know if Juliet told you that I'm managing the Candy Cane Exchange."

He nodded. "She did mention that, and she was quite proud of you for taking it on when Bailey could not."

I smiled when he said that. "Well, I wanted to ask Juliet about the notes she gave me from the church. She said they were collected on Sunday."

His brows went up. "Is there something wrong with the notes? Did someone short you the money? I was very careful to tell the congregation that the exchange is a fundraiser, and it's one dollar per candy cane note. I believe it was in the Sunday bulletin as well."

I shook my head. "*Nee, nee*, they're fine, and I think your church alone raised over half of the money that Margot will need for the new costumes. Everyone has been very generous. Several people gave more than a dollar to deliver their candy cane, as a donation."

He smiled. "The congregation is always willing to step up and help the community. I'm very proud of them for doing that."

"My question is: Are all the notes from your church members?"

"What do you mean?" he asked.

"Do you know for sure that all the notes from your church came from the congregation, and not from someone who might not attend here?" *Like an Amish person*, I wanted to add, but I stopped myself.

He frowned. "I have no way of knowing that. We didn't limit it to just the congregation. We made an announcement the Sunday before last, so people could have brought in notes from friends and neighbors for the box. There's really no way to know if all the notes were from the congregation. We just had members put their notes in a basket at the back of the church. No one was standing there to see who put the notes in the basket, or who the notes were from."

"Does that include Amish friends and neighbors?" I asked.

He looked surprised. "Of course. We're in Holmes County, after all. I would be surprised if there weren't any Amish notes in the ones Juliet gave you. We have Amish neighbors who come into the church all the time. I'm sure they might have added a note to the pile if they thought about it."

"Right," I said and frowned. It looked to me like I was back to square one. I had thought by coming to the church I could eliminate all the potential Amish suitors, but from what the reverend said, that wasn't the case.

He frowned. "Is that a problem? Is there something wrong with the Amish participating? I will be the first to admit that I don't understand all your rules and edicts, but I wouldn't think this would go against the teachings of your faith."

I shook my head. "It doesn't. In fact, the way it's being done is very Amish-friendly."

"If it's so Amish-friendly, why are you worried about Amish participation?"

That wasn't a question I could answer just then, if ever.

Chapter Seven

The walk back to Swissmen Sweets was cold and dark. It was well after six in the evening now, and this late in the year, the sun had set over an hour ago. Despite the darkness and the cold, I felt myself drawn to the candy cane box again. I was no closer to finding out who my secret admirer was than I had been when I discovered my first note.

I knew if I spoke to Cousin Clara about it, she would ask me why I needed to know who it was. Maybe she would even tell me that I should just enjoy being admired. But that wasn't how I was. It was why I had never fit well in my old conservative district. I had this need to know and ask *why* and *how*. I was like Bailey in that way. I wished that I had told Bailey about the note before she left for New York. She was so clever. I knew she would have been able to solve the case, if I could even call it a case, in no time at all.

Did it matter? I wondered. If I had a suitor, a real suitor, he should have the nerve to come up to me and tell me how he felt instead of sending me ambiguous notes. Did I really want to be courted by a coward? But was the person being cowardly or romantic? If romantic, of course I wanted to know who it was. I sighed. It was so infuriating. I wasn't sure how to go about finding out.

I had checked the candy cane box less than an hour ago, but I was so close to it, so I couldn't resist checking it one more time before I went in for the evening. I had many candy cane notes to prepare.

I lifted the latch and put my hand in the box. There was another note there. It was amazing how many notes appeared in the box. I thought by this point Margot's idea had raised over one hundred dollars. That was over one hundred notes. The church youth group was going to be very busy on Christmas Eve delivering all those candy canes; that was for sure.

I pulled out the note, and in the glow of the red and green twinkle lights that had been wrapped around the gazebo, I could see that the envelope was addressed to me. My breath caught; it was in the memorable, slanted handwriting of my secret admirer.

My heart soared, but then it came crashing back to earth as I glanced across Main Street at Esh Family Pretzels. What if Abel had sent the notes as a cruel prank? He did seem to know something about the Candy Cane Exchange. Or had he been bluffing to get under my skin? I couldn't be sure.

With more unease than I had felt when I opened the other two notes, I opened this one.

"Sweetest Charlotte, You are a bright light in the village. Always be yourself. You are loved for the person you are. Your secret admirer."

Loved? *Loved?* My hands shook as I reread the note in the light of the gazebo. Could my secret admirer love me? Or not just love me, but be *in* love with me? I felt this had gone too far.

"You look like you're frozen in place," a man's voice said.

I jumped, and the note fell from my hands into the snow. "Uriah, I didn't see you there."

He scooped up the note, and before I could stop him, held it close to his face.

"Oh my!" he said. "I'm sorry, I took a peek at your private letter." He handed it back to me.

Red-faced, I folded up the note and shoved it into the pocket of my cloak. "Do you know who it's from?" he asked.

I frowned at him.

"I am sorry. I shouldn't have asked. You have just been going to the box so often. I couldn't help but wonder if you had found notes for yourself there."

My mouth fell open. "How did you guess?"

He smiled. "Every time I come upon you, you shove a white note in your pocket. It does not take much imagination to assume there are notes addressed to you."

I had to tell someone or I would burst. Maybe Uriah, as an impartial person, would be the best one to talk to about it. "Can you keep this a secret?" I blurted out before I lost my nerve.

"*Ya*, you can trust me not to tell a soul." He folded his arms and leaned in.

I nodded, and before I could change my mind, I said, "Someone has been sending me notes through the Candy Cane Exchange. I don't know who it is, and it's driving me crazy. For the last several days, I have been trying to figure it out, and I have gotten absolutely nowhere. I don't even know if the person is Amish."

He nodded. "I thought it might be something like that. I didn't think that someone would want to empty the candy cane box as often as you have unless she had a very *gut* reason."

"I don't know if whoever is sending these is serious, or if maybe they're playing a prank."

"What makes you think it might be a prank?"

I hesitated. I had told Uriah too much already and was wondering if I'd made the right choice in telling him anything at all. I certainly didn't want to name Abel Esh as a possible suspect in such a prank, at least not yet. I took a breath and whispered, even though there was no one else on the square. "The notes were signed 'Your secret admirer.' I don't have a secret admirer. Why would anyone admire me?"

"Don't be so hard on yourself. I'm sure there are a lot of bright young men in the district who have shown interest in you."

As soon as he said that, Bernard Lapp's face popped into my head. Bernard was nice enough, but... well, I just couldn't picture him as husband material. At least not for me.

"Perhaps the young fellow is just shy."

"Maybe," I said slowly. "That doesn't change the fact that the mystery is driving me crazy, and I want to know who this person is."

"I can see that it is. You are quite worked up about it."

I frowned at him.

He held up his hands. "It's only an expression. We all get worked up from time to time, and there's nothing wrong with that."

I nodded, appeased a little.

"Are you sure you don't want the young man to reveal himself in his own time? It might be a wonderful surprise."

"*Nee*," I said with much more force than I'd intended. "I don't know when he will do that, if ever, and I just can't wait."

He pulled on his long, white beard. "All right, then, it seems to me that you do need to get to the bottom of this. It's clear to me that's what you really want."

"It is." I squeezed my gloved hands together. Even wearing the gloves, my fingers were beginning to sting from the cold. "What do you think I should do?"

"If you have to know his identity, there's only one thing to do." He paused. "Run a stakeout."

I blinked at him. "A what?"

He cocked his head. "I would have thought that you would know what that is because you have spent so much time with Bailey King and her extracurricular sleuthing."

I shook my head.

"A stakeout is when you hide near a spot where a crime has been or will be committed and wait for the culprit to arrive and reveal themselves."

"Is the note a crime?" I asked.

"It might not be a crime, but it is keeping you up at night, isn't it? So it is disturbing your peace, is it not?"

He had me there. After finding the first note, I had tossed and turned all night long. I'd also reread the note countless times. I'd analyzed it for clues as to who the writer of the note might be. But in vain. I finally fell asleep sometime after one in the morning. Just thinking of it made me tired. I had to be up for work in the candy shop at four in the morning. I was going on very little rest.

"It is keeping me up at night," I admitted. "I just don't know why someone would do this. I'm not scared, if that's what you are thinking, just extremely curious. Why doesn't the person talk to me, tell me how he feels, if we are assuming that it's not a prank?"

"It is more difficult than you think to tell a person how you feel. I have loved someone from afar for a long while myself. It's hard to deal with at times." He smoothed his beard. "Take care not to break this young man's heart. This might be the only way he can work up the courage to tell you how he feels. View the notes as a sweet gift, not as a failing."

I wondered if the person Uriah had loved from afar was matchmaker Millie Fisher. I hadn't seen anything in Millie's behavior that told me how she might feel about Uriah's extra attention.

"Can I tell you what I'm afraid of?" I asked. He'd confessed something to me, and now it was my turn to do the same for him.

He cocked his head, and the red and green lights from the gazebo reflected off his snow-white beard. "Of course, your secret is safe with me."

"I'm afraid that it's not real." I couldn't believe that I was admitting this to him, or even to myself. "I'm afraid it really is some sort of prank. Maybe it's better not knowing for sure, and thinking it's something nice."

"You need to take the risk to find out whether the notes are real or fake. If you don't discover the truth, you will always wonder. If you always wonder, it won't sit well with your soul."

I knew he was right. My own curiosity would bother me for years to come if I didn't find out what was going on, and the sooner the better. "So what does it take to do a stakeout?"

He smiled.

Chapter Eight

The next morning, Cousin Clara let me take a quick break to walk to the Harvest Market. I was all out of candy canes, and according to Margot's very explicit instructions, I was to go to the market to collect more.

When I stepped out of Swissmen Sweets, I saw the village square was a beehive of activity. It was Thursday afternoon of the last weekend before Christmas, and the village was preparing the Friday and Saturday Christmas parade. Uriah and some other Amish men were putting up the manger scene where the Holy Family would stop and greet their visitors after traveling around the square twice in the parade. Two other Amish men were penning the farm animals that would be in the pageant. One of those animals was a camel. I recognized Melchior the camel from last Christmas's parade. I wasn't surprised that Margot had booked him again for this year. He had been a crowd favorite.

Melchior was tethered to a tree near the gazebo and the candy cane box. I wasn't sure what all this meant for my stakeout that night.

I shook my head. I couldn't worry about that now. I had to get to the market and back so I could help Emily and Cousin Clara with all the new Christmas orders that had come in. Worries about the stakeout and the camel would have to wait until after the shop closed.

"Charlotte!" Bernard smiled at me brightly as he always did when I walked into the market. Could he be my secret admirer? I studied him with renewed interest.

"Are you here for candy canes?" he asked in his cheerful voice. His black hair was cut in the standard Amish bowl cut, but that did nothing to tame the cowlick that bobbed on the back of his head. He had soft, brown eyes that reminded me of milk chocolate and just about the brightest smile

I had ever seen. He was an attractive young man. Any Amish girl in the district would be proud to be courted by him. Then why was I worried he might be my admirer?

I blinked at him. "How did you know that's why I'm here?"

His smile widened. I hadn't known that was possible. "Margot told us that you took over the Candy Cane Exchange, and that there had been so much interest, you would need more candy canes because Swissmen Sweets would not have time to make any more. We have been holding some back for you!" He said all of this in one breath. "I'm glad you came in or the boss might have made me put them out for the customers. I told him that wasn't a *gut* idea. If you make a promise to Margot Rawlings, you have to keep it or suffer the consequences."

I smiled. He had a point there.

"I'm glad you did."

"I think it's great that you have taken on the Candy Cane Exchange. I am particularly aware that the new costumes are needed. I was a shepherd last year, and I can vouch that those costumes are threadbare. I was cold out on the square night after night. My costume was the worst of the lot."

"Why?" I asked. "What happened?"

"The camel stepped on it."

I blinked at him. "Melchior?"

"Yep, that's the only camel I know. He stepped on the edge of my costume with his hooves. I kept going, and the fabric was so thin it was torn right off my body. You should have heard the gasp from the crowd. I have to tell you, Margot was not amused. Thankfully, I was fully dressed under the robe because it was so cold. So no one saw too much."

I winced at the very idea.

He sighed. "I would love to be in the pageant again, but Margot said they don't need any more actors to play the parts. I think she still holds me responsible for what the camel did. It doesn't matter how many times I tell her that he stepped on my robe. It wasn't like I asked him to do it. She still thinks it was my fault."

I shifted my feet. "I really should get back to the shop...."

"Oh, I know. I'm sure you're busy at Swissmen Sweets *and* with the Candy Cane Exchange. I think it's a lovely idea to send a candy cane to another person in the village who you admire."

I eyed him. "Have you sent one?"

He grinned. "That's only for the person I sent the note to know." He shook his index finger at me. "I hope you've not been reading the notes, Charlotte."

My face flushed to the same color as my hair. "Of course I haven't."

"Unless it was addressed to you, I would guess. Then, you'd read it many times over." He laughed. "Let me go get those candy canes for you." Before I could question him further, he disappeared.

As I waited for Bernard to return with the box of candy canes, I fidgeted from foot to foot. Bernard could be the type to write a secret admirer note. He always went out of his way to speak to me when I came into the market. In the past, I had seen him completely ignore other customers who had been waiting much longer than I to help me. I wrinkled my nose. I wondered if I was reading too much into this. Uriah was right; I had to find out who was sending me those notes. If I didn't, I would suspect every young man who smiled at me.

Two Amish women walked past me with their heads together. They didn't even look at me as they moved by. I recognized them as ladies from my Cousin Clara's district, but I knew they didn't recognize me. I had on my black bonnet and it covered my red hair. That was what people most often remembered about me.

They whispered to each other in Pennsylvania Dutch. I knew that they hadn't recognized me, but I knew who they were. And they were talking about *me*.

"Charlotte Weaver needs to make a choice," the first one said. I knew her name was Gail. "One cannot straddle the fence for this long. It's not natural."

"I agree," her friend Jeanine replied. "It makes our district look bad to other Amish communities, having people her age not baptized into the church. If she doesn't want to get baptized, she should leave."

I covered my mouth to stifle a gasp. I knew Ruth Yoder, the bishop's wife, wasn't happy that I hadn't been baptized into the church yet. But Ruth was always complaining about someone or something in the district, so it was hard to take her seriously. What I didn't know—until now—was that others in the district were talking about me, too.

"But why are people talking about her now?" Jeanine asked.

"She's doing the Candy Cane Exchange, you know. Ruth Yoder believes that's more proof that she's bound to go *Englisch*. It was Margot Rawling's idea, and no one is more *Englisch* than Margot Rawlings."

Jeanine nodded. "So true. She would turn the village into an amusement park if she could get away with it."

Gail clucked her tongue. I assumed that meant she agreed with Jeanine's opinion of Margot, and of me.

"It's been over a year since she left her home district, well over a year," Gail said. "Don't you think by now she could have made up her mind? I have no respect for people who can't choose one side or another. Making that choice is what it means to be Amish."

Sides? Who said anything about sides? No one said to be a *gut* Amish person I had to be around only other Amish. That wasn't even possible. Bailey was my cousin and my boss, and no one would think she was tempted to convert to the Amish way of life.

"I spoke with Ruth about it," Gail went on. "And told her that I thought it set a bad example for a person from our district to be as involved with the *Englisch* as Charlotte is."

"I'm sure Ruth agreed with you."

She loosened her bonnet ribbon. "Of course she did, because she is a wise and devout woman."

"Maybe if Charlotte found an Amish man to settle down with, she would make her choice once and for all. Is she courting with anyone?"

"Not that I know of. I think Ruth would have told me. I'm sure the young men in the district are leery of her. You know she was on television as part of *Bailey's Amish Sweets.* The bishop allowed it. Ruth was very upset over his decision about that, as you can imagine."

"Oh, I can," Jeanine said.

I wrinkled my nose. Why did they think Ruth would know who was courting me, if anyone? I rarely spoke to the bishop's wife, and any time I did, it was about the candy she purchased at Swissmen Sweets.

"You know what I think?" Gail said. "Abel Esh."

I thought my eyes would bug out of my head.

"Abel needs to settle down, too," Gail went on to say. "It's different for young men, you know, but he *is* over thirty. If he had a wife, he might stop sulking around the village and causing trouble."

"And you think Charlotte is the one to do that? I think the two of them would be a very poor combination," Jeanine disagreed. "What about the bad blood between the King and Esh families over Emily's wedding?"

"Maybe this will be just the thing to bring peace to the families. I might suggest it to Ruth, and she can ask the bishop to encourage Abel to court Charlotte." Gail sniffed. "Charlotte is no longer young, and she should be happy for any Amish man to consider her as his wife at this point."

"I know Clara might be more lenient because she has an *Englisch* granddaughter, but it puts her and her granddaughter in a bad light to have Charlotte living and working at Swissmen Sweets with not even a hint that she plans to be baptized in the faith."

"Clara really should do something about it. It's as much her responsibility as the church elders' to lead Charlotte in the right direction," Gail said.

I balled my fists at my sides. How dare these two women who barely knew me speak about me like this! They thought they had the right because I had not yet been baptized into their Amish district? Why would I be baptized into a district that was so judgmental and mean-spirited? That was why I'd left home—to escape harsh criticism like this—and now I was running into it yet again. Maybe they were right, and I just wasn't meant to be Amish.

Furthermore, I wouldn't be courted by Abel if he were the last Amish man on the planet.

"Well, Abel needs to find *someone*," Jeanine said. "So I see your point about putting the two of them together. He has been single far too long. It's not *gut* for a man to be alone like that."

"He's living with his sister."

"You and I know that's not the same thing. It's my opinion that Esther Esh is part of the problem. Have you ever seen such a sour-looking young woman? Nothing makes her happy. She's not married, nor do I ever expect her to be married. She's quite a bit older than Charlotte, so she's a lost cause."

I winced. Esther wasn't the nicest person I knew. The ladies were right about that, but I felt bad for her that women in the district thought so poorly of her. For all her faults, no one could say she wasn't a hard worker. Since Emily had left the pretzel shop, she'd been running the place single-handedly. Her brother was no help. It seemed to me that no one was safe from Gail and Jeanine's sharp tongues.

"Charlotte," Bernard said loudly, "I have the candy canes for you right here. Now, there are three hundred in this box, and that should be enough to get you through to the end of the exchange. No one thought this fundraiser would be quite as popular as it is."

"I–I—" That was all I could get out because the two women who had been talking about me a moment ago were now staring at me openmouthed. At least they had the decency to look horrified when they realized I'd overheard everything they had said.

I grabbed the box from Bernard's hands. "*Danki*! I have to get back to the shop. I know Cousin Clara will be wondering what's become of me." I ran to the door. When I reached it, I paused, struggling with the huge box. Instead of asking for help, I awkwardly opened the door with one hand while balancing the box on my knee. I hoped that none of the candy canes were broken in the process because I didn't want to set foot in the market again for a very long time.

"Is it something I said?" Bernard hurried over to me and pushed open the door when it was clear I couldn't do it on my own.

"*Nee!* I just have to go." I clumsily escaped.

"If you need anything, Charlotte, you let me know. Anything at all—I'm happy to help you!" Bernard called out to me as I ran to the sidewalk.

The soles of my black boots slipped on the icy pavement.

Chapter Nine

While I had been in the market, it had begun to snow again. It would most definitely be a white Christmas, and Margot would welcome the snow for her Christmas pageant as well.

I ran down the block in the direction of the square. I heard the candy canes bouncing up and down in the box as I went. I slowed down. I couldn't afford to break any of them. If I did, I would have to go back to the market, which was the last place I wanted to go.

I was panting by the time I reached the square, and there were tears in my eyes. How could those women say such things about me, and about Cousin Clara, too? Cousin Clara had nothing to do with the fact that I hadn't made a decision about whether or not I wanted to remain Amish. She had said to me countless times that the decision was mine to make, and I had been so thankful to her for not adding any more pressure.

Bailey told me once that people my age in the *Englisch* world rarely know what their life will be. I didn't know what I wanted to do with my life either, so maybe I should be *Englisch*? Maybe it would be easier for everyone if I got the decision over with? I didn't want Cousin Clara's standing in the community to be impacted by me.

When I heard someone walking down the sidewalk behind me, I brushed the tears out of my eyes.

"Are you all right?" Deputy Little asked.

"I'm fine," I said, but there was no way for me to hide the fact that I had been crying. My fair skin was always a giveaway to embarrassment and all my other emotions. It was maddening.

"Are you sure? Did someone hurt you? Was it Abel?" He glared at the pretzel shop across the street. "I've been wanting to arrest him for a long time. If he did something to hurt you, that's all the reason I need to do it."

"*Nee, nee*, it was nothing like that. I just overheard something that I shouldn't have and it hurt my feelings." I tried to wipe the tears from my cheeks. "I'm not sad. I'm madder than anything else. Sometimes people can be so, so..."

"Judgmental?" he offered.

"*Ya*, that's the word I was looking for. How did you know?"

He shrugged. "I have dealt with the same."

"What do you mean?"

"It's not always easy being the youngest person in the department. Sometimes the other deputies don't listen to my ideas, or they mock my decisions."

"People judge you because of your age. Me too." I swallowed. "But in my case, I'm too old."

"Too old—you are in your early twenties! That's not too old for anything."

"It is if you have been in *rumspringa* since you were fourteen. There are many—more than I thought, actually—in my Amish district who criticize me because I have not yet been baptized into the faith." I shook my head. Why was I telling him any of this? He didn't care. He was an *Englisch* sheriff's deputy. Our lives and our paths could not be more different from each other.

"If I could make it right, I would." He peered down at me with real concern in his eyes. "Can I help?"

I shook my head. "Only if you could arrest a couple of old, gossipy Amish women."

He looked me straight in the eye. "Yes, yes, I would."

I blinked at him, taken aback by the sincerity in his voice. "Well, you shouldn't. That would cause a lot of trouble between the police and the Amish in Holmes County."

"Do you—" He paused, as if he was wondering whether he should go on. "Do you want to talk about it? About what they said?"

He had kind hazel eyes, and a compassionate ear. He was easy to talk to, and he wasn't critical, like some of the people in my Amish district. I could talk to Bailey about anything, of course, and she would give me an honest answer. But she was in New York for one more night, and I didn't want to burden her when she came home. There would be so much to do before Christmas and she was already stressed.

"They think I should marry Abel Esh," I blurted out.

Deputy Little stumbled off the sidewalk onto the snow-covered grass of the square. Behind him, the Amish and *Englisch* volunteers were putting up the last of the decorations for the parade and nativity scene that would happen the next day. The farm animals that had been brought to the square for the nativity scene snoozed together inside the shelter Uriah and the other Amish men had made for them. The only one standing outside the scene was Melchior the camel, who looked as if he was trying to catch snowflakes on his tongue.

"I–I didn't know that you liked Abel. I'm sorry if complaining about him upset you." Deputy Little looked pained as he said that, as if he were embarrassed by the number of times he'd said he wanted to arrest Abel.

"That's not it at all!" I exclaimed. "I would never marry Abel. I would never marry him even if he were the last man on earth. He's not even my friend."

His shoulders sagged, as if he had been holding his breath during this entire conversation. "I'm glad to hear it."

I frowned at him. "You are?"

His brow went up. "Yes, I'm glad to hear it because Abel is not a very kind man. He wouldn't make a good husband for you—or for anyone." He looked me in the eye for a long moment. "You deserve better than Abel Esh."

"I think everyone deserves better than Abel." I broke eye contact with him. "I'm nothing special in that regard."

"That's where you're wrong, Charlotte. You are someone very special. More special than you can even know."

"If I deserve someone better, is that someone like Bernard?" I said to myself.

"Bernard?" Deputy Little asked. "What on earth are you talking about?"

"Never mind." I wouldn't go into telling him about my secret admirer. He would think I was crazy for trying to find out who he was or he would want to find the person himself. I couldn't let anything mess up my stakeout that night. I glanced at Melchior. Not even a camel.

Chapter Ten

I said goodbye to Deputy Little and said that I had to return to the shop, which was true. But also, I wanted to move away from the deputy. Some of the things he had said had gotten to me. What did he mean when he told me that I was very special? I wasn't sure it was safe to dwell on those words for long. If I did, I would become even more confused about the Candy Cane Exchange and what I should be doing with the rest of my life.

I stepped into the candy shop and was startled at how busy it was. True, it was the last week before Christmas, but I had never seen the shop this busy. There was a line that went all the way to the front door.

"Charlotte, you're back," Cousin Clara said from the front counter while she handed a tall *Englisch* man a large white box that I was sure was filled with Swissmen Sweets' very best fudge. "Can you take over at the counter so I can run to the back and grab some more fudge? We've just about been cleaned out."

"*Ya*, of course," I said. I tucked the box of candy canes in the hallway that led up to the apartment and, as quickly as I could, removed my cloak and bonnet and then washed my hands. I donned an apron.

I was still tying the apron when the man in front of me said, "I would like some of your peppermint fudge."

I blinked when I saw that it was Abel Esh. Abel never came into Swissmen Sweets. *Never.* He and Esther had sworn that they would never set foot in the shop because of Emily's betrayal. I peered over my shoulder to see that the door between the front room and the kitchen was closed.

"Are you out of peppermint fudge?" he asked.

"*Nee.*" I shook my head. "How much would you like?" I thought it would be best to keep this as businesslike as possible.

"A half pound, please," he said with an insincere smile.

I nodded. As I cut the fudge and packaged it, Abel said, "How is the Candy Cane Exchange going? I see you going over to the box quite often, checking for new notes. There must be something in there that causes you to go back so often."

I set the fudge in the box and taped it closed. I handed it to him, taking care not to touch him in the process. "The Candy Cane Exchange is an important fundraiser for the village and I take my responsibility as coordinator very seriously."

He took the box. "Oh, I thought you were taking finding your secret admirer seriously. My mistake." He turned and pushed his way through the people waiting in line to the door.

I watched Abel walk out of the door and my heart sank. I believed that my suspicions were right. That he was the one who was putting those secret admirer notes in the candy cane box, and he was only doing it to torment me. I felt sick to my stomach for thinking that the notes were anything other than a joke.

If I had not been trapped behind the candy counter, I might have run out of the shop right then and made Abel tell me what he thought he was doing by writing those notes to me. I couldn't do that, though. Emily and Cousin Clara were in the kitchen scrambling to make more candies to fill our orders and I was the only one available to work the counter.

I smiled at the next customer. "May I help you?"

* * * *

Late in the afternoon, the crowds in the shop subsided.

"Phew!" Emily said as she ran her delicate hand along her smooth brow. "That was a crazy day. I know it's *gut* for the shop, but I hope every day leading up to Christmas will not be like this. Between my work here and the busyness of the Christmas tree farm, I might sleep through Christmas Day and all the way to New Year's."

"I believe the orders will begin to slow, but we will have more foot traffic from the pageant," Cousin Clara said.

"At least Bailey will be back," Emily said.

Cousin Clara patted her prayer cap, as if to make sure it was still in place. "*Ya*, Bailey will be home late tonight. I know we all will be happy to see her."

"Very happy," Emily said. "Oh!" She pointed out the window. "There's my husband in his buggy to pick me up and take me home." She took off her apron and grabbed her cloak and bonnet from the coat tree at the front of the shop. "I will see you tomorrow!"

We said goodbye to Emily, and Cousin Clara sighed as she looked at the mess on the counter. We had been in such a rush to serve the customers that there hadn't been time to keep the counter as neat as we usually did.

"Cousin Clara," I said, "why don't you go upstairs and put up your feet? Have a cup of tea. The shop closes in a half hour. I can clean everything up and wait on any last-minute customers."

"But you have the candy canes to worry about."

"And I will," I said. "But I can do this, too. It won't take me long to tidy this up, and by the time I do that, it will be five o'clock. Then I can work on the candy canes."

She pressed her left hand into the small of her back. "I am tired. I hate to admit it, but I am. It would be a great help to me if I could go lie down for a little while. I will come down later and make sure that everything is restocked in the kitchen for tomorrow morning."

"I can do that, too, Cousin Clara."

"*Nee.*" She shook her head. "You have to let me do something so I don't feel bad about leaving you alone for the last part of the day."

I smiled. "Okay."

After Cousin Clara went upstairs to rest, I began cleaning off the counter. I didn't mind the work. There was something about making a space neat and tidy that calmed me, and I had cleaned so much in my life, it took no time at all to finish the job.

It was just five minutes before we closed and I was polishing the glass-domed candy counter with a mixture of water and vinegar when the shop door opened. I looked up from my task and was surprised to see Bernard Lapp standing in the doorway in a long, black winter coat, holding his black stocking cap in his hands. Because he had just removed his hat, his cowlick was worse than ever and stood straight up in the air.

"Bernard!" I said.

"Is this a bad time? Are you closed?"

"*Nee, nee.*" I grabbed my rag and spray bottle and hurried to the other side of the counter. "We are still open. I'm sorry if I sounded surprised. I just didn't expect to see you in the shop this late." I cleared my throat. "Can I get you some candy?"

"*Nee,* I didn't come here for candy. I'm glad you are here alone. I wanted to speak to you in private."

My mouth fell open. Was Bernard Lapp about to tell me that *he* was my secret admirer. It wasn't Abel after all?

"I just wanted to make sure that you are all right. Another customer who overheard Jeanine and Gail told me what they said about you and why you ran out of the market so upset. I was worried that you were hurt by their talk."

I folded the rag I had been holding in my hand and set it on the counter. "It's very kind of you to check on me. I'm all right. I know that there are many people in the district who aren't happy with me because I haven't yet been baptized into the church."

"It's your decision to make. You shouldn't let them pressure you." His voice was firm.

I raised my brow. That wasn't the typical response from the Amish men I knew. "*Danki.* Can I at least give you a bag of the peppermint popcorn we made today?"

He grinned. "Well, I wouldn't turn that down. It's one of my favorite holiday treats."

Mine too. I filled a plastic bag to the brim with peppermint popcorn and closed it with a twist tie. I handed it to him. "Enjoy."

"I will." He looked as if he was about to leave, and I realized that this might be my only chance to ask him the question that was burning in the back of my mind.

I took a breath. Sometimes the best way to find out the truth was just to ask. "Bernard?"

He turned with a questioning expression on his face.

"Did you send me any notes through the Candy Cane Exchange? Notes that you didn't sign?" I couldn't bring myself to ask him straight out if he was my secret admirer.

He honestly looked confused. "*Nee*, I haven't put any notes at all in the candy cane box."

"Oh." Did that mean I was right in thinking Abel was my secret admirer? I wished that was not the case.

"Why do you ask?"

"I–I, well, someone has been putting notes to me in the box, and I'm just trying to find out who it is."

He shrugged. "It's not me." He smiled. "If I sent you a candy cane, Charlotte, I would be sure to put my name on the note." He held up the bag of popcorn. "*Danki.*" He went out the door.

Now I knew I would worry about his last comment for the rest of the evening.

Chapter Eleven

I was almost certain that Abel Esh was my fake secret admirer and he was doing it as a joke. Even so, I'd told Uriah I would do a stakeout that night, and a stakeout was what I would do.

It was nine in the evening when I slipped down the stairs from the apartment to the candy shop. Cousin Clara, who was exhausted from the long day's work, was already asleep. Even so, I was very careful as I made my way down the steps.

Nutmeg the cat sat at the bottom of the steps and meowed at me. I held my finger to my lips. "Shhh! I'm going on a stakeout."

The orange cat cocked his head as if he was trying to understand what I'd said. I slipped by him. Rather than go out the front door, I went through the kitchen and out the back door of the shop. I found myself in the alley that Swissmen Sweets shared with Esh Family Pretzels next door. This would be a *gut* place to run into Abel, so I quickly made my way to the front of the candy shop. When I reached the sidewalk, I gasped as I looked at the square. It was so beautiful.

Millions of twinkle lights were wrapped around the trees and the gazebo, the manger scene stood ready for the parade the next day, and the nativity animals, including a sheep, a goat, and a donkey, huddled together on a pile of straw and blankets in their pen. Someone had made a tent for them that covered half the pen so that they would be protected from the elements. I would not be the least bit surprised if it was Uriah who'd made that tent for them.

Melchior stood by the gazebo, a colorful blanket draped over his hump, chewing on feed from a trough at his feet. His majestic frame was silhouetted against the trees by the twinkle lights. It was indeed beginning to look a lot like Christmas, as the *Englisch* song claimed.

I crossed Main Street and hurried toward the candy cane box. Melchior, who was only a few feet away from the box, loomed overhead. I stuck my hand into the box and came up with more notes. I held up the battery-powered lantern I had brought with me and turned it on. I would only need it to read the fine print on the notes. Between the twinkle lights and the moonlight reflecting off the snow, there was plenty of light to see by.

I had stopped at the box right after closing and there had been a number of notes there then, but there were only three in the box now. Two were to Amish families in the village and the third—I swallowed—the third was made out to me. I took it out.

I opened the note. "To the sweetest girl in the village. May your Christmas be half as sweet as you. Love, your secret admirer."

I crinkled the note in my hand and scowled in the direction of Esh Family Pretzels. Abel might think his prank was funny, but I wasn't laughing.

"If you crush that note any harder, you're going to rub the words right off," a gravelly voice said behind me.

I jumped. "Uriah! How long have you been here?"

"Just arrived. I thought you might need help because it's your first stakeout."

I shoved the note into the pocket of my cloak and turned off the lantern. It took a moment for my eyes to adjust to the dimness again. "This isn't your first stakeout?" I asked.

"*Nee.* I have done this a time or two before."

I wanted to ask him what he meant by that.

"I hear something!" Uriah said in a harsh whisper, and he pulled me around the side of the gazebo.

"I didn't get the other notes out of the box," I said.

"You can come back for them. We have to move!" he hissed.

Melchior snorted as we ran by, and I really hoped I didn't have camel slobber on the top of my bonnet. I ducked around the side of the gazebo with Uriah.

"Shh!" he whispered with his finger to his lips.

Slowly, we both peeked around the side of the gazebo, and I couldn't believe what I saw. "He's not putting a note in the box. He's taking them out," Uriah whispered.

I gasped when I realized that Uriah was right. Abel stuck his hand in the box, removed the two notes I'd left there, and put them into his pocket.

"He can't do that!" I said and marched around the side of the gazebo.

"Charlotte," Uriah hissed as he tried to grab my arm.

But I was too quick and too angry. "What are you doing?" I shouted at Abel.

"Charlotte, it's so nice to see you. Did you find any love notes in the candy cane box from your secret admirer?"

Then it hit me. Abel hadn't written those notes, but he had read them. I flushed at the thought of Abel reading the words written by my secret admirer. I felt all the blood rush to my head.

"You awful man," I said. "How could you steal from the village like that? And how could you—"

I didn't finish the rest of my sentence because a deep voice called, "What's going on here?"

A bright flashlight caught Uriah and me right in the eyes. We threw up our hands to block the light.

"Lower your light," Uriah cried.

Deputy Little lowered the beam to the ground, and after blinking a few times, I saw that he wasn't alone. Margot Rawlings stood next to him.

"Margot, what are you doing here?" I asked, still seeing white dots in my vision.

"Someone called me to say people were running around the square. I was afraid it was some kids messing with my manger scene, so I called the sheriff's department. Deputy Little and I came straight here." She glared at us. "And I'm glad I did. What's going on?"

"Uriah and I were on a stakeout because we knew something odd was going on with the candy cane box." I didn't add that the odd thing was the notes from my secret admirer. "And it's a good thing we did. Because we saw Abel stealing notes and money from the box."

"What?" Margot cried.

If I didn't know better, I would have said the curls on the top of her head got bigger when she shouted like that.

"It's true," Uriah said.

"They're lying," Abel said.

Deputy Little stepped forward with a pair of handcuffs in his hand. "I think you're the one who's lying."

Abel saw the handcuffs and took off. He didn't make it very far because Melchior the camel kicked out his hind leg, hitting Abel in the side as he ran by. Abel flew into a fresh pile of snow.

"That's one way to stop a culprit," Uriah said.

It sure was, I thought.

Chapter Twelve

Groaning, Abel rolled onto his back. He rubbed his side. "That camel kicked me."

Margot stood over him with her hands on her hips. "You're lucky he didn't do more than that." She nodded to Melchior. "Good camel."

Melchior spat on the ground.

Deputy Little stepped forward

"*Nee!*" Abel cried. "You can't arrest me."

"I can," Deputy Little said. "And I will."

"Please." Abel looked to Margot for help. "I made a mistake. I won't do anything like this again."

Margot glared at him. "I'm pretty sure that's what everyone who is about to be arrested says." She turned to Deputy Little. "Can you arrest him if I don't press charges?"

"I can, but it would be helpful to have your support."

"Please," Abel said. "I am truly sorry." He was still on the ground.

Uriah folded his arms and said to me out of the side of his mouth, "He doesn't look so tough now, does he?"

Nee, he did not.

Margot put her hands on her hips and glared at Abel Esh. "I won't press charges as long as the money and all the notes are returned." She paused. "Right now."

Abel licked his lips and struggled to his feet. He was truly scared about being arrested. He should have thought of that before he stole the notes and money. It wasn't a kind thought for me to have, but I couldn't believe what he had done while calling himself an Amish man.

"They are in the pretzel shop. I have all the notes and I haven't spent any of the money. You can have it all."

"All right," Margot said. "If you can bring me everything..."

Deputy Little frowned. "Are you sure? He broke the law."

"It's Christmas, Deputy. The time to practice a little bit of forgiveness."

Deputy Little nodded, even though he didn't look pleased with her decision. He then took Abel by the arm. "We will go get those right now."

Abel glared at the sheriff's deputy but went along with him to the pretzel shop across the street with no further protest.

Margot watched them walk across Main Street and turned to me. "Well, Charlotte, I'm surprised at you. I think you got some of your detective skills from Bailey."

"I guess so," I agreed.

She pressed her lips together. "I trust that you will get the money and notes from Deputy Little when he comes back. I'm late for a meeting at the church. Uriah, I would like it if you'd walk with me to the church. I have a few points I want to go over with you about tomorrow's parade."

Uriah nodded. "Will do." He looked at me. "Are you all right to wait here by yourself?"

I smiled at him. "I'm fine. I have Melchior as backup."

Uriah laughed. "*Ya*, you do."

After Margot and Uriah walked toward the church, I tentatively approached the camel. "*Danki,* for what you did. You saved the day."

He bowed his head and, after a second of hesitation, I scratched his nose. He leaned into my caress. He wasn't so bad for a camel.

I don't know how long I had been standing there with the camel before I heard a voice behind me. "Looks to me like you have a new friend."

I turned around and saw Deputy Little smiling at me.

He held out a rumpled stack of notes. "Abel claims this was all he had. I tend to believe him. For all his bluster, he was very afraid of going to jail for the night." He shook his head. "I checked to make sure there was still money in each envelope. It's all there."

"There must be seventy dollars' worth of notes here. I can't believe he would take that many." I looked up at the deputy. "And if he was going to steal from the box, why didn't he just steal them all?"

"He said he didn't want to make it look obvious. When he saw how popular the Candy Cane Exchange was, he decided it would be a quick way to make a little cash. He would have taken more if you hadn't checked the box as often as you did. He said you walked over to the candy cane box from Swissmen Sweets every few hours."

I shivered at the thought of Abel watching me closely enough to know how often I visited the candy cane box.

Deputy Little swallowed. "He will slip up again, and when he does, I will arrest him. Margot can't stop me then."

"Maybe this will make him change his ways. Maybe he was scared enough by the thought of going to jail to turn his life around," I said.

The deputy shook his head. "I wish I had your faith in people. You really are the sweetest person I know."

As soon as he said "sweetest," something fit together in my mind. Every note from my secret admirer had the word "sweetest" in it. Deputy Little was the one!

"You," I said. "You're my secret admirer!"

He stared at me. "What?" His face turned red all the way up to his hairline. "I don't know what you mean."

"*Ya*, you do. You said I was the 'sweetest.' All the notes said that. You were the one sending them."

In the white twinkle lights surrounding the trees, I could see his complexion flush red. I was right, and I was smiling.

"It was me. Did you like the notes?" he asked in such a quiet voice he reminded me of a little boy.

I let out a breath. He'd admitted it. "I loved them. It drove me crazy not knowing who they were from, but I loved them. The only time I didn't like them was when I was afraid they were part of a prank Abel was pulling."

He shook his head. "They weren't a prank. I meant every word."

"But you're *Englisch*." My breath caught in my throat.

He laughed. "I know."

"And I'm Amish." Couldn't he see the problem?

"I know that, too."

"If…" I trailed off. "I will have to make a decision."

His face fell. "I know, and that's why I have hesitated for so long to tell you how I feel. I didn't want to put pressure on you one way or another." He sighed. "Then I heard about the Candy Cane Exchange and couldn't resist. I thought it was a way to tell you, but I lost my nerve and didn't sign my own name. That's why I ended up writing 'secret admirer.'"

"Maybe it's *gut* that you did. If you hadn't written those notes, we never would have known what Abel was up to. I would have had no reason to stake out the candy cane box to see who it was."

Deputy Little made a pained expression. "Please don't call it a stakeout. If the sheriff got wind that the Amish were doing stakeouts in Harvest, we would never hear the end of it."

I laughed, and then the laugh died on my lips. "I still don't know what to do." My voice was low.

"I'm not asking you to do anything. You know how I feel, and I'm relieved that you know. You don't have to make any decisions today, or even in the days to come. I can wait."

I nodded, but I already knew the direction my heart was leaning.

Epilogue

I woke up Christmas Eve morning and there was light streaming in through my bedroom window. It was after eight. How could I have slept in so late, and why had Cousin Clara let me do it? Then I remembered. The shop was closed today.

But I still had to get up. I had the candy canes and notes to deliver to the church by eight thirty in the morning. That was when the church youth group members were going to start their deliveries. I jumped out of the bed and looked out the window. There was fresh snow on the ground. This evening would be the last Christmas parade, and Melchior and the other animals were snoozing on the square below.

I dressed quickly and found Cousin Clara in the apartment's small kitchenette.

"Would you like some breakfast?" Cousin Clara asked.

"No time! I have to get the candy canes to the church. I can't have another mishap or Margot will never ask me to do anything for the village again."

She smiled. "There are many, Bailey included, in the village who would be happy not to be asked by Margot to do her a favor."

"I enjoyed it." I paused. "It was enlightening." I turned away before she could see my blush as I thought of Deputy Little—Luke. It was hard for me to think of him as Luke. Luke was a normal man. Deputy Little was a police officer.

"I should be home in an hour or two." I hurried down the hall.

"Take your time," she called after me. "It's a holiday, after all!"

Thankfully, I'd had the *gut* sense to load my little foldable push cart with the candy canes and notes the night before. All the notes with their attached candy canes were in three large boxes in the wagon waiting by the front door. There were many more than I'd thought there would be. I still couldn't believe that Abel had stolen from the candy cane box like that. It was such an underhanded thing to do. It made me gladder than ever that he wasn't my secret admirer. Although I still didn't know how I felt about the man who *was* my secret admirer. But as Deputy Little—Luke—had said, I didn't have to make any decisions today.

I hurried out the door and waved to Melchior and the other animals as I pushed my cart through the snow and across the square. The church parking lot was half full, but I didn't stop to look around for who might be there. I had to get the candy canes into the church fellowship hall fast. I skidded around the back of the building and through the back door of the church. I clattered through the vestibule.

"It's 8:29," Margot said as she looked at her watch and tapped her foot. "You just made it."

I let out a breath that I hadn't known I was holding.

A half dozen teenagers came forward and took the boxes of candy canes from my cart. My job was done, or almost done. I let go of the cart handle and walked over to Margot. I reached into my cloak pocket and pulled out the thick envelope of bills that I had collected from the candy cane box over the last week. I held it out to her. "Five hundred thirty-two dollars."

She took the envelope from me. "Really? That's much better than we could have hoped for. You did a fine job, Charlotte."

"*Danki.*"

I stayed in the fellowship hall for a little while in case the *Englisch* teenagers had any questions about my notes, but when it was clear I was no longer needed, I took my cart and slipped out of the back door of the church again. The Candy Cane Exchange had been a success. I couldn't wait to tell Bailey about everything that had happened surrounding it, but I thought I would leave out one important piece of the story until I made up my mind about him.

I pushed my cart away from the church, happy that it was a successful fundraiser and for my part in it.

"Charlotte," a voice called.

I looked to my right and saw Luke standing by his department car.

I felt myself blush as I walked over to him. "Hello." I couldn't think of anything else to say. I was tongue-tied. He had been so easy to talk to before, and now I found that I couldn't even say a sentence.

"You missed a candy cane," he said. He pulled a candy cane from the pocket of his coat. There was a note tied to it with a red ribbon. He held it out to me.

I hesitated for a moment and then took the candy cane from his hand. With shaky fingers, I read the note. "Merry Christmas to the kindest, prettiest, and *sweetest* girl in the village. Your admirer, Luke."

I smiled up at him. "I hope you have a Merry Christmas, Luke."

He rocked back on his heels. "I think I will."

Chapter One

Lois Henry pulled at her multicolored geometric print blouse. "It's so hot this evening, I feel like I'm bak- ing bread in my shirt. When is this concert over? Is it run- ning long? Or is that just me because I'm perspiring like Jethro the pig in the noonday sun?" She fanned her red face with the concert program.

Lois and I sat side by side in lawn chairs on the Har- vest village square just before twilight. Around us, other villagers both *Englisch* and Amish shifted in their own seats as the middle school band concert dragged on. I felt the hair on the back of my neck curl from the humidity that at last report was at sixty percent, making the warm night air feel that much hotter. It was one of those few times that I saw the benefit of Lois's air-conditioned house and car.

The businesses that encircled the square—the candy shop, cheese shop, and pretzel shop—had long been closed for the night. The only business still open was the Sun- beam Café, which was trying to take advantage of the Harvest concert series for a few extra sales. The large white church next to the café glowed in the sunset, looking more like a painting of a church than the real thing.

I patted away the dew on my forehead. "Pigs don't ac- tually sweat," I said. "That's why they wallow in mud and water on hot days to cool down."

"I didn't say it for an animal husbandry lesson," Lois said. "Did you see what this humidity is doing to my hair?"

I turned in my lawn chair to have a better look at her. The chair, which Lois had purchased at the local flea market, was far from sturdy. In fact, I had a feeling it might break apart any second. I stopped twisting.

Lois's typically upright red-and-purple spiky hair drooped to the left side of her head. I didn't say it, but it reminded me of a grassy field that had been bent over by the wind. "Your hair looks different from usual." I felt this was the nicest way to put it.

"It's going to take me an hour to set my hair again after tonight. People really don't know how hard it is to look like this." She picked at her hair with her long pur- ple fingernails, but it did little to put her hair upright again.

I certainly didn't know how hard it was. Lois's appear- ance and mine could not be more different from each other. Although we were the same age, nearing the end of our sixties, and had grown up on the same county road, our upbringing had been very different. I grew up Amish, and Lois grew up *Englisch*. Even so, we had been the best of friends as girls and remained the best of friends to this very day.

However, I knew to many people we appeared to be an odd pair. I wore plain dress, sensible black tennis shoes, and a prayer cap. My long white hair was tied back in an Amish bun. Lois wore brightly colored clothes, chunky costume jewelry, heavy makeup, and had that striking haircut.

She leaned across the arm of her chair, and the seat made a dangerous creaking sound. "Did I sweat my eye- brows off?"

I shook my head. "Nee, they're still there." I did not add that they were looking a tad more wobbly than usual. It was certainly due to the trickle of sweat running down the side of her forehead. I had to agree with Lois: It was a hot night, and the concert should have been over an hour ago. We weren't the only ones who thought it had gone on too long—several couples and families had gotten up and left.

Lois shifted her folding lawn chair, and I found myself wincing with every creak and rattle the chair made. I didn't want her to be hurt if it broke. Even though we were sit- ting on the grass square in the middle of the village of Harvest, anytime you fall at our age, it can leave a mark.

"Careful, Lois, that chair is not as sturdy as you think it is," I warned.

She bounced up and down in the chair. "Don't be silly. It's as sturdy as they come. They don't make chairs like this anymore." With her final bounce, there was a loud crack, and Lois and the chair went down.

I jumped out of my seat. "Lois, are you all right?" The children playing in the band froze and stopped playing. The leader held his hands suspended in the air. Lois waved from the grass. "Keep playing. I'm fine."

Several people from nearby blankets and chairs ran over to us. Two *Englisch* men helped Lois to her feet.

"Are you hurt?" I asked.

"Nothing more than a bruised ego, and that stopped bothering me twenty years ago." She smiled. "If I became upset every time I fell over, I would be in a perpetual state of nerves." She smiled at everyone who'd rushed over to help. "Thank you, you're all too kind. Now, hurry back to your seats, so the concert can continue."

After they were out of earshot, Lois said, "Because we need to move this concert along. It's going on forever." She rubbed the side of her leg. "I spoke too soon about not being hurt."

"What's wrong? Should we find a doctor or nurse?"

"No, no, it's nothing as serious as all that. I just banged up my knee."

"Let me at least get you some ice for it, and here—" I moved my chair next to her. "Sit in this until I get back." My chair was as unstable as hers had been, but it had

to be better than her standing if her knee was bothering her. "Stay there. I will find the ice."

She rubbed her knee. "We can only hope by the time you return, this concert will be over," she whispered. Well, mostly whispered, but luckily the band had re- sumed playing, making it hard to hear much of anything over the cymbals and drums. "I don't know how much more of this I can take."

"All right," I said. "Please, stay there, and I will find some ice."

On the far side of the square there was a small conces- sions booth. I thought I would start there. If I didn't have any luck, then I would run across the street to the Sunbeam Café and grab a cup of ice from Lois's granddaughter, Darcy Woodin. I didn't want to scare Darcy until I knew how badly Lois was hurt.

"Excuse me," I said to the man waiting in line. "Can I just ask for some ice? My friend fell out of her chair and bumped her knee."

The *Englischer* stepped aside. "I saw her go down. It looked like a nasty tumble."

The girl inside the food trailer handed me a cup of ice and a fistful of paper towels.

I smiled at her. "*Danki*, this is so kind of you."

"I'd hurry back to your friend, if I were you. Margot Rawlings is headed this way, and she's staring right at you."

I looked over my shoulder and found that she was right. I thanked her again.

"Millie Fisher, can I have a word with you?" Margot called.

I sighed and stopped in the middle of the grass. Margot walked up to me and put her hands on her hips. Margot was an *Englisch* woman who was just a few years younger than me. I had known her most of my life. Although she was *Englisch* like Lois, their appearances were very different. Margot wore her hair short like Lois, but it was a pile of soft curls, which she had a habit of patting and pulling when she was frustrated. She also had a much simpler wardrobe of jeans and plain T-shirts. She was a no-nonsense woman who was doing everything within her power to make sure that Harvest, Ohio, became the number one tourist destination in Amish Country.

The concert tonight was one of her events. Throughout the summer she had been hosting a concert on the village square every Friday evening from seven to eight. It was almost nine now. The concert had certainly outlasted its allotted time. I had heard from Lois that Margot thought these concerts would bring people back into the village in the evenings. Typically, everything in Harvest closed at five or six, even in the summer. The concerts were popu- lar, and tonight's had had a nice crowd before the perfor- mance ran a little too long.

Margot tapped her sneaker-clad foot in the grass. "What is this I hear about Lois Henry falling out of her chair?"

I held up the cup of ice. "She's not seriously hurt. We're taking care of it."

"What happened?" she asked.

"Lois found the chairs we're using at the flea market for what she calls 'a steal.' I think they were past their prime when she got them. I'm very careful when I sit on them and try not to breathe."

Margot shook her head and her curls hopped in place. I would never say it to her, but her signature curls always reminded me a little bit of tiny baby bunnies skipping up and down on the top of her head. I didn't think it was a comparison she'd appreciate.

"Lois and her flea-market finds. Her house is just one big warehouse. You can barely walk through the living room, it's so jam-packed with her yard-sale and flea-market finds. She needs to purge some of those pieces."

I made no comment because Lois was my friend, but at the same time, I agreed with Margot. Lois had an ad- diction to shopping and shopping for furniture in particu- lar. She loved to collect interesting pieces, but she really didn't have anywhere to put them in her two-bedroom rental house on the edge of downtown. She lived alone and her collection wasn't hurting anyone; it made her happy, so who was I to offer criticism? It wasn't like she was a hoarder. Lois was a collector.

And she was one of the most giving people I knew. If someone needed a piece of furniture, she wouldn't think twice about giving it to a friend, no matter what it cost her to buy it.

Margot looked over her shoulder at Lois. "It's not the village's fault she bought a rickety chair. I hope she doesn't think she can file a complaint."

"I don't believe she's planning to do that."

"Hmm."

"And if you are so concerned about Lois, why not go speak to her? She's sitting right over there. This ice is for her, and it's melting quickly in the heat."

Margot seemed to think about my suggestion for a mo- ment. "Well, I'm glad she's all right. I'll check on Lois later. You know when there is an event on the square I'm very busy. I always have to run from one thing to the next."

I pressed my lips together to keep myself from saying something I would regret. I still thought she should ask Lois how Lois was doing.

"But I am glad I caught you alone. I very much wanted a word with you in private."

I shook the ice in the cup and listened for the rattle. At Margot's raised brow, I steadied my hand. I wasn't shak- ing the ice to wave her off. I only wanted to know that it had not completely melted away. I had no idea why Mar- got would wish to speak to me alone. As an Amish per- son, I could not be on any of her village committees, and I did not have a business or service that would lend itself to events on the square. I was a quilter by trade and a matchmaker by avocation. I subsisted on my small in- come from selling quilts to local shops and from special orders, and I helped the young Amish men and women in the county to find their matches at no cost. I have had this gift since I was a small child. I knew in my heart when two people were right for each other. I also knew when two people were wrong for each other.

I didn't charge for the matchmaking because it was a gift from *Gott*. It was not meant to be a business venture but an adventure in true love.

"What can I help you with, Margot?" I asked in the friendliest manner I could manage. Because if Margot was asking you something, most likely she wanted you to do something for her. She always did.

"When was the last time you saw Uriah Schrock?" Margot asked in her businesslike way.

"Uriah?" I asked. That was not what I'd expected her to ask at all.

I knew Uriah, of course. We had gone to the same Amish schoolhouse as children, and when we were young, he had been sweet on me. But that made no difference to my feelings. I'd only had eyes for Kip Fisher. Kip and I were married young and had twenty wonderful years to- gether, but then he passed away from cancer when he was in his forties.

Today, Uriah was the groundskeeper of the village square, and that made Margot his boss. If anyone should know where he was, it was she. It made me very curious as to why she was asking me where her employee was. Shouldn't she be the one who knew his whereabouts?

"Uriah was supposed to be here today to set up for the concert as usual." Margot tugged on her curls. "But he never showed up. I called the shed phone at the farm where he's been renting a room, and there was no an- swer."

My stomach dropped. That wasn't like Uriah at all. He was typically a very responsible man. He would not ig- nore his work.

"I just wondered if he said anything to you about going back to Indiana. I know the two of you are special friends." She narrowed her eyes at me when she said that last part.

I pressed my lips together and willed myself not to blush. I was far too old for blushing. I wasn't sure what "special friends" meant, but I did not like the sound of it. Special or not, he was my friend, and it worried me Uriah hadn't shown up for work. It was not like him at all.

"Where is he renting a room?" I asked, realizing for the first time that I didn't know where Uriah had been liv- ing since he'd returned to Ohio. Had I never asked him?

"He's renting from the Stollers. They are a young cou- ple who live on an alpaca farm."

"Alpaca?" I asked. "I didn't know people in our com- munity were farming alpacas."

"It became very popular in Ohio while you were away."

Ten years after my husband died, I moved to Michigan for a decade to care for my ailing older sister, Harriet. Only after she passed away did I return to Ohio.

I nodded, feeling a little surprised that Uriah had never mentioned that he lived on an alpaca farm. I would think that would be an interesting bit of information to share.

"So have you seen Uriah?" Margot started tapping her foot again. Apparently, it was taking me far too long to give her a straight answer.

"*Nee*, not for a few days. I expected to find him at the concert tonight."

I did not admit to her that I had been looking for him when I first arrived. Usually when Lois and I came to the square for an evening concert, Uriah made a point of stopping by our chairs and saying hello. Months ago, Uriah had asked me to accompany him on a buggy ride. I had been so taken aback by the request that I declined. Somedays, I wished I had the nerve to tell him I had changed my mind.

Margot tugged on her curls, and like some miracle, every time she let them go, they bounced perfectly back into place. "It was very poor form not to tell me that he wouldn't be here tonight. I had to scramble and tell everyone where to put the chairs and where the band should set up. In the past, I have always relied on Uriah to do that sort of thing. You don't think he found himself in some kind of trouble, do you?"

I folded my hands on my lap and held them tightly. "Trouble? What do you mean when you say *trouble*?"

"Could he have gotten lost or hurt? He's just not the type to blow off work. I expect that sort of behavior from the high schoolers we hire during the summer to help out with the grounds, but not from someone like Uriah."

"*Nee*, it does not sound like him." My worry grew. "There must be some sort of explanation. Maybe his buggy broke down."

"Maybe," Margot said. "I'd be lying if I didn't say I'm more concerned than ever now that I know you haven't heard from him either. I thought if anyone in the village would know of his whereabouts, it would be you. He mentioned that he wanted to move back to Indiana this summer, but I can't believe he would do so without telling me first."

My chest tightened. "I did not know that was his plan. When did he tell you?"

"A week or two ago," she said as if the exact date did not matter. "It was always his plan to go back. All his children and grandchildren are there. What would keep him here?"

"Nothing, I suppose . . ." My voice trailed off.

"He said he wanted to tell me"—Margot stopped tap-ping her foot—"so that I had plenty of time to find a re-placement caretaker for the village square. That doesn't sound like someone who would leave without a word."

She was right, it didn't. "Then it can't be that. He'd tell you he was leaving. I'm sure it's something else." I hoped he would have told me too, but I didn't say that.

She stood up. "Well, if you hear from him, let me know. And he'd better have a good reason for not being here tonight. I won't be happy if he doesn't have a good excuse."

I swallowed hard and watched her walk away. At the time, we didn't know how *gut* his excuse really was.

About Amanda Flower

USA Today bestselling and Agatha Award–winning mystery author **Amanda Flower** started her writing career in elementary school when she read a story she wrote to her sixth grade class and had the class in stitches with her description of being stuck on the top of a Ferris wheel. She knew at that moment she'd found her calling of making people laugh with her words. She also writes mysteries as USA Today bestselling author Isabella Alan. Amanda lives in Northeast Ohio. Readers can visit her online at www.amandaflower.com.